THE EXPERT AMBUSH

Phoebe was quite unfamiliar with the winding paths of Vauxhall Gardens, as well she should be. For this was the most notorious place of improper pleasure in London, out of bounds to young ladies without escorts.

But now Phoebe was fearfully alone on a garden path as daylight dimmed—and the shocking stories she had heard came true. An arm snaked around her waist, and she was pulled to one side of the graveled walk.

Her scream was cut off when a firm hand was clapped over her mouth. Then that hand was replaced by a warm mouth.

Even as her senses swam, she recognized the man who held her so closely and kissed her so skillfully—Lord Latham, who would stop at nothing to ruin her reputation. Seduction was a sport at which he reigned supreme, and this was his favorite hunting ground for fair prey. Here Phoebe knew she was at his mercy—and as far as she was concerned, the lascivious Lord Latham had none. . . .

THE CONTRARY CORINTHIAN

by

Emily Hendrickson

A SIGNET BOOK

SIGNET
Published by the Penguin Group
Penguin Books USA Inc., 375 Hudson Street,
New York, New York 10014, U.S.A.
Penguin Books Ltd, 27 Wrights Lane,
London W8 5TZ, England
Penguin Books Australia Ltd, Ringwood,
Victoria, Australia
Penguin Books Canada Ltd, 10 Alcorn Avenue,
Toronto, Ontario, Canada M4V 3B2
Penguin Books (N.Z.) Ltd, 182–190 Wairau Road,
Auckland 10, New Zealand

Penguin Books Ltd, Registered Offices:
Harmondsworth, Middlesex, England

First published by Signet, an imprint of Dutton Signet,
a division of Penguin Books USA Inc.

First Printing, January, 1995
10 9 8 7 6 5 4 3 2 1

Printed in the United States of America

Chapter 1

Val accepted his elegant, ebony walking cane from his portly butler, Priddy, then stepped from his residence with a satisfied air. Deciding he would walk the few blocks to the important part of town—Bond Street—he had not ordered his carriage, preferring to savor the sights and sounds of the city. He set off in that direction with a firm stride and a jaunty swing of his cane.

It was good to be back in London, no matter that the city would be a trifle thin of company just yet. With the Christmas season past and Parliament soon to sit, the peerage and gentry would slowly return to their imposing town houses and rented quarters for the Season to come.

It had been good yet somewhat sad to see his best friend, Lord Norwood, succumb to the bonds of matrimony. Following the marriage of Blaise and Hyacinthe, now the dashing Viscountess Norwood, Val had wandered off to his own property, ostensibly for a bit of shooting, but really for a period of quiet and reflection.

His shoulder, injured when Hyacinthe had shot him while mistaking him for a villain, had healed nicely. His valet, reliable old Rosbert, had earned himself a raise for his excellent care during the recovery period. The elderly housekeeper at Latham Hall had known better than to offer her services, aware her master disliked being fussed over by some ministering female.

Reflecting on his friend's obvious happiness, Val wondered. Was it time for him to settle down at long last? The heir to an immense fortune and a family name of somewhat ancient stature, he supposed it was inevitable. After all, every fellow met his fate sooner or later. As a noted Corinthian—one of those men of great style and *ton*—he had a certain standard to uphold. Val resolved to survey the latest crop of marriageable misses at Almack's with a less jaundiced eye, with a view to finding a young woman to gracefully fill the position of Lady Latham. While he had no elevated peerage, many women would not look amiss at the title of baron, particularly when it came with abundant funds. And thanks to prudent investments and careful management, he was extremely well to grass.

All went well with his morning until he chanced to meet Lady Marshton while strolling along Bond Street. She looked straight through him—a cut direct! He could scarce credit the matter. A cut direct? Incredible! He had never been so insulted. If it had not been that her ladyship had a daughter making her come-out this year, he would have thought little of the matter, but no mother snubbed an eligible peer of any age under those circumstances.

Suddenly uneasy, Val sauntered along, pausing to study the contents of various windows while casting glances at those passing by. Had he been away too long? What could have happened to change his position in Society? Furthermore, something he knew nothing about. He caught sight of another woman he knew slightly. She had a niece she intended to sponsor this Season, if his memory served him right.

"Mrs. Bottomley, how charming to see you again. I trust you are looking forward to the coming Season with pleasure?" Val smiled just the proper amount, bowing to the lady with just the right degree of propriety.

"Indeed, Lord Latham," the good lady replied with a distinct frostiness that had not been present when they last met. She looked a trifle flustered, as though torn between her recollection of his title and wealth and something else that appeared most unpleasant, judging by her troubled manner.

"And you anticipate a lively time of it with your charming niece?" Val felt frustrated that he simply could not come out and ask the woman what was amiss. His very bones told him something was wrong here.

"Indeed, my lord. Miss Pringle is a well-behaved young woman with a lovely face and an excellent dowry to match, who ought to do well for herself." Mrs. Bottomley fiddled with the strings of her reticule, then took a deep breath."Excuse me, sir, for I must hurry along. So many things to tend to these days, you know."

Val watched her nod politely, then almost fly away from him as though he had suddenly sprouted a sign proclaiming him afflicted with the plague.

With a frown settling over his handsome brow, he sauntered along the street in the general direction of his club. Something was afoot here and he intended to find out what. Swinging his cane to and fro with a casual air, he made his way directly to White's.

Once inside those hallowed halls, he inquired of the porter as to whether his particular friends were about. When assured that at least one of them should be present, he marched up the stairs, intent on his mission, ignoring the fine portraits that frowned down upon him.

He checked the room, noting that while there were acquaintances, there were none who were close to him, who might reveal the truth—whatever that might be. A feeling of dread crept over him. What had happened?

He was greeted with jolly smiles and obvious enthusiasm by those he knew fairly well. Knowing grins and chuckles were sent his way, with muttered comments about one's youthful follies finding one out, he heard to his utter bewilderment.

Ferdy. Where in the blasted world was Ferdy Andrews? Val was about to query a mutual friend when an older gentleman, a gamester who would bet on any likely prospect, accosted him.

"Well, well, Latham," Lord Dakin said with a decided twinkle in his gray eyes, "I must say I admire your dash and daring. Not many chaps have your audacity, young fellow. Good to see the new generation ain't all milk and water, eh? The bets are out, y'know. Odds as to whether or not your credit will survive this. My money is on you, my boy. Don't let me down, you hear?" He bestowed a jovial punch to Val's shoulder, chuckled in an almost suggestive manner, then strolled off to confront another member over a wager involving the matter of a flock of geese and a carriage.

Another fellow entered the room, and clapped Val on the back while uttering much the same sentiment.

Utterly baffled and vaguely alarmed, Val found a secluded seat by one of the front windows, ordered a bottle of wine, then sipped from his glass as soon as the waiter had poured out the claret for him. He stared pensively at the carriages passing the club and then off to the bustle of Piccadilly Street. What had occurred while he was away?

If Ferdy was not to be found, Val would have to solve the mystery on his own. But it would be a help to have his good friend at his side, someone who might have a clue regarding the mystery. That is, if he was still his good friend!

The notion that something might have happened to mar an association of many years standing so concerned Val that he left his wine unfinished and strode from the room and down the stairs, fully aware that a good number of amused glances followed him. Whatever had occurred must be such that it entertained the men while angering the women. To Val's experienced mind that not only spelled trouble, it spelled feminine trouble—the very worst sort.

Since he had walked this morning, he hailed a hackney of reasonable quality and ordered the jarvey to convey him to Curzon Street and Ferdy's chambers at the Albany, that elegant establishment for bachelors.

While the horses clip-clopped over the cobbles, Val tried to recall if there was a woman alive who had any claim on him, and could think of none. He had no present mistress, was extremely prudent in his brief liaisons, and in short, was not vulnerable in that sphere. So what could have happened?

Paying the man handsomely for his speedy trip, Val entered the building and marched up the stairs to find his good friend.

He was found to be home. Ferdy's man grudgingly allowed Val to enter the pleasingly arranged chambers. Ferdy lounged in his very masculine sitting room, reading the morning paper. He lowered it to give Val a troubled look, then set the paper aside, rising to greet his old friend.

"Val." There was a distinct pause before Ferdy continued in a restrained manner. "So you are back. I trust all is well with you? How was shooting this year?"

Ferdy, usually the most easygoing of all the chaps Val knew, was now obviously ill at ease.

"Cut line, Ferdy. Else I shall believe I am sunk beyond all hope of redemption. What is going on? Lady Marshton gives me the cut direct. Mrs. Bottomley nearly freezes me with hauteur—and her with a niece to present this Season." Val ignored the table where wine bottles sat invitingly and paced about the room with angry strides.

"Well . . ." Ferdy hedged.

"Old Dakin called me daring and dashing and that new fellow—what's his name—clapped me on the back as though I had won some sort of prize—in a contest I'd not entered. And why are bets being placed regarding my retaining my credit with Society?" Val stopped in his tracks and fixed his friend with a hard stare. "Tell me all you know."

Ferdy strolled across the room to look absently out of the window. Then he turned around to give Val an apologetic grin. "It's the woman, you see. While it ain't unusual for a fellow to keep his doxy in London, I don't know of a one who will parade his by-blows in Hyde Park."

Val felt as though the air had been punched from his chest. "By-blows? What are you talking about, man?"

"That pretty little minx who takes her twins for a walk in the park every day. Boy's the spitting image of you, Val. Pity he's not yours legally, y'know. Fine-looking lad." Ferdy paused a moment to reflect. "Girl looks more like her mama." Then he frowned again. "But, Val, it ain't the done thing, to have your doxy walking the children in the park with all the other proper governesses and nannies. The women are all upset, I can tell you." He grinned at his friend and added, "I must say, I don't know where you've hidden this paragon, Val. She's a beauty, make no mistake on that. Won't talk to anyone and that's the rub. No one can learn a thing about her."

Val sank down on a chair that most fortunately was close to hand, a dazed expression momentarily crossing his face before he gathered his wits about him. "I am not the least aware of any by-blows, twins or otherwise. I have never been one much for chasing petticoats—you know that. The few mistresses I have had over the years have been most discreet. I imagine that were one of them to produce an offspring, I would be petitioned for its keeping posthaste. I assure you that has not been the case. Whoever they may be, those twins are not mine!"

Ferdy gave a sigh of relief, then frowned. "Well, if that's the situation, who is she? I tell you, Val, there is something smoky about this business."

"Indeed! We had best get to the bottom of this mystery before my name is totally destroyed. I came to London with the intent of finding myself a proper wife and this will scarcely lend me any credit."

"You, leg-shackled? That *will* set the *ton* on its ear." Ferdy crossed from the window to ease himself down into the facing chair, no small feat given the tight fit of his pantaloons. "But how could there be a child who is your spitting image without being related to you?"

"It's a mystery to me. You say this paragon of doxies parades her charges in the park every afternoon?" Val glanced at his pocket watch, then rose. "What do you say we have a spot of nuncheon, then make every effort to locate this young woman. You did say she is young?"

Ferdy gave a reflective smile and sighed."Not only young but dashed attractive." He stabbed a finger in Val's direction, adding, "Everyone says you are one lucky chap to have found a mistress who is so loyal. She'll not so much as look at another man, much less speak to one. Prim as a pin. You are certain she is not in your keeping? For I must say you are the envy of half the *ton*, my friend—the male half, that is."

"And I appear to have angered the female half," Val countered, with no amusement in his voice. "The worst of it is that I have not the faintest notion of whom this woman might be! This is not a good thing when I intend to find myself a suitable wife." He rose and made his way toward the door, glancing back to see if Ferdy was following him.

"I will believe that when I see it," Ferdy muttered before joining Val in exodus from the Albany chambers. They ignored a hackney, preferring to speculate about the identity of the paragon who had turned Val's life upside down, while strolling back toward the club where they intended to eat.

During their light meal, it was decided that Val would haunt the area of the park where the young woman appeared with the children in tow.

"Once I have a chance to see her, I can decide whether or not I know who she is and how best to proceed," Val explained, his dark eyes exchanging a knowing look with Ferdy.

"I must say that I'm glad to know the tots aren't yours," Ferdy said, after a sip of his wine. "Hate to think of a chit trying to rear them on her own." With a quick frown he added, "Come to think on it, they are dressed right well and she is garbed all the crack—respectable, if you know what I mean. You don't suppose she might be, well, someone you met at a house party and er, entertained while in your cups, or something of that sort?"

"Ferdy," Val groaned, "you pain me. Do not even think of such a thing. I might have my share of the grape, but never so much that I do not know what I'm about. The last house party I attended was so proper that not a soul could complain, other than of boredom."

With Ferdy's prodding, Val launched into the tale and soon had his friend chuckling over Val's description of the dry-as-dust affair.

They managed to leave the club without being accosted by any more of the amiable gentlemen intent upon finding out the identity and location of Val's supposed doxy.

"Think it will rain?" Ferdy said with a glance at the lowering sky.

"It wouldn't be so cruel," Val said without much conviction. The London weather was notoriously nasty in late February. While snowdrops and daffodils might be nodding their heads in various gardens, a fellow could expect a chilly rain to dampen his day with distressing frequency.

Having taken a hackney to the edge of the park, they began their prowl of the paths that ran across the greens and along Rotten Row. Carriages had begun to roll along the way, although the ladies were bundled up warmly, and hurried when they saw the area thin of company. The few on horseback were intent on their exercise and ignored the two men who marched along the paths.

At long last, Val turned to his good friend. "I begin to

think you have fabricated this creature of whole cloth, Ferdy, old boy."

"Can't understand it," Ferdy said with a rueful shake of his head. "She's been here every day that I've come here the past two weeks." He frowned, then brightened. "Maybe something happened to her or the children."

"I had no notion you were such a fiend, Ferdy, to wish my nemesis ill." Val bowed to two older women who sailed past in a landau, who in turn cast him speculative looks.

"What do you suppose they were thinking?" Ferdy mused as the carriage disappeared from the park.

"I have the idea that they were trying to decide if the tale offered by their husbands was true or if the gentlemen were making it up," Val said in disgust. "Look, 'tis beginning to rain in earnest. We had best find a hackney before we are drenched and catch our death." They hurried to find an available carriage and were shortly on their way across town.

Discouraged but not deterred, Val dropped Ferdy off at the Albany before continuing on to his home. He needed to think and plan his strategy. Clearly if there really was a young woman in London who took twins for walks in the park—one of whom appeared to resemble Val—he needed to uncover the truth of their identities.

Val would have chalked the entire matter up to momentary madness were it not for the number of people who had, one way or another, demonstrated that the woman existed. As he saw it, what he had to do was locate her first, then tackle the matter of the children.

Deciding the best procedure was to brazen it out rather than hide in his house, Val took himself off for the evening, determined to enlist Sally Jersey's help in learning how extensive the damage to his good name might be.

He had attributed the scarceness of invitations to the lack of people in town, and that those who were here were not aware of his presence as yet. He was quickly disabused of that notion.

"Sally, I appreciate your invitation," he murmured to his hostess when he had a chance to speak with her off to one side of her drawing room.

"And so you ought. I mean to show the tabbies they should not judge until the true facts are known. Exactly who is she, Lord Latham?" Lady Jersey bestowed a curious look on Val while remaining a discreet distance from him, quite as though he was dangerous.

"I am wounded," Val protested. "Since when have I been reduced to Lord Latham?"

"Since you became a dangerous rake, a man a woman dare not trust," Sally said with a flirtatious wave of her fan and a sly smile.

"Of all the utter rot," Val muttered, then apologized for his language. "According to Ferdy, there is a female in London who walks a young lad in the park who resembles me somewhat. I have no idea whom she might be—although I certainly intend to find out. I do not claim to have a monopoly on brown hair and brown eyes nor a slim build. And I declare that I have no children—baseborn or otherwise," he concluded with a wry grin.

"Well that is a comfort to all the hopeful mamas in town with chits to present to Society. Do you intend to visit Almack's when we resume our little Wednesday evening affairs?" Her expression was calculating, as though she dared him to cross some invisible line of her devising.

"If you permit, madam. I am not so foolish as to think I am invulnerable." Val bowed to her in admiration of her ploy.

"Oh," Sally cooed, "I do adore a vulnerable rake. That is the most attractive male alive—far more interesting than a Corinthian." She batted her long lashes at Val, amusement lighting her face.

"Every man, no matter how strong or powerful, becomes a trifle vulnerable when under the spell of a beautiful woman," Val murmured.

"I shall help you," she declared quietly. "I can spread the tale of your innocence, you know, and I shall. I daresay there is not a gossip in town who is not eager to listen to anything I have to offer in the line of a delicious tidbit. And this is quite the loveliest bit of gossip."

Val couldn't suppress a true grin at this bit of understatement. Sally's love of gossip was legendary. He could not have found a better partner to spread his account of mistaken identity as a father of twins.

"I mean to find out who this young woman is. I find the assault on my good name intolerable," he added with a shared look of understanding. Both members of the *ton* knew only too well how fragile that thing called reputation was, and how easily it could be destroyed by vicious rumors and wicked tongues.

"I wish you the best of luck, *mon ami*." Aware that to spend another minute in conference with her shocking guest would court the sort of gossip not to be desired, Sally tapped Val's shoulder with her fan, bestowed on him a somewhat enigmatic smile, then wandered off to tend to her other guests.

Val watched her move gracefully through the throng of the very upper crust of English society. Did it really matter if he lost entrée to this group? Was it truly important that he be able to mingle with these aristocrats? Indeed it was, he decided after a moment's reflection. It was the life he was born to and he knew no other. His entire future depended upon making a suitable alliance with a young woman of impeccable virtue and proper origins—the precise opposite, clearly, of the woman in the park.

Across London, the young woman in question sat at the bedside of a rather small lad with tousled brown hair and fevered brown eyes. He gave an impressive sneeze and reached for the proffered square of linen so as to blow his nose.

"I am very sick," Anthony said, with not a little satisfaction. "I am much sicker than Doro."

"Indeed you are, love. And sick little boys need to drink their broth and sleep," his Cousin Phoebe reminded him.

"We cannot walk in the park tomorrow," he said with a woeful shake of his head. "I am too sick."

"The weather is dreadful, so you will not miss a thing," Phoebe said with a half smile, knowing Anthony was determined to reap as much attention as possible from his cold. Not that it couldn't yet turn nasty, but at present he needed rest and chicken broth.

"I do not like to miss our walks. Do you think the man with the monkey will be there tomorrow?"

"Not in the rain, love. Besides, I would not walk in the park without you, not even if Doro could go with me. And I would not dream of taking her out in this chill. No, we will have to wait for you to be all better first," Phoebe assured her charge, caressing his head lightly with a gentle touch.

"I will try hard," Anthony promised, looking not the least like a peer of the land, the Viscount Waring, but rather a little boy who just needed a bit of loving and care.

Once she had soothed him to sleep, Phoebe left a nursemaid to keep watch, and returned to the drawing room to find her hostess, the twins' charming and not-very-elderly great-aunt, the Dowager Lady Latham.

"And how does little Anthony fare?" Lady Latham demanded when Phoebe had joined her.

"He is not seriously ill, but one never knows about a cold. Without warning it can turn into a putrid sore throat, or even pneumonia. I promised him that I would not walk in the park without him tomorrow. Indeed, if the rain continues that will be no hardship." Phoebe stood by the window of the large, attractive room, staring out into the falling rain seen by the light of the torches across the street. A gust of wind spattered raindrops against the windowpane and she shivered, wrapping her arms about her waist.

"Here, put on this shawl," her ladyship commanded with concern. "It will never do for you to take ill as well. And Dorothea? Is her cold better?"

"Indeed, ma'am. Doro rarely takes ill and recovers with a rapidity that irritates Anthony no end." Phoebe smiled and then crossed the room to take a chair by the fire where Lady Latham sat, accepting the fine cashmere shawl with gratitude.

"It is a good thing you wrote me of your difficulties regarding the children's inheritance," her ladyship said with a nod of her head. "I am come to think all solicitors are nincompoops. Fancy frightening you like that—making you believe all their funds would be cut off unless you found a husband. What utter nonsense. And just how do they think widows cope with raising a family once their husband is buried?"

"As to that, I do not know. I confess the missive was most intimidating. I thought perhaps your word might carry far more weight than mine." Phoebe exchanged a wry look with the older and wiser woman.

"The most sensible thing my nephew George ever did was to appoint you the guardian of his children. Never mind that you are the only one they have, you have cared for them since they were born. I know how Camilla and George liked to go haring about hither and yon. I would wager that you saw more of Doro and Anthony than their parents ever did."

Phoebe shifted uneasily in her chair. "What you say may be true, my lady, but they did love their children very much."

"So much so that they had to tear off to some silly party and be shot coming home by some miserable highwayman. Bah!" Lady Latham declared. She stretched out an arthritic hand to the fire, obviously enjoying the warmth.

"Would you like to soak your hand in a lovely herbal bath I know about? It would take but a few moments to find the herbs and it is a most soothing feeling." Phoebe jumped up, intent on changing the subject for the moment and wishing to perform a kindness to the woman who had done so much to help Phoebe in her distress.

"You will spoil me so that I shan't wish to ever let you go back to the country," her ladyship grumbled, but nodded her agreement to the notion nevertheless.

When Phoebe returned with a fragrant basin of steaming water and herbs, her ladyship found to her amazement that the soak felt quite wonderful and sighed with pleasure at the relief offered.

"I shall make you a lotion which I can massage into your hand. I think you will see a slight improvement if you do this regularly, although I cannot promise anything," Phoebe said while keeping a careful eye on the basin and her ladyship.

"Which is more than the doctors do. Those quacks offer ridiculous nostrums at outrageous costs, while promising the moon in return. What they want is the moon in their pocket!" her ladyship complained.

"Yes, ma'am," Phoebe said, concealing a smile behind a quickly raised hand.

"What do you intend to do now that I have managed to straighten out that fool solicitor? I will not have you leaving so soon. You have just barely arrived. I insist you remain until summer. There is much for the children to see and do in the city, you know. There is the Tower, and the animals at the Exeter 'Change, and the museums, not to forget the occasional balloon ascension in the park."

"The children would dearly love to see as much as they could," Phoebe said wistfully, thinking that the children would benefit from any sort of cultural activity, having been confined to the country all their young lives.

"And what about you, young woman?" her ladyship demanded when Phoebe leaned over to check the temperature of the water. "I would see you do a bit of socializing as well. In fact, as soon as Anthony is feeling more the thing, I believe we ought to attend the theater."

"The children would enjoy a pantomime," Phoebe said with a grin.

"They will see one. I was thinking more of you. To my way of thinking, you deserve a bit of pleasure. And a few new gowns. Tell me, does the money allotted you in compensation for caring for the children permit a decent wardrobe? You look more like a governess than a lady."

Accepting Lady Latham's interest as giving her the right to ask outrageous questions, Phoebe answered her with more truth than usual when queried about her status.

"I have been given no compensation, my lady. But please understand, I care for the twins because I love them, and who else would tend to them if I failed them?"

"What? No compensation? That is the outside of enough!" With her good hand her ladyship reached for a small bell and rang it with an indignant shake. When her butler entered, Lady Latham said, "Send for that old fool of a solicitor, Smedley. There is a wrong that needs to be corrected at once. Oh, and send for Madame Clotilde as well. We will need her immediately if we are to be in time."

"But, dear ma'am," Phoebe protested.

"If there is anything I detest it is a young woman in drab gray who looks depressingly proper. When Madam and I are done with you, you will be a new woman. Just see if you won't." Her ladyship withdrew her hand from the soak, blotted it in the towel proffered by Phoebe, and looked much like a puppy that has managed to tree a cat.

"Oh, dear," Phoebe said, sitting down abruptly. "What next?"

Chapter 2

It rained for days, that misty, cold, dreary sort of rain that chills one to the bone. Though Phoebe scarcely noticed the state of the weather. What with a meeting with Mr. Popham, the elderly solicitor who permitted Aunt Annis—as Lady Latham asked Phoebe call her—to browbeat him unmercifully and the confrontation with Madame Clotilde and tending a fretful Anthony, her days were full to overflowing.

The solicitor—a grayish, thin man who could easily disappear into the mist given a chance—ultimately agreed it was most unfair to expect Phoebe to care for the children without some sort of fund for expenses. He had muttered something about the estate, the proper allocation of funds, and other legal sounding things. All objections were swept aside by the force of Lady Latham's displeasure.

"For, good sir," she exclaimed, "as guardian and cousin of Viscount Waring, she must present a proper picture to Society. She can scarce do so without a farthing to her name." Which was an exaggeration Phoebe said later, since she had a modest stipend from her father.

"I agree, madam," Mr. Popham finally said with a sigh. "I shall see to a generous allowance for Miss Thorpe immediately." Looking sadly harried, he discreetly blotted his brow with a square of white cambric when Lady Latham turned her attention elsewhere for a few moments.

When her ladyship returned her sharp gaze to the solicitor, he almost seemed to shrink. Phoebe silently admitted she would hate to do any sort of bargaining or business with her ladyship. Her powers of reasoning were formidable indeed.

"See to it that there is enough for good clothing for Miss

Thorpe, not to mention those little necessities that set the well-bred lady apart from the ordinary miss," Lady Latham insisted.

"Indeed, Madam. I would never think of being niggardly in my arrangements for Miss Thorpe," he replied with quiet dignity. He left shortly thereafter, looking immensely relieved to be spared additional scoldings and orders.

Once those arrangements were settled, it only wanted for Madame Clotilde to make her appearance.

Phoebe almost chuckled when the fashionably, yet quite judiciously, gowned woman with the most improbable shade of red hair swept into the morning room where Phoebe and her ladyship sat reading the newspapers. She was trailed by two assistants bearing boxes of pins, stacks of fabric samples, and books of designs.

Apparently, Aunt Annis had sufficient standing to be able to summon a premier mantuamaker to her home on a moment's notice. Phoebe wondered precisely what that message sent to Madame Clotilde had contained.

"Well, I can see I shall have an excellent form upon which to work my magic," the little French woman—if she was indeed that nationality—declared after inspecting Phoebe from every angle. "The soft black curls, large blue eyes, and such creamy skin—ah, that makes my task easier," Madame declared with her hands clasped before her. "Not too tall, slender and shapely . . . you will take the *ton* by storm."

When Phoebe insisted she had no desire to take the *ton* or anything else by storm, Lady Latham overrode her protest and commanded they proceed. The following two hours were extremely wearing. Later, Phoebe left the morning room feeling as though she had done battle, and knew a bit of sympathy for Mr. Popham. She suspected it was a bit like having a very large dray wagon run you down—overwhelming.

Caring for a fretful little boy was a distinct pleasure after the time spent selecting colors and fabrics and styles that Phoebe declared too fashionable and thought too expensive. She entered his room with distinct relief.

"Am I not getting better soon?" Anthony demanded in a near-whine when Phoebe settled by his bed.

"Why do we not have Doro join us for a game?" Phoebe countered. "The rain is quite dreadful, you know, and she is near bored to tears with being alone. Do you suppose we might entertain her?"

Intrigued with the notion that he might help amuse his younger—by twenty minutes—sister, Anthony loftily assured Phoebe that her proposal would be just the ticket.

The trio happily settled into an afternoon of games, with much gleeful laughter from the winner and big sighs from the loser, who most often happened to be Phoebe.

Phoebe cherished these times of warmth and closeness, particularly since she had been so worried these last months that Mr. Popham would take the children from her care and place them with strangers. She could thank Lady Latham—that is, Aunt Annis—for that reprieve.

"Bloody rain," Val muttered before resuming his pacing across the Turkey carpet that covered his study floor. His dark brown eyes revealed vexation, and he ran impatient fingers through the thick, dark hair that was now in total disarray. His garb had less than its usual elegance.

"Finding the mystery woman elusive?" a sympathetic Ferdy inquired.

"I roamed the park this morning, as I have every morning since I last spoke with you, and finally decided that only a fool would be out in this weather."

"And you doubt she's a fool." Ferdy settled back into the sturdy wing chair by the fireplace, relishing the warmth and comfort on the unpleasant day.

"Well, it was a mere drizzle when I left the house," Val said, with a touch of defensiveness. "There were a goodly number of nannies marching along with well-covered tots in tow."

"Cheer up, the rain cannot last forever," Ferdy offered by way of consolation. "What do you say we toddle off to White's—unless," he said with hope, "you would rather eat here." He leaned forward as though to rise.

Knowing that his friend far preferred the quiet of the town house and the ministrations of Val's first-rate cook, he gave Ferdy a wry grin. "I am being a gudgeon. I suspect I have become obsessed with that woman, whoever she might be. As a matter of fact, I ordered our dinner when you arrived."

"Good fellow," Ferdy murmured, settling back against the softly cushioned chair with satisfaction.

"You haven't learned anything more about her and those twins, have you?" Val inquired with deceptive casualness. The entire matter was beginning to drive him around the bend. As he had admitted to Ferdy, he was becoming obsessed with her—and he hadn't even the faintest idea what she looked like!

"Not a thing," Ferdy admitted.

"It would help if I could describe her more clearly. You said she is pretty. Could you be more specific? Heaven knows you can describe the newest opera dancer down to the measurement of her ankle."

Ferdy grinned at this acknowledgment of his capabilities, then thought for a few moments. "Like I said, she gives the impression of a pretty woman. Hair is always covered by a bonnet, so that ain't a clue. Never looks at a chap, so I can't say to her eye color. Nice skin, though," Ferdy said in reflection.

"Do you have any notion how many females there are in this city with nice skin?" Val said with derision.

"You did ask," Ferdy pointed out mildly. He placed his hands over his somewhat ample stomach and gave Val a righteous look. "Ain't as though anyone else has offered to help you."

Val gave his friend a contrite look and ceased his pacing. Dropping into the chair opposite Ferdy, he contemplated the nicely blazing fire. "There has to be someone who knows of her. Blast it all—she cannot live in the air, she must have a home."

"I gather you tried the agencies?"

"Every one of them. The first time I said I was looking for a woman and her twins, I garnered such a look as to put me in a temper. The next time I inquired for a friend of my sister's."

"But you do not have a sister," Ferdy reminded him with a puzzled look.

"I know that. It made the query seem less suspect," Val

said, with more patience than he had shown to the agency man.

At that point Priddy entered the cozy room to inform the gentlemen that dinner was served.

Val and Ferdy promptly—Ferdy was always prompt to meals—rose and went along to where the table was nicely set for two gentlemen to dine in comfort and pleasure.

It would be wrong to think of Ferdy as fat, for he was never that. He was big—there was no other word for him. Sandy hair flopped over a broad brow above kind hazel eyes set in a usually genial face—all of a large size. His perfectly fitting coats took far more fabric to make than the average, and he towered over the tailor who had the making of them. His mere size was sufficient to prevent any sprouts of nobility from challenging him to anything—not that he was inclined that direction, being of a most easygoing nature.

They chatted easily the remainder of the meal, then decided that it was dashed dull to sit around the house.

"I promised Mrs. Bottomley I'd attend the little party she is giving her niece, to more or less introduce her around. Sally Jersey's gossip proved effective—at least for her. Won't give a ball for a niece, it seems. Shall we head that direction?"

"Why not?" Ferdy said, while casting a longing look at the last piece of Madeira cake that reposed on the sideboard.

"After you finish your cake, of course," Val concluded with an understanding smile.

"Good," Ferdy said, helping himself to the cake and gesturing toward his cup. The butler, knowing Ferdy well, was ready with the coffeepot and filled the cup to the brim.

"And tomorrow I shall be stationed in the park at an early hour. Pray it does not rain," Val said fervently.

"I've a cousin who is a bishop. We might ask him."

"To look for the woman?" Val said, quite confused by this turn of conversation.

"No, to pray it stops raining," Ferdy replied, then rose from the table with a satisfied air and not a crumb of cake remaining on his plate.

* * *

"I would rather have cake, if you please," Anthony said politely.

"If you wish to venture outside come the morning you had best eat your potatoes and fish," Phoebe said to the disgusted boy.

"I would rather have cake," he repeated firmly.

"So would I," Phoebe said in a reasonable tone, "but one cannot always have what one wishes."

"What do you wish for, Cousin Phoebe?" little Doro inquired between nibbles of her buttered potatoes.

"Oh, nicer weather and our walks in the park."

"I will pray for sunshine," Doro offered, quite certain she would be heard.

"You do that, love. Now, what fascinating thing shall we do before bedtime?" Phoebe saw to the last bite of fish into her charge's mouths, then gestured to the maid to bring in the pudding.

"Great-aunt Latham bought us a game today. May we learn it?" Doro said in her sweet little voice.

"Oh, jolly good. I'll wager I can beat you, Cousin Phoebe."

"You are so good at games, I have no doubt but what you will, love." Phoebe smiled fondly at the children, who were near as like being her own.

"So here you are," Lady Latham said from the doorway of the nursery. "Once your new clothes are delivered, there will be an end to this sort of thing."

"Indeed not, ma'am. If I cannot spend time with the twins, the other affairs will have to go. Doro and Anthony come first."

"Not even a parent is that devoted," her ladyship observed. "You owe it to yourself *and* to them to get out a bit now and again. I would not want you to end up an embittered old maid. After all, they will grow up before you know it and then where will you be?" Lady Latham said with perfect logic.

The quietly spoken words unsettled Phoebe. Had she so wrapped herself up in the children that she was in danger of losing her own identity?

"Allow me to spend the days with them and I will be happy to attend you come the evenings," Phoebe said at last.

"Well, if you desire to wander in the park come the day, see to it that you have a maid along. I should hate to have anyone think you less than you are."

"And what am I, dear ma'am?" Phoebe inquired with a trace of amusement.

"You are a young lady, and do not forget it." With that final pronouncement, Phoebe was left to join the children in a rousing game of Mother Goose and the Golden Egg, played on a board before the fire. Since there were any number of penalties and much gleeful laughter, Phoebe was able to put aside her disturbing thoughts until she went to her bed.

Then they surfaced again. Was she giving the children too much attention, spoiling them? She did not think it possible, but perhaps it was.

When the morning dawned bright and clear, she forgot her worries of the night before. Nothing would do but for all to be dressed in warm clothing and to head for the park as soon as was reasonable.

Doro danced at Phoebe's side along the path that led toward the Serpentine River. Anthony raced here and there, eager to examine everything he saw. Frequently they paused to exclaim over some discovery and admire the amazing items uncovered—like the empty shell of a bird's egg and a very large black bug that Doro decided was "horrid" while Anthony declared it "smashing."

Phoebe held tightly to Doro's little hand, glancing around her and noting the park was thin of company this morning. The Season was upon them and most likely there were more demanding things to be done. She pitied the maid who had been ordered to go along with the trio; the girl looked chilled and bored.

"Oh, ducks," Doro cried with delight, freeing her hand to caper along the path until she stood at a safe distance from the water's edge.

Phoebe undid the paper parcel of old bread and offered the contents to the children. Soon the twins were happily engrossed in dividing bits and pieces of bread among the collection of ducks.

"That one is very greedy, Cousin Phoebe," Doro observed after a particularly pushy duck had driven her to take a step backward.

"Ducks are like that at times, I expect. They like not having to ferret out their own food."

Anthony stamped his feet at the obnoxious duck and, with a triumphant whoop of delight, drove it back into the water.

"Be careful, love," Phoebe admonished.

Some distance away, the little scene was closely watched by a fascinated Val. This had to be his quarry—a young, neatly dressed woman accompanied by a pair of twins. She seemed to be genuinely caring for the children, laughing and watching over her charges with more solicitude than the nannies and maids he had observed elsewhere in the park in the past few days.

When she turned and he was able to see her face, he was agreeably surprised to note that she possessed a pretty countenance, with a dainty nose, rosy cheeks, and a pleasing mouth that appeared to be made for laughing. She seemed to do quite a bit of that.

While he strolled a bit closer, he surreptitiously studied her garments. She wore simple, yet well-made clothing of obvious quality. And, he admitted reluctantly, she did not have the look nor the demeanor of a doxy. His theory on that appeared to be all wet.

The piping voices of the delighted children turned his attention to them. The little girl glanced his way and he could detect a faint resemblance to the woman. The boy kept his back to Val, so it was impossible to determine whether or not there was the strong resemblance that had been asserted.

Suddenly the lad turned and Val found himself quite stunned. At Latham Hall there was a painting done of himself at about the same age and this child might have posed for it, so alike were they. Val took back every unkind thought he had nurtured about those who had twitted him. They had every right to be suspicious about the boy's paternity.

Why had this boy been kept hidden from him? Val *knew* he had never seen this young woman before in his life, yet there was no denying the incredible similarity between himself and the lad. So . . . how did one account for the likeness?

He pretended an interest in watching the antics of the ducks while continuing to edge closer. How could he strike up an acquaintance with the trio? He dismissed the proper-looking maid who huddled some distance away as being of no importance. There had to be something he could do. He reflected it was rather amusing that a gentleman of the *ton*—a noted Corinthian and member of the peerage, in fact—accustomed to having women seek him out, should be in this predicament.

"Look, Cousin Phoebe," cried the lad, "this duck likes me. I should like to have it for a pet!"

Phoebe? Not at all an unusual name, Val thought, but he knew he had never spent time with a woman by that name. But the boy called her Cousin. Cousin? That made it even more curious and opened the door to an alarming number of possibilities. It meant that the mother was someone else! How dreadful.

"I fear that her ladyship would not approve of that, Anthony. A kitten or puppy is more the acceptable pet."

"May I have a puppy, then? Please Cousin Phoebe?" the lad wheedled.

"We shall see."

"That means no," the little girl observed sagely. "Cousin Phoebe always says that when we ask for something we ought not have."

The woman laughed, a remarkably delightful sound that reminded Val of music.

"I fear you have caught me out, young lady," the woman said. "I expect we had best save the puppy for when we return home." She offered the lad a comforting pat on the arm and smiled at the little girl in such a way that Val felt a tightening in his throat. He decided that she couldn't be a harpy, given her fetching ways.

"You promise I may have a puppy then?" the boy artfully begged, obviously determined to nail down this auspicious opportunity before it was lost.

"What sort?" their cousin asked.

"A beagle," the lad replied promptly, clearly having given the matter some thought.

"Well, I've no doubt that might be arranged." She handed the children the last of the bread, then watched the ducks press closer.

"That nasty duck is here again, Cousin Phoebe," the girl complained.

"Shoo," cried Cousin Phoebe, to Val's amusement. She took her umbrella and waved it about, irritating the bird, who cleverly dodged it in hope of more bread.

Determined to lure the bird away from his sister, the boy charged forward with a fat crumb—with disastrous results. He fell into the Serpentine and rapidly disappeared beneath the surface of the muddy water!

The splash stirred Val into action. Stripping off his coat and tossing it aside, he ran forward and plunged into the Serpentine. Finding the lad wasn't quite as simple as he expected. The boy had floundered about and sunk to the bottom in what seemed like seconds. The ducks had roiled up the water—which was already quite muddy—so that Val couldn't see a thing.

On the shore the little girl and the Cousin Phoebe creature cried in alarm while Val made another attempt, this time with success.

He hauled up the dripping, bedraggled child from the mud, and carried him to where the others anxiously waited.

Glancing quickly at the little girl, he turned to the woman and tried to keep his voice calm. "Here, let me put him on his stomach. We have to force out as much water as possible, else he'll suffer from all that he's swallowed." The woman and girl stood back, allowing Val to gently pummel the boy, encouraging the removal of all the filthy water.

When the child had coughed up an alarming amount of liquid and was more himself, Val sat back on his heels and shivered while he watched the boy closely to see how he'd fare.

"Here, sir, your coat," the woman named Phoebe said with clear concern in her voice. "Though I fear you may ruin it if you put it on. But I most heartily thank you for saving Anthony from a watery grave. I had no idea the water was that deep so close to shore." She dropped to her knees beside the child, her concern for the lad overriding any interest she might have otherwise shown in the stranger who had appeared so suddenly.

"I suspect it varies a good deal," Val said while stuffing his arms into the sleeves of his coat and giving thanks that he had not adopted the extremely tight fit favored by so many of the masculine members of the *ton*.

"Anthony has been ill, sir," observed the girl.

"Permit me to present Dorothea, sir. And this is her twin, Anthony. We are very grateful to you." Miss Phoebe had wrapped a thick shawl about the boy and now hushed him to silence when he would talk. "And, indeed, the boy has been most ill. I can only hope that he does not suffer a reversal from this wetting."

Even if he had saved the child's life, good manners did not permit them to introduce themselves—more's the pity, Val thought. He studied the boy, then looked at her, wondering what it would take to find out more about her.

It was at that moment that she looked at Val, really looked at him. He found her reaction amusing.

"Oh, my," she said in amazement. "I declare, you two look alike." She picked up the tightly wrapped boy and clutched him to her while staring at Val.

"Yes, I noticed that," Val said wryly.

Phoebe whoever-she-was merely looked amused rather than alarmed or horrified, as he thought might have been the case. She gave him a quick smile, then turned her attention to the boy.

"Well, the important thing at the moment is to take Anthony home and see that he has a hot bath and dry clothing. And if I may say so, that is what you need as well, good sir," Phoebe concluded, distracted with worry.

She was quite lovely, he decided. Several lustrous black curls had escaped from the confines of her bonnet, and she had entrancing blue eyes that crinkled in the most delightful way when she smiled. In all, she was a pretty, graceful creature. And when she had clutched the boy to her, a part of Val could not fail to note that she was nicely endowed as well. Her charming figure certainly qualified her for the role of a doxy—although her speech proclaimed her in possession of a good education, and her manner was exceedingly well-bred.

He wanted to learn more about her. "Could I not assist you? Surely the boy is heavy for you to carry. You need help," Val insisted.

"The maid went for assistance immediately, sir. But I am most grateful for your offer when you must be chilled to the bone." Phoebe paused, turning her head to look along the road that paralleled Rotten Row. "Ah, here comes the carriage now." She gave Val an anxious smile when he gently took the boy from her, moving toward the carriage.

"If you would be so kind as to help me place him inside, I would appreciate it. And then, if I may repeat myself, you really need to return to your lodgings at once. I am greatly indebted to you and I would not wish you to suffer in return for your noble deed."

Her earlier amusement had fled and was replaced by her real concern for the boy. The morning sun scarcely warmed him, and the lad trembled with the aftereffects of his cold bath.

"I trust we shall meet again, good lady," Val persisted, hoping she might reveal something. "I should like to call—to find out how the boy does."

"She isn't a lady, she is our Cousin Phoebe," Doro said, quite diverted with the handsome gentleman who was eyeing her cousin with avid interest.

"But *which* Cousin Phoebe, that is the question," Val said, determined to learn more if possible. While she would do nothing so improper, one of the children might reveal her last name.

"There's only one like her," the lad piped up.

"I am certain Anthony will be fine, sir. There is no need for you to concern yourself, although it is most kind of you." Dismissal rang clear in Cousin Phoebe's voice.

Then the maid, who had silently stood waiting for some signal, clambered into the hackney and closed the door. Val shivered as the vehicle bearing the trio disappeared from view.

Val suspected that the boy was right. Certainly he had never encountered anyone quite like Phoebe in all his days.

A violent shiver and the approach of several men on horseback reminded Val of his condition. Fortunately, another hackney approached and he hailed it with relief.

"You be the gentleman who needs a ride home?" the jarvey queried.

"I am," Val confirmed, surprised the maid would have the forethought to send another carriage after him. Or had Phoebe paused in her hurry home to consider his state? He preferred to think that Miss Phoebe of the black curls and delightful blue eyes had thought of him.

At least he hoped it was *Miss* Phoebe. Armed only with her first name, he was little better off than before. But he had met the chit and she was not at all what he had expected. He was determined to discover more about her.

Once home, he bathed and changed clothing with dispatch, then sat by his fireside while contemplating what little he had learned. It had taken a ruined set of clothes and the loss of a favored pair of boots to find out that Ferdy was right, that one of the twins was a dead ringer for himself and that the young woman who seemed to be in charge of them was a very pretty miss.

But he would wager all of his considerable fortune that she was no doxy. But if not that, *what* was she and *where* could he find her? And what could explain the boy's eerie resemblance to himself? He would not rest until he knew more about Miss Phoebe—for, as the boy said, there was only one like her.

Chapter 3

Her name is Phoebe and I couldn't find out another thing about her," Val said with disgust. "You were right about one thing, though—the boy looks amazingly like me. She is not their mother, however. They referred to her as *Cousin* Phoebe, which makes the situation all the more difficult." Val paced up and down before his drawing room window, ignoring the passing scene below. "How do I locate a mother when all we know about is the cousin?"

Ferdy leaned back in his chair, looking thoughtful. "Couldn't see if she was married, I suppose."

"Not while she was wearing gloves. Can't tell whether or not a woman is married as long as she's in gloves—I've had a bit of practice in that line," Val admitted with a rueful glance at his friend. Val supposed his past history as a bit of a rake would not help his credit in this matter in the least. Women in particular were inclined to believe the worst about a fellow who was in the petticoat line. And, he had to confess, he did like the ladies.

"And another thing," Val said consideringly, "she was not the least flirtatious. Oh, I know the lad had taken a wetting, but most of the women I have met would have taken advantage of the situation to further our acquaintance. She scarcely looked at me. And when she did, I'd swear she was amused!" Val concluded with a touch of injury. "Imagine, looking at me with amusement."

The more Val thought on it, the more his feeling of ire grew. Just who did this . . . this nobody think she was? She had not appeared the least impressed with his rescue. But then, perhaps she didn't realize precisely who he was—he also had the lowering notion that she cared not a whit.

"Could be she is their mother and has raised them to call

her cousin—if she is unmarried. Neater that way . . . fewer complications," Ferdy said with a raise of his craggy brows.

"Possibly. However, I would stake my reputation as a connoisseur of the feminine line that 'Cousin Phoebe' is the single sort. She did not *look* married. Didn't have that smug glow you would normally see on a young married woman who has produced twins."

"You are the expert," Ferdy said with a grin. Then he added somewhat pensively, "Sometimes I believe the main reason I remain at your side is to learn more about the fair sex. You are a prime one with the ladies."

"You are an apt pupil if that is the case—even if you do limit your attention to opera dancers. My vaunted expertise is not of much help in this instance. Apparently this paragon among women does not go anywhere save the park and is unknown to anyone I know in London. Surely she does not hibernate between visits to Hyde Park. She *must* do something else!"

"What do you plan to do next, now that you have seen her and the twins?" Ferdy asked.

Val ran a hand over his face, admittedly frustrated. Nothing had gone his way in this matter. The worst of it was that although he tried to make it known that he was not the father of the delightful—and he supposed that they were—children, no one, especially the women, seemed to really believe him.

Oh, they made noises like they did, but he suspected that inwardly they believed that where there was smoke, there was fire, or something of that nature. If the lad were not his duplicate, it would be far easier to deny having sired the pair. But as it was, Society was holding him responsible for the supposed by-blows.

It was one thing for old Billy to have a raft of children by Mrs. Jordan, the actress; a king's son might scrape by with that sort of behavior. It was quite another for a baron from a respectable family line to behave in so reprehensible a manner. Never mind that such things happened with distressing frequency and were hushed up by all concerned if possible.

"You could try Bow Street."

Val shook his head. "No, that is a last resort. It would be bound to leak out that I was trying to hunt the girl down. I suspect that would only fuel more gossip. However"—and he stabbed the air with a well-manicured finger—"Rosbert has always served me well when I desired a bit of information. There have been times," Val said with a grin, sharing a meaningful look with his friend, "when I wanted to find out vital facts."

Ferdy chuckled at the delectable memories of what that information had produced for his friend.

Val crossed the elegant, although simply furnished, room to tug the bell pull. Within minutes, his valet entered with a questioning expression.

"You rang, milord?" Rosbert, a slim, graying man in his late thirties, stood at attention, his bland expression concealing everything he thought. Val always had the feeling that Rosbert knew what was wanted even before asked.

"Indeed, Rosbert. I have a mission for you. I want to find out where a certain young lady resides. You are the most discreet person I know. She is in the park of a morning. I shall go there tomorrow and point her out to you—providing she comes, that is." He turned to an interested Ferdy and added, "When the lad took a wetting she murmured something about his having been ill."

"That explains why she was not to be seen when you first went looking for her," Ferdy said with satisfaction. It had irked him to tell Val about the girl only to have her fail to appear.

"Very good, sir," Rosbert replied with proper enthusiasm. "I will be ready to go with you in the morning. Anything unusual about the case, sir?"

"There are twins involved, one of whom looks remarkably like me."

"It was the oddest thing, Aunt Annis," Phoebe told Lady Latham over a cup of tea. She had settled Anthony into his featherbed with a hot brick at his feet and a mustard compress on his chest, and was grateful for a quiet coze, "the gentleman who rescued Anthony from the Serpentine looked amazingly like him, enough to be his father." Phoebe recalled the stunned expression on that handsome face. At the time it had amused her that such a polished gentleman should be shown to such a disadvantage.

"Did he, now? That *is* interesting," the older lady replied in considering tones. She sipped her tea, a sly smile crossing her face, as she contemplated this bit of information. Unfortunately, Phoebe missed that look.

"Do you know something about him?" Phoebe asked when she glanced up from her teacup. "Or whom he might be?"

"I doubt it. With my hand aching so badly these past months I have been inclined to remain at home. However, that potion you gave me has helped. I believe that when your new clothes arrive, we ought to accept a few invitations. I have put it about that I am feeling better. In fact, I intend to have a small gathering here quite soon."

"I am so pleased, my lady," Phoebe said, moved by the generosity of the dear woman who had taken her and the twins into her home with so warm a reception. "I know you do not wish payment, but I am delighted if I may help you in any way."

"You will, dear girl, you will," Lady Latham said in the oddest and most obscure manner.

Phoebe ignored the peculiar comment, chalking it up to the peculiarities of aging.

Within several days, during which Phoebe remained at home to keep a close eye on Anthony, the pretty gowns began to arrive—rich rose sarcenet, deep blue jaconet trimmed with what seemed like a mile of delicate silver lace, and the loveliest white muslin, with rows and rows of tucks around the skirt that made it bell out most prettily.

She was not surprised when her ladyship announced over a late supper that they would have a few close friends in the following day.

"You are to wear the rose sarcenet and that string of pearls you brought with you," Lady Latham ordered nicely. "Most acceptable for a proper young woman."

"I would never wish to look improper," Phoebe reproved.

"Nor shall you. And I think it would be charming for Anthony and Dorothea to pop in to make a curtsy. Such lovely children. You have done exceedingly well in raising them. What a pity you do not have little ones of your own to train." The older woman narrowed her eyes in speculation when she saw Phoebe's cheeks pinken.

"Is there a gentleman you fancy, my dear?" Lady Latham inquired, her gaze sharpening while she watched Phoebe.

"What a shocking thing to say," Phoebe declared with a chuckle. "How am I to answer such a question?"

"The truth. Always tell the truth, even if you feel you might not be believed. For a lie will out in the end, believe me." Lady Latham gave a firm nod of her head to underscore her conclusion.

Surprised at such a stout declaration, Phoebe gave her a troubled smile, then replied, "The vicar at the village church is most charming, if ineligible. I doubt Aldous Clark has two spare farthings to rub together. But . . . he is exceedingly kind and wonderfully good to the children. He has given Anthony lessons, you see. I enjoy his company."

"I see a great deal more than you think. You may as well forget about the man, for he will not do for you," her ladyship declared in a crisp voice. "I feel certain that together we can find you someone who will be acceptable."

"He would have to love the children as I do, you know that," Phoebe cautioned.

"As to that, few men pay any attention to their brats, more's the pity. If they see them upon the rare occasion it is not at all unusual. But if you wish a doting father, I will see what can be done. It will make it next to impossible, you know," her ladyship cautioned, another sly look crossing her face. "Doting fathers are not at all fashionable these days—can't recall when they were."

The following afternoon, a sizable number of women of the highest standing in Society gathered in Lady Latham's drawing room for an afternoon of tea and music and gossip. The little party was going well, with Phoebe feeling as though she had made a favorable impression, when it came time to have the twins make their curtsy.

"My grand-niece and nephew, Dorothea and Anthony," her ladyship announced, omitting last name or title, which Phoebe thought odd. Anthony—by now much recovered from his wetting—entered the room, tugging a curious Doro behind him. Both were dressed in their finest. Anthony made a creditable bow, thanks to Smedley's instruction. Doro curtsied just as Lady Latham had coached her to do and a very pretty job she made of it, too, in her delicate white muslin sashed in blue satin.

Silence fell over the room as one by one the ladies took note of the twins, stared at Phoebe, looked to the very smug Lady Latham, then back to Anthony and Doro.

"You are their cousin?" Lady Jersey asked with a skeptical note in her voice, which could be forgiven, seeing how much Doro resembled Phoebe.

"First cousin, once removed, actually. My cousin and her husband died after being shot by a highwayman. My cousin's husband lived long enough to grant me custody of their twins," Phoebe explained with the ease of one who had had to do this recitation a goodly number of times.

"I see," said her ladyship with a confused expression on her face, indicating that Phoebe's simple answer had raised more questions than answers.

"Shot by highwaymen?" murmured one of the ladies to another. "What a sad story." Her dubious expression made it clear she disbelieved the tale.

"How very convenient for some people," murmured another, arching her brows.

Phoebe hastily excused the children, then looked in confusion to Lady Latham. This was a most peculiar reaction to the twins. Had her ladyship expected something of the sort? She wore a suspiciously satisfied expression.

"Indeed, I am very pleased that dearest Phoebe brought the children to me," her ladyship said in an oddly bland voice. "There was a silly fuss over the custody, you see. I declare, solicitors are such fubsy creatures. As though a girl as proper as Phoebe would not make the dearest guardian for the twins. She has seen to Anthony's training, and Doro is a bright little thing. They love their cousin deeply."

"You must admit it is highly unusual for a young woman to be given custody of a pair of children," Lady Jersey said, with more than a little curiosity.

"I have every confidence that Phoebe will be an excellent mother to Anthony and Dorothea," Lady Latham said with a touch of aggressiveness in her voice. "When it comes time for the boy to go off to Eton, we will have nothing to be ashamed of, I assure you. He will take his rightful place as Viscount Waring. I feel certain that his vast estate will be properly managed, for the solicitor is quite zealous in that regard."

"The Waring estate?" Lady Jersey said, her eyes widening at this bit of news.

"Of course. Beeches has been in the family for ages."

Her ladyship turned away to request another pot of tea and the subject was abandoned, although Phoebe felt certain that any number of the women burned to inquire more closely as to the children's background. Viscount Waring and his lady had been much about in Society, but never with their children. Phoebe suspected that most had never learned of the twins' birth, since neither George nor Camilla had bothered to send a notice to the London papers.

Feeling rather muddled, she withdrew from the general chitchat, and merely listened. This was a different world, an alien one. Yet for the twins' sake, she thought she must become better acquainted with it. Compared to these women, she felt vastly provincial, even with the rose sarcenet and her single strand of pearls.

At first it had been amusing to watch the women assess her gown and the quality of her jewelry. Before long it began to irk her. How dare they think ill of her!

Then her mind slipped to the gentleman who had saved Anthony from the cold waters of the Serpentine. Even dripping wet, he'd had a self-possession that bespoke enormous confidence. Had she not been so worried about Anthony taking a turn for the worse, she would have been utterly speechless in the face of such polish and aristocratic good looks. And how he had stared at her, much like these women.

Then she realized that one of the women had addressed her. "I do beg your pardon. I fear I was woolgathering."

The woman smiled and a few chuckled when Lady Latham smirked and inserted, "Thinking of a certain gentleman, I make no doubt."

As Phoebe had been thinking of a certain gentleman, although it was not Aldous Clark as Lady Latham most likely thought, she blushed a delicate rose and the subsequent laughter made her turn an even deeper hue.

"Aha! We will not tease you for his identity. I fancy I know who it is. Not one of us has been immune to his charms, my girl. Just do not raise your hopes too high, for no one has captured his heart as yet," Lady Jersey cautioned with a wry smile.

Phoebe was now quite thoroughly confused, for she doubted that Lady Jersey knew of Aldous Clark's existence, much less of her own preoccupation with the unknown gentleman in the park.

"Well, I have high hopes, you may know," Lady Latham declared with a coy smile. "I had thought to venture out again, Sally, my dear," she said in a soft aside to that lady. "Perhaps Almack's?"

"And you wish a voucher for your guest?" Lady Jersey said with barely concealed surprise.

"She will occupy a secure position as my heiress," Lady Latham whispered, deciding on the instant to make this a reality. "After all, she is exceedingly close to Viscount Waring."

"Indeed," breathed Lady Jersey, taking another look at Phoebe, who was now chatting comfortably with Lady Sefton and in glowing good looks in her pretty rose gown. "And what of Lord Latham? I had always understood Val was your heir."

"Val is well to grass—he don't need my money. But a gel needs a comfortable dowry in this world," observed Lady Latham with a fond smile at Phoebe. "Besides, with only his foolish brother, Robert, as heir, Val will most likely wind up as the next Duke of Thurlow."

Lady Jersey digested this bit of information, then said, "I must admit I am a trifle confused. I thought your nephew died a few years ago. I was unaware he had a son." She edged closer so to assure that she alone heard what was to be said. She hated to admit that there was a peer in this world of whom she was ignorant.

"George was a nodcock, I must admit. But the lad *is* his, I assure you." Lady Latham gave Lady Jersey a beseeching look, having been sure to inject a calculated trace of anxiety in her declaration so as to produce the desired effect.

Still at sea but not about to admit it, Lady Jersey breathed a sigh of delight. She was in possession of a juicy tidbit and would decide just how to use it later on. For now, she chose to set the cat among the pigeons.

"The vouchers will be sent to you immediately after I return home. I feel that after Maria"—and she nodded to Lady Sefton, another of the formidable patronesses of Almack's—"has enjoyed such a delightful chat with dear Miss Thorpe that she will agree with my decision and I feel certain the others will as well."

"I count on you to help me in my plan," Lady Latham said quietly before politely turning to answer a query that had arisen from another of the ladies present.

When Phoebe learned later that she was to enter the hallowed halls of Almack's, a social height to which she had never dared aspire, she was speechless.

"But dear ma'am, I shan't know what to say or what to do, and I doubt if I know a single gentleman in London." The elegant man in the park could scarcely count. He might be a lion of Society for all she knew, but she did not even know his name!

"Pish tosh," Lady Latham decried. "I know everyone worth knowing. Just remember that I have your best interests at heart, dear girl." And with that enigmatic smile again fixed on her face, her ladyship announced she would retire for a rest.

Phoebe watched her go up the stairs, a feeling of disquiet stealing over her. Lady Latham appeared to be far deeper than she'd suspected.

"I tell you it is dashed maddening," Val confided to Ferdy while they strolled along to White's that evening. "Sally Jersey gave me a thoughtful stare that had me quivering in my shoes. I fear she has a bee in her bonnet that bodes ill for my future—if she has her way, that is."

"What did she say?" Ferdy dutifully inquired.

"Asked if I intended to grace Almack's this Wednesday, but I've a mind to keep my distance; Sally put me on my guard. Tell you what, you go and report to me if anything interesting or curious happens."

"You know how I detest those affairs. Those twitty girls make me feel like a great bear. I do not want any mother thinking I am on the lookout for a wife."

"Ha!" Val said, then chuckled at the idea of his good friend being leg-shackled. "All the more reason that you attend. Learn what you can, and I will not have to worry about you turning into a moon calf over some chit barely out of the schoolroom."

"The things I do for you," Ferdy said with a good-natured sigh.

"You know I'd do the same for you," Val reminded him, which was true. The unlikely pair had been fast friends for so long that it was unthinkable for one not to help the other when in a pickle.

"Too true," Ferdy said with another sigh, then proceeded to do all he could to forget the Wednesday night obligation with a round of gaming and excellent wine.

Phoebe could not decide whether she was in the doldrums or merely terrified. Wednesday evening had arrived. In spite of repeated urgings to eat, for Lady Latham declared the place offered rather dreary refreshments, Phoebe could barely nibble at the delicious food set before her.

Almack's. The very name gave her shivers.

"You will be as fine as fivepence, my dear girl," Lady Latham admonished.

"I wish I were as convinced of that as you appear to be," Phoebe admitted with a hesitant smile.

"Perfectly painless."

Phoebe studied her ladyship. The older lady—whose age Phoebe had never quite determined, but who appeared very well preserved—looked as though she were hatching some devious plot in her head. What that might be, Phoebe could not begin to hazard, but it made her uneasy.

Long before Phoebe was ready to leave, Lady Latham bore her off in a cloak trimmed in ermine and a delectable evening cap over her dark curls. The white muslin had been a dubious, if agreeable, choice given her age of twenty-two.

"I am not making a come-out," Phoebe had reminded

her. "I scarce qualify as a young miss direct from the schoolroom."

"You have been cheated, then. I mean only to see you have what you deserve."

Innocent words, Phoebe thought as they were whisked along through the streets of London to King Street and Almack's. She glanced out the carriage window as they passed White's, the more elegant gentlemen's club of the city. Traffic had come to a crawl, so she had a chance to peer most closely at the establishment that women were forbidden to enter and where so many gentlemen took refuge.

Was he in there, the gentleman from the park? Her thoughts had turned to him far too often, recalling the way his breeches had clung to rather nice legs and his shirt—plastered to a manly chest—had revealed too much for maidenly sensibilities. She hadn't swooned, for she'd been too worried about Anthony—but she had noticed. Oh, she had noticed. Aldous Clark could not hold a candle to the unknown cavalier.

At last they left the carriage, Phoebe being none the wiser as to the whereabouts of her secret fascination. Her heart fluttered as they climbed the stairs to enter the high-ceilinged room.

Five crystal chandeliers glittered with the light from more candles than she cared to count, and at the far end of the ball room, an orchestra played a boulanger. Phoebe felt her spirits rise at the sprightly music. She told herself that no one could harm her here with Lady Latham to guard her. While the room was not magnificent, as one might have expected of so lofty a place, what it lacked in looks, it made up for in company. The cream of English Society was gathered before her.

"Delighted you could join us, my dear," Lady Jersey purred to Phoebe before introducing her to Lady Cowper.

She thanked her ladyship politely, then accompanied Lady Latham down the length of the room until they found a bench quite obviously meant for the dowagers and chaperones.

Word of the mysterious newcomer to Society had obviously filtered throughout the *ton*. Those ladies who had been present at Lady Latham's afternoon gathering had not remained silent. And as for Lady Jersey, well, she might be teasingly called "Silence," but everyone knew she adored gossip, carrying her bits and scraps about London with delight, and oftentimes not a little malice.

Phoebe was bewildered to find herself besieged with partners. She was more than delighted to discover that she could conduct herself agreeably on the dance floor. Her cousin had entertained often, and had performed all the latest dances from London, and Phoebe had learned them. But learning is one thing; practicing and performing is quite another. She was thankful she'd not forgotten a step.

The evening was well along when Ferdy presented himself to Lady Sefton. She was the patroness who daunted him the least.

"Lord Andrews," she cried with pleasure, "it is a long time since you have joined our little group. We have missed you."

Ferdy gulped and managed a creditable bow. He was not permitted to escape, however. Lady Jersey glided forward to place her slim hand on his arm and gaze up at him with a smile that made him suspicious.

"I have just the partner for you. Allow me to introduce you to Lady Latham's protégé, Miss Thorpe. She will not alarm you in the least," her ladyship added, knowing full well that the very large and impressive Lord Andrews retreated at the sight of a damsel making her come-out. "I am surprised that Val is not with you. He usually supports you when you join us of an evening. Tonight in particular—since Lady Latham would undoubtedly welcome his assistance in launching her charge. Not that the girl has needed his polished presence. She does very well for herself."

"He was busy," Ferdy managed to say in his pleasant tenor voice.

Just then the country dance being performed concluded. Before Phoebe could make the customary walk around the room with her partner, Lady Jersey crooked her finger at the young man, who immediately obeyed her summons.

Once he was excused, Lady Jersey gave Phoebe a rather feline smile and said, "Allow me to present Ferdinand, Lord Andrews as an acceptable partner for the next dance. I believe you two will find a good deal in common." With that enigmatic remark, she glided away to confront another bachelor who had obviously hoped to escape her matchmaking attentions.

Phoebe placed her hand on the peer's proffered arm and walked onto the dance floor. Lord Andrews was, without a doubt, the largest gentleman she had ever met. He would make two of Aldous Clark. She was quite certain she had seen him while walking the twins in the park—he would be difficult to miss—although she had taken care never to allow any of the men who had so openly stared at her the satisfaction of knowing she was aware of them.

"Miss Thorpe, I believe I have seen you before. Do you not frequent the park with a pair of twins on occasion?"

She curtsied to him in the pattern of the dance, then accepted his hand to twirl about in the next step. When facing him again and able to speak, she said, "Indeed, sir. I have that pleasure."

Ferdy had been quite sure that this young lady, despite her surprising appearance at Almack's, was none other than the woman with the twins, but he'd had to make certain of it. "You know Lady Latham?" That piece of information had near flummoxed him. Val's aunt was sponsoring this girl? Impossible. He must have heard wrongly.

"Indeed, dear Lady Latham has been most generous with her time and care of me and the twins, even inviting us into her home. I am very grateful to her ladyship."

Ferdy almost stopped in his tracks. What a pity Val had played chicken this evening. There was little doubt that this is what Lady Jersey had hinted at when teasing Val about coming tonight. And Val was off to the opera, no doubt watching the latest dancer.

Somehow Ferdy managed to slip past that pitfall and make agreeable conversation. In his determination to be pleasant to the girl and hopefully learn more about her, he completely forgot to be his usual subdued self—a fact not missed by the ladies of the *ton*, who had all but given up on the handsome but elusive gentleman.

When the dance ended, he returned Phoebe to Lady Latham, noting the obvious fondness that dragon of Society directed at her guest. For once, he didn't run when he saw Sally Jersey descending upon him.

"I vow, you have restored my faith in my instincts. You made a charming partner for our latest lovely."

"What do you know about her?" Ferdy said in his usual direct way.

"She is guardian to those adorable twins and heiress to Lady Latham's fortune," Lady Jersey said with delight.

Ferdy nearly dropped his jaw. Heiress to all that money? He had to find Val immediately. He bid Lady Jersey a hurried farewell and left with as much aplomb as possible under the circumstances.

Val was in his box at the opera, looking rather bored. He looked up in surprise when Ferdy charged into his box.

"We must talk," Ferdy insisted, his urgency stirring Val from his chair. The two of them left the opera, and were soon jogging along in Ferdy's carriage.

"Well?" Val inquired once settled against the squabs, designed for a man of Ferdy's size and weight and thus exceedingly comfortable.

"Pity you didn't go with me this evening. You missed precisely what you have been looking for—Miss Phoebe."

"Never say that woman showed up at Almack's! Was she admitted?" Val asked, quite astounded.

"You would never guess if you lived to be a hundred. It seems that the young woman is not only accepted in proper Society, but she is the protégé of your own aunt!"

Chapter 4

If that is your notion of humor it is not appreciated," Val said with an offended glance at his friend.

"Not humor," Ferdy insisted politely. "Sally Jersey introduced me to her—and I must say, she is a pretty-behaved gel and an excellent dancer. At any rate, Sally said that not only is Miss Thorpe—for that is her last name—the guardian of those twins, but Sally took malicious pleasure in telling me that Miss Thorpe is your aunt's new heir, or heiress in this case. I thought you were to have all that lovely money?" he concluded with a puzzled expression.

"So did I," Val said, rubbing his chin in a reflective gesture. "I had best present myself in my dear aunt's drawing room tomorrow. I would like to know what is going on in her little world. Last I heard, she was not even going about, her arthritis was plaguing her so."

"Want company? Support, as it were?" Ferdy offered with a grimace. While he would always help his good friend, Lady Latham made him uneasy. She seemed to him to be the dangerous sort of woman . . . another matchmaker. Although in his experience it appeared that most women were born with that instinct—bound and determined to make a chap's life miserable.

"No, but thank you for the offer. I had best confront her alone." Val stared glumly out of the carriage window until they reached his town house.

Ferdy came along with him into the house, where they sought the comfort of the library, a blazing fire, and an excellent bottle of port.

"Cheers," Val said in an effort to improve his mood.

"You know, it might be all a hum," Ferdy offered hesitantly. "I mean, Sally loves to tease a fellow. Maybe that is what she did this time. Putting me on about Phoebe Thorpe and her being your aunt's heiress and all that."

"You know it is not as though I need all that money," Val said. "I have sufficient for my wants. I simply do not like to see the old lady imposed upon. Lord knows she's a schemer and not to be trusted an inch. Still, she is my aunt and there are times—which I admit are few and far between—when I actually enjoy the old dragon."

Ferdy scratched his head, then sank deeper into his favorite chair, a very large high-backed chair with deep cushions and broad arms. "I hope you will not regret my not coming with you—as witness and all that sort of thing."

"I have no doubt I will vanquish the dreadful Miss Phoebe Thorpe on the morrow." Val raised his glass in a toast. "Here's to Miss Thorpe, may she slink back to wherever she came from with speed and silence." He thought a moment, then said quietly, "Pity, that. She has a smashing figure and her looks are quite appealing. No refinement at all, however."

"She had sense enough to ignore you," Ferdy reposted with a grin. "You know you are the very dickens when it comes to fascinating females."

"I do seem to have that ability, true," Val said modestly. "I suppose if I were cagey I would charm Miss Phoebe of the pretty black curls and bright blue eyes right back to the country and avoid a conflict." He had not forgotten that flash of blue he'd seen in the park—Miss Phoebe Thorpe had the most striking eyes he'd ever seen.

"You mean to send her fleeing in alarm for her virtue, I suppose, seeing how she is a gently bred female."

"Since when have I ever had a woman reject my advances?" Val queried with a hint of affront.

"About time you get a taste of what all the other chaps know. Not every female will fall at your feet, Val," Ferdy cautioned.

"Nonsense. 'Tis merely a matter of the right approach," Val said with the confidence of a male who has charmed every female he has met from the time he was in the cradle.

Ferdy just smiled and enjoyed his port. He had the oddest notion that the following days would provide more entertainment than the latest rage on the London stage.

Val glanced at his good friend, noted the amused expression, and grimaced. Although he would never admit it, he had an uncomfortable feeling about this situation.

Later when he went up to his room, he turned to his valet and said, "Rosbert, I have learned the identity of the young woman I seek. Phoebe Thorpe is her name. And she resides at present with my aunt, of all things."

"At present, my lord?" Rosbert replied, quick to catch a nuance in his employer's voice.

"I intend to see her gone as soon as possible. I will do everything in my power to thwart Miss Phoebe Thorpe."

Rosbert gazed at Lord Latham with concern. Then he quietly went about assisting him into his nightclothes before taking himself off to bed.

"Yes," Val said to the night sky beyond his upper-floor window, "Miss Thorpe will be sorry that she ever came to London, much less tried to cozen an old woman out of her money."

"You were a quiet sensation, my girl," Lady Latham crowed in the carriage on the way back to her town house. "Always best to take Society in a roundabout manner. Had everyone there guessing and itching to know more. As my dear mama once told me, it is best to always leave them wanting."

"Wanting what?" Phoebe wondered. The evening had been a revelation to her. While she had never expected to make a splash in Society, she was gratified to find she did well enough. Her parents would have been proud of her had they lived to know she reached that pinnacle of the aristocracy: attendance at Almack's.

How grateful she had been when her cousin had taken her in following her parents' demise from smallpox. It had been a pleasant enough life. Never had she anticipated that she would become the twins' guardian, and subsequently be taken to Lady Latham's bosom, as it were. But wanting?

"Wanting whatever they wish—whether it be knowledge or whatever 'thing' they cannot have," her ladyship said with a crafty smile. "Be careful what you offer to others; withhold until you are certain that what you have to give will be properly received."

This advice seemed so obscure that Phoebe decided she must be tired. Perhaps it would make more sense tomorrow.

She followed her ladyship into the house and up the stairs, not bothering to stifle a yawn—although she did properly cover her mouth with her beautifully gloved hand.

At the top of the stairs, she paused and gave her ladyship a troubled look. "One of the gentlemen acted most strangely when we were introduced. A Lord Andrews. Do you know him? I recall that Lady Jersey introduced us and that after he left me with you, he sought out her ladyship for a small conversation. He seemed astounded that I am residing here with you."

"Find him interesting, do you?" Lady Làtham said with a frown. "He is a nice enough boy, but not worth your time. Ferdy Andrews balks at the mere idea of wedded bliss. You'll not see him walking down the aisle unless he finds a woman who takes him unawares."

"And when did I ever say I am *looking* for a husband?" Phoebe demanded with more spirit than she usually displayed to the awesome Lady Latham.

"Pish tush," her ladyship said with a wave of her hand and a canny smile. "Every woman alive wishes a husband if she knows what is good for her."

"You arc single," Phoebe pointed out with a shrewd look.

"I was married for many years. I have earned a respite. Not but what I might not consider that state if the right gentleman presented himself for my approval."

"I thought the gentleman had the choosing, as it were," Phoebe said. Her fatigue faded while sparring with Lady Latham. There was something about the older woman that made one alert and on one's toes. She was a wily creature, and more and more, Phoebe sensed that she had to exert caution when dealing with her.

"We allow them to believe that, my dear," her ladyship said with a sage nod. "There is only one path to freedom for a woman, and that is the altar. Once safely married, she may do anything—provided, of course, that she has had the good sense to find a man who is captivated by her or one who is sensible."

"What an interesting point of view," Phoebe said politely. "However, I find I am too tired to think clearly, and I find I need that facility when we have our little discussions."

"The younger generation has no stamina," her ladyship declared before walking along the hall to her rooms.

Phoebe watched until the older lady disappeared. Then, quite pensive, Phoebe made her way to her own room.

What her ladyship said was true. The path to freedom—whatever it might be—should be found in marriage. Phoebe suspected that was not always the case.

Come morning Phoebe found herself involved with selecting several new muslin dresses for Doro, who was growing nicely as a child ought. And Anthony begged to have a new skeleton suit, that clever all-in-one garment little boys wore once they left off short-coats.

"I would like blue, if you please, Cousin Phoebe," he pleaded. "And a dark jacket, too."

She had intended to purchase just such a thing for the lad and was only too happy to know his wishes. To Doro, she said, "And I suppose you would like white muslin with a pink sash?"

"And a blue print as well, please?" Doro said before crossing the room to peer out of the window at the street below. "Come, Cousin Phoebe. See that little girl on the corner. What is she doing?" Doro pointed a fat finger at a child in a threadbare garment, who held a basket in her hands.

"Selling flowers, I expect," Phoebe said. It saddened her to see a child put to work, but she knew that most likely every penny helped that child's family survive.

"She looks about my size. Might I give her one of my dresses? I think her dress is not very good."

"We'll see, love. Perhaps we might find a way to help her," Phoebe offered. "Would you like to buy some of her flowers?"

"Oh, yes, please," Doro replied with a smile. "I like flowers very much."

Sad to say, Phoebe soon forgot about the little flower girl, what with the press of herding the children off to the shops, where they were to purchase their new garments.

There were lists to consult and ribbons to be matched and she decided that Doro simply must have a new bonnet and pelisse, as her old one was just too skimpy for propriety.

When they drove off, Doro poked her head out of the carriage window to look back. She wore an exceedingly thoughtful expression the remainder of the trip.

Val waited until he thought his aunt would be up and about before presenting himself at her front door. The area was quiet save for a carriage disappearing down the street.

Smedley ushered him up the stairs and into the drawing room with what seemed like more than his usual dispatch.

"Good day, Aunt," Val said, smiling at the demure picture the old lady presented with a lady's magazine on her lap. Why, she looked as sweet as a comfit.

"What brings you to my door, Val? Haven't seen you in an age." She gave him an uncomfortably sharp look.

"Rumors," Val said, deciding to come directly to the point. He had no desire to spar with his crafty aunt. She too often got the better of him because, he assured himself, he was too much of a gentleman to argue with a lady—especially when she was his wealthy aunt.

"And what rumors might those be? Most of the time they are a lot of humbug. Once in a while they are true. Come, join me by the fire and we shall have a comfortable coze." She gestured to the chair across from her, close to the gently blazing fire and where she could watch him without tilting her head at an angle, for her nephew was dreadfully tall.

Aware he was in for a grilling, Val gingerly seated himself, then eased back when she failed to pounce on him at once.

"Now," she prompted quietly, "you said something about rumors." Placing her magazine on a table, she relaxed against her chair, giving the impression of a lady at ease.

"I heard the most absurd thing from Ferdy last evening. He was at Almack's and said he was introduced to a young woman who claimed to be living with you. A Miss Phoebe Thorpe." Val watched his aunt's face for a clue to her thoughts. Nothing was revealed, which did not surprise him very much.

"So? May I not invite someone to stay with me if I please?" Lady Latham leaned forward with a narrow gaze that pierced the comfortable armor Val wore.

"Of course, of course. You may invite anyone you please, I suppose," he concluded with a frown. "Providing they are not taking undue advantage of you. Sally Jersey told Ferdy that this young woman has been made your heiress. Is this true?" Val inquired a trifle more forcefully than he'd intended.

"What if it is?" Lady Latham shot back. She had the look of a judge who has just been presented with a felon charged with stealing from helpless creatures.

Val jumped up and began pacing back and forth across the exquisite Turkey carpet. "I did not believe it. I really did not believe Ferdy when he told me about it. I thought it was all a hum." He pointed a finger at his aunt and said, "How could you allow this stranger to take you in like this, to cozen you into willing her your money?"

"Well, you certainly don't need it and she does," the old lady snapped.

"That is your criteria? That she *needs* the money?"

"I like the gel. She amuses me. And her potions have done more for my aches and pains than the best physicians in all of London. She cares about me, truly cares. And do not think for a moment I am not aware of the difference between true caring and the fake sort of lip service I often receive." She glared at him until Val felt about as small as a mouse.

"What about her twins?" he said, recalling that vital bit of information against the chit.

"They aren't hers," Lady Latham declared so positively that Val wondered if he dared challenge that statement.

"How do you know for a fact?" he ventured to ask.

"Because I know whose children they are," she said with distinct satisfaction. "I summoned her here from Little-Moreton-Under-the-Marsh because I wanted to meet them. She had written to me seeking advice about a small matter. I liked the tone of her letter and I could see she had received a good education. Lovely hand," Lady Latham said with a sigh.

"I would like to meet this paragon," Val said, using the

persuasive charm that usually worked such wonders when dealing with females.

"You cannot," Lady Latham declared.

"Why?" Val inquired with suspicion. It was too convenient for Phoebe Thorpe to be gone from the house when no one knew he would be calling.

"She has gone shopping, I believe. Children tend to grow like weeds. They needed some new toggery." Lady Latham smiled at Val as though she found great pleasure in thwarting him.

"And you finance the clothing?" Val hazarded.

"No. Bills are paid by their solicitor," she replied with glee. "They cost me little enough for the pleasure they all give me. *Her* expenses are paid by the new Viscount Waring," Lady Latham concluded softly.

Val frowned. "I had a cousin who bore that title. Didn't he die a few years back? I confess I have not kept track of that branch of the family. The chap preferred the society to be found in the country." Val paused, trying to call forth a mental picture of his cousin. "I knew him at school, but we did not get along very well," Val admitted.

"Ought to have. Interesting thing, families. If you learn what the parents are like, you will most likely know how the children will turn out. Phoebe's parents were fine gentry of highly suitable stock. As I recall, her mother was a famed beauty of her day. Pity they both died of the smallpox. Hard on the girl. Lucky for her that her cousin took her in. I feel certain that it helped Phoebe understand the importance of assisting others less fortunate."

"I had heard she was the twins' mother," Val said.

"Rubbish. Since when did you believe everything you hear? Do not be a nodcock, Valentine Latham."

When his aunt tilted her head and peered up at him with those glittery eyes, Val sensed his battle was nearly lost.

"I would like to meet her, dear Aunt," Val said through gritted teeth. Good lord, his aunt would drive him around the bend if he had to deal with her on a daily basis. She knew precisely what irritated him.

"And I wager you would also like to send her packing. You act as though I was born yesterday. You shan't see Phoebe . . . unless you chance to meet her while we are out and about. For instance, I plan to attend the theater this evening. Phoebe has never seen a play before. I thought to give her a little treat."

"You went to Almack's last evening. Isn't that treat enough?" Val said, giving his aunt a disapproving look for being such a gullible creature as to fall in with the tale offered by this cozening female.

"Why, Valentine . . . are you begrudging my enjoyment in entertaining Phoebe? I assure you that my coffers can stand it. Now be gone with you. It is time for me to take a beauty nap. How else can I keep going as I do?"

Knowing when to retreat, Val bowed over his aunt's gnarled hand, then beat a hasty departure. He had an uncomfortable feeling that his aunt was chuckling all the way up to her room while he marched down the stairs to the front door.

There he paused. "Smedley, do you by chance know where Miss Thorpe went to shop? I need to see her about something and my aunt could not recall the name of the place."

"I believe it was to Grafton House first, then to the mantuamaker. Her ladyship wished the children to have their clothing items made up, rather than Miss Phoebe sew them as has been her wont in the past."

Amazed at this loquacity from the normally taciturn butler, Val said, "I take it that Miss Thorpe is a great favorite among the staff?"

"Indeed sir," Smedley said with what almost amounted to a smile. "She is very good for your aunt. And she cares for the children as a mother, maybe better than some."

After learning the direction of the mantuamaker's establishment, Val thanked him and left the house. He was more determined than ever to track down the elusive Miss Phoebe Thorpe.

Grafton House was overflowing with females of every sort imaginable. Val took one searching look and gave up. If Miss Thorpe was in there with the twins, he doubted he would find her. Next he directed his carriage to the mantuamaker's place and sat there for a time.

He was about to leave when, as luck would have it, Miss Phoebe and the twins appeared. Val contrived to exit his carriage on the far side and then saunter along the walk until he chanced to meet her face-to-face.

"Ah, we meet again. And still no one to introduce us. I fear we are destined to go through life never knowing each other's names. Yet I have found you out," he said with a most charming smile. "You are Miss Phoebe Thorpe, lately of Little-Moreton-Under-the-Marsh."

"Then you have me at a disadvantage, sir. But I must thank you again for all you did when Anthony fell into the water." She bestowed a sincere smile on him that was so polite it might be used as a model for correctness.

"I trust he did not suffer too harshly from his wetting?" Val said, with a quick look at the lad who was so like himself.

"A few days in bed and he was as good as new." Miss Thorpe gave her charge a fond look, one that held pride mingled with love.

Anthony advanced a few steps while studying Val with that sharp, intense stare a child often has. "Did you know that we look much alike, sir?"

"So I see. How do you account for that?" Val said with a wry twist of his mouth.

"Cousin Phoebe did not not answer when Doro asked about it. I do not know. Do you?" the boy inquired.

"I suspect," Val said, while adding two plus two, "that we are related. Unless I miss my mark, your papa was a cousin of mine. How did you come to live with them, ma'am?" he asked Phoebe.

"I was invited," Phoebe said, studying the man who had rescued Anthony. He was even more polished and perfect than the day he had plunged into the Serpentine. He certainly knew how to dress to advantage without making himself into a dandy. He also seemed uncommonly certain of himself, wearing an air of self-confidence like a cloak about his well-tailored shoulders. Her reaction to his splendor was to become more formal and withdrawn.

"Invited? As my aunt invited you to live with her?"

"Your aunt?" Phoebe asked, feeling quite at sea. Then little remarks began to return to her, comments about a nephew in London.

"Lord Latham at your service," he said with a bow that seemed to mock her.

"Yes, well, then it is your aunt who invited us to spend some time with her so she might know the children better. She is a remarkable woman." Phoebe unbent enough to offer the gentleman a hesitant smile.

"Indeed, she is. May I add that I believe you also are a remarkable woman, Miss Thorpe?"

Not much liking the tone that had crept into his voice, Phoebe stepped back and placed her hand on the knob of the door that led to the mantuamaker's establishment. "I believe we are attracting undue attention, my lord. I would bid you good day."

"See . . . I said you are remarkable. Most women would demand to know why I thought them unusual," he said in a teasing sort of voice.

Phoebe relaxed a trifle, thinking that perhaps she had overreacted to that first tone. "Very well, then, why?"

The teasing smile left his face and he took a step toward her that she instinctively felt was threatening. She refused to retreat, facing him with a lift of her chin, while placing the children behind her.

"Because, Miss Phoebe Thorpe, you are a cozening female of the worse sort. You worm your way into my aunt's heart and trick her into willing you her vast fortune. Any woman who can manage to accomplish that with my foxy aunt merits more than a modicum of regard. Be aware that I intend to take legal steps to prevent this dastardly deed from happening. I am on to your intrigue, Miss Thorpe."

Before an astounded Phoebe could inform this odious and most perfect gentleman that he was a totally bird-witted twit and quite wrong about her reason for coming to London, he had nodded his head in a barely civil manner, and marched up the street to enter a carriage. She glanced back while entering the shop, to see the carriage disappear around the next corner, then breathed a sigh of relief.

"Mercy," she said to herself. "What a dreadful man." A very *handsome*, dreadful man, honesty compelled her to add.

"Why did Lord Latham say those nasty things, Cousin Phoebe?" Doro inquired.

Fortunately, Phoebe was spared an answer when the mantuamaker came forth to greet her. If Madame Clotilde was offended by the request that she produce some children's garments, she did not reveal it. Doubtless she felt that any woman who paid her bills when they were presented was so eccentric that she must be humored.

Sometime later, Phoebe and the children left the shop with the order placed to everyone's satisfaction. Doro was to have her several muslins with various hued sashes and a blue print dress. A delighted Anthony skipped along at Phoebe's side as he contemplated the notion he was to have two skeleton suits—blue and brown—plus two nice jackets to keep him warm.

Doro had insisted upon a little jacket as well for, as she said, "I am cold at times, Aunt Phoebe."

Looking at the lightweight muslin dress with the wide, low neck that was practically a uniform with the younger set, Phoebe could see how that might be. She had agreed to the request.

But once they left the mantuamaker's, the humiliating scene returned to bedevil Phoebe's mind. The very idea that she would cozen Lady Latham out of a fortune was revolting in the extreme. First of all, Phoebe would never think of such a scheme, indeed—this was the first she had heard of it. Secondly, she doubted if anyone could trick Lady Latham out of a farthing by nefarious means or any other. The old woman was simply too sharp.

When they reached Lady Latham's home, an indignant Phoebe paid the jarvey, then marched her charges up the steps. At the door, Doro paused, peering behind them to where the little flower seller stood across the street. She tugged on Phoebe's shawl.

"Please, Aunt Phoebe, may I buy some flowers? That little girl is there again." Doro cast a distressed look at the child not far from her own age.

A chagrined Phoebe put her troubles aside and handed Doro several coins more than originally intended so that she could do as she pleased.

Doro's sigh of satisfaction when she returned with a bunch of dainty violets in her hand was more than worth every penny spent.

Doro marched up the stairs until she reached the drawing room. She made her way past the lady who visited with her ladyship, then came to a halt.

"I have some flowers for you, dearest great-aunt." Then she offered the little bouquet with a butterfly kiss on the old lady's cheek.

"A pretty-behaved child," Lady Cowper said with approval."Is this one of the twins I have been hearing about?"

"Indeed. And here is the other, along with Miss Thorpe. Phoebe, love, was your mission successful?"

"I found the proper fabrics and persuaded the mantua-maker to cut them as we wish."

"Then why do you look as though you would like to do battle with someone?" Lady Latham said, her eyes narrowing.

" 'Tis your nephew, dear ma'am," Phoebe declared, forgetting there was another in the room. "He accused me of cozening up to you merely to inherit your fortune! As if I would do such an appalling thing. Oh, I've a mind to teach him a thing or two, the odious court-card!" Then she remembered the other present and blushed, while stammering a very judicious apology.

"What an amusing event," Lady Cowper declared. "Val, a court-card! You could not call him a more crushing thing, dear girl." She exchanged a knowing look with Lady Latham, then added, "Could it be that our Val has met his match?"

Lady Latham looked at Phoebe and said softly to her younger friend, "Do you know that this is the first time a woman has failed to adore him on sight?"

Phoebe, sensing that she was among friends, and could speak without being too much on her guard, said, "If Lord Latham desires a war, he has one. I have never been so insulted in my life."

Chapter 5

I do believe I have found the ideal candidate for the position of the next Lady Latham," Val reported to his good friend. He poured out two glasses of fine claret, then offered one to Ferdy.

"I know you said you were looking, but I was not aware you were quite that serious," Ferdy replied while settling back in his favorite chair. He sipped appreciatively at his wine, then watched Val.

"Time I settle down," Val said, avoiding his friend's searching gaze and staring at the flames. They were decidedly less challenging.

"And where did you locate this paragon, may I ask?" Ferdy inquired in a lazy tone that might fool anyone else. Val knew his friend was a trifle offended at not being made aware of the choice earlier and most assuredly desired more information to satisfy his insatiable curiosity.

"Miss Eustacia Oliphant appears to have all necessary qualifications. She is well-bred—comes from a fine old family. She also possesses a tidy dowry, and seems to have a gentle nature . . . although I cannot say I have heard her speak above ten words. Seems to be struck dumb whenever we chance to meet." He gave Ferdy a look that commingled frustration with amusement.

"You do appear to have a decided effect on the female population," his friend said with a grin.

"Perhaps it is my imagination, but it would seem that that effect has altered. In spite of Sally Jersey doing her best to circulate the truth of the matter regarding Miss Phoebe Thorpe and those twins, I find fond mothers still looking at me somewhat askance. It is as though they try to decide whether or not to believe the scandalous stories they have heard about me."

"You must admit that you have not led a precisely blameless life until now. I can see why a mother desiring to protect her precious daughter would be hesitant to believe you are serious in the pursuit of a wife. Remember, you are a Corinthian of the first water. A few parents do look askance at us. It is not just our superb attire but our dash and élan that elevates us. We are known for wooing but not marrying," Ferdy concluded wryly.

Val studied Ferdy for a few moments, then said, "You could let it be known in certain ears that I am serious. It might not do any harm to also drop a reminder regarding the state of my finances. I have found that does tend to have a bit of influence," Val said ironically. "Perhaps it would even overcome the status of Corinthian?"

"If you had a daughter, would you not try to find the best situation you could for her? Money and position go a long way to offset an outrageous reputation." Ferdy leveled a look at Val, one that dared him to deny this truth.

"Are you saying that my reputation is such that a parent would not wish to ally their house with mine?" Val said with rising ire.

Ferdy was well aware of the dangerous waters he sailed upon. Yet he also felt it important to let his best friend know the depth of his dilemma. "I am trying to tell you that it is not a simple matter of selecting a woman—as you might a carriage or horse—and offering for her. From what I have heard, she may not be permitted to voice her feelings in regard to the matter, but rest assured that her mother will sniff out all gossip and look for the truth. Which 'truth' she finds will depend upon who reaches her ear first. Do you have any enemies?"

"Oh, good grief," Val murmured, sinking back on his chair with a frown creeping over his face.

"You begin to comprehend what I mean, I take it," Ferdy said, in a voice that clearly commiserated with Val's predicament.

"Do you know Miss Oliphant?" Val asked, peering at his friend in an unusually hesitant manner.

"Cannot say that I do."

"She has delicate blond hair that resembles gold and silver spun together to create a halo about her head. Her eyes are the pale blue of a winter sky. I fear she seldom betrays an emotion, so I have never observed her expression alter from the polite, bland one I have seen to date. However, her oval face has clear skin with a rosebud mouth and a straight little nose."

"In short, she is the paragon I mentioned earlier," Ferdy said with a grimace. "I would be uncomfortable with such perfection. I far prefer a flesh-and-blood woman in my bed and at my table."

"I suppose you refer to a woman such as Miss Phoebe of the black curls and blue eyes," Val retorted.

"Tell me, since Miss Thorpe also has blue eyes, what makes her different?" Ferdy asked, looking at Val with a thoughtful stare.

Val recalled his last confrontation with Miss Thorpe in front of the mantuamaker's establishment. "Her eyes are the gentian blue of summer and can smile with simple pleasure or flash with anger—although her expression when directed at me seems more like outrage. You are not left for long to wonder what goes on in Miss Thorpe's mind. Her eyes tell you a great deal, most of which in my case is not what one might wish from an admittedly pretty woman."

"I gather you had a bit of a clash with her to learn all that. You certainly didn't discover her character over tea in Lady Latham's drawing room," Ferdy hazarded.

"At first my aunt flatly refused to let me see Miss Thorpe, then admitted the chit had gone shopping for the twins. New clothing, she claimed. I suspect that my aunt foots the bill, although she insists that their solicitor handles all those sort of arrangements."

"Solicitor? And who might that be?" Ferdy asked, sitting upright in his chair, looking unusually alert.

"I suppose it would be the same man who handled my late cousin's estate. Cannot think of the fellow's name, but I imagine my secretary has it somewhere. If not, it should be a simple matter to locate him. Why?" Val leaned forward, intent on his friend's line of thought.

"I should think it would be vastly illuminating to find out the terms of that will. Did you not tell me that the reason

Miss Thorpe wrote to your aunt was to seek her help and advice about a matter? Perhaps it had to do with the estate, or the will, or the raising of the children?"

"What a brilliant thought, Ferdy, old chap." Val settled back against his chair, raising his glass in a silent toast. "Yes, that must be the case. Cannot think why it did not occur to me before. I believe I will do a bit of investigating. I need more ammunition to rout the lovely Miss Thorpe. I will not allow my aunt to squander her fortune on such a designing female. If there is the slightest chance that this solicitor holds the key to that defeat, he must be found."

"And you think Butterworth can do that?"

"Butterworth can do anything!" Val declared, hitting the arm of his chair in emphasis. His secretary was the most reticent man on earth, but Val had long insisted that the fellow learned more that way.

"Very well, then," Ferdy said, rubbing his large hands together in anticipation. "I confess I do not like to see your aunt be tricked into bestowing her money on an undeserving woman—even if the old lady is a veritable dragon."

Val shared a look of amusement with his friend, then said, "Do you go to the Elsworth ball this evening? I believe Miss Oliphant is to attend. I should like you to meet her."

"Indeed. I believe I received an invitation and if I am tardy with my acceptance, most hostesses forgive a single gentleman of means."

The two men burst into laughter at this truism, then marched off to Ferdy's house so he might hasten his belated acceptance to Lady Elsworth immediately. After this was accomplished, they strolled on to Bond Street.

"This is a shocking gown, Aunt Annis. The neck is much lower than I have worn before," Phoebe insisted while studying her reflection in the looking glass.

"Pish tush," her ladyship decried. "You will have the men buzzing around you like bees intent on making honey."

"Lady Latham!" Phoebe cried, slightly shocked, although admittedly amused at the old lady's speech.

"Lady Elsworth is always up to the minute on every

fashion. When Madame Clotilde said this gown is the very latest in design, you may be certain that her ladyship will notice. First impressions are so important, my dear girl."

"I am still upset over my confrontation with your nephew, ma'am." Phoebe turned away from the image of the questionable gown of blue-and-silver tissue silk and sat down to face her benefactress. "Why did he accuse me of such a dreadful and untrue thing? I have no interest in your fortune, whatever it may be. To charge me with trying to cozen you out of your money was the worst thing anyone has ever said to me. I simply do not understand him. He has a *most* absurd notion in his head."

"No man is perfect," her ladyship said with amusement. "And what I do with what is my own is none of his business. Although I dote on Valentine, I would never tell him so. I like to shake him up once in a while."

"You intended to shake *him* up? Well, I *had* formed quite a heroic notion of him after he dove into the Serpentine to rescue Anthony. At first I pegged him a mere man of fashion, a Corinthian or dandy, if you will. When he recovered Anthony in such a fine manner, I thought better of him; he seemed most noble and good. Then, to have him appear out of nowhere and charge me with such a plan! Well, 'tis a good thing I am not given to the vapors or I would have been prostrate on the ground. What a contrary man!"

Phoebe jumped up from the tufted bench at the foot of her bed and began to pace about the room, the pretty gown swishing about her slim figure in a rather fetching way.

"Enough of that. I might choose to bestow a trifle on you, 'tis nothing to fuss about. It will serve no purpose to rile your nerves with what happened. Let us have our dinner, then go off to Lady Elsworth's ball. I am determined to introduce you to gentlemen who are worthy of your charms and talents. You certainly have proven what a fine mother you would be. Those children are delightful—and I do not particularly like children."

"Ma'am?" Phoebe said, not certain she had heard right.

"Most children are noisy and disobedient and altogether a bother. These little ones actually appeal to me."

Diverted from the matter of the inheritance, Phoebe digested this peculiar remark while following her ladyship down the stairs to the dining room. When they were seated and had been served a simple meal, Phoebe gave Lady Latham a judicious look and pronounced her final observation on the nephew.

"As to Lord Latham, ma'am, I think he is touched in the head. If that upsets you, I am sorry. But I care for you, *not* for some paltry sum of money, but because you are a dear lady who is all that is kind."

Phoebe cast her gaze at her plate and thus missed the surprised look on Lady Latham's face that was immediately followed by one of wondering pleasure.

Just as they were preparing to depart, Smedley proffered a posy that had been delivered for Phoebe from an unknown admirer. Lady Latham crowed with delight and happily spent the time in the carriage hazarding guesses as to the identity of Phoebe's mysterious swain.

Lady Elsworth's ball was one of the highlights of the Season. She always entertained lavishly, but this year she had clearly outdone herself, and the affair promised to establish a precedent that would set other hostesses to grinding their teeth in frustration. Anyone who was anyone was there.

Ferdy ascended the grand staircase with Val, looking about with a cynical gaze. "And just how many young ladies making their come-outs do you suppose will grace these rooms this evening? The cream of the crop, so to speak? Or the entire lot?"

"As many as can wangle an invitation, I suppose. I say, is that actually my aunt up ahead of us?"

"Indeed," Ferdy said, his cynical expression changing to one of sly amusement. "And I believe I also detect a young woman at her side—one with black curls dressed in a blue-and-silver thing. Fancy Lady Elsworth inviting a nobody to her ball."

"As to that, if my aunt sponsors her entry into Society, she cannot be considered a nobody—even if we might call her that," Val admitted, compelled to be honest in this instance. "Aunt Latham came from the junior branch of a ducal family and married into one—Thurlow, you know. She reminds one of her background in the event one might forget it." Val omitted mention of his own expectations in regard to the ducal title, preferring to hope his elder brother might marry and produce an heir before popping off.

"Which lends credibility to a young woman you suspect of being a cozening female of the worse sort," Ferdy concluded with a grimace.

Val was unable to reply as they had now reached Lady Elsworth.

"Dear boy, I am so pleased you and Lord Andrews could attend my little ball," the lady said with a wry smile.

Val bowed low over her hand while he endured her inspection of him and Ferdy. She was a noted arbiter of fashion, in addition to being an outstanding hostess.

"As usual, you are dressed in the height of Corinthian elegance. How fortunate you have the figure to carry it off." To Ferdy she added, "You may be a large person, sir, but you do well enough in your own way. Now enjoy yourselves and try not to break too many hearts."

She had already turned to the next in line before Val had a chance to ask her about Miss Thorpe. He was not quite sure what he wished to know, but he would appreciate the opinion of an astute woman such as her ladyship.

The two men strolled along the edge of the ballroom until Val paused, nudging his friend in the ribs. "There she is."

"Since the woman I note is a delicate blond, I assume you mean Miss Oliphant, not Miss Phoebe of the black curls and blue eyes."

"You could refrain from that description, I believe. I am all too aware of Miss Thorpe's attributes."

"Indeed," a very pensive Ferdy said. Then he focused his attention on the blond beauty and nodded slowly. "I believe she might do."

"I should think so," Val muttered. "She is the top of the cream in my book."

"It would appear that a good many others have the same book," Ferdy countered.

Val revealed none of his inner dismay at the cluster of first-rate gentlemen around the ethereal Miss Oliphant. In the past, his pursuit of a fair damsel had been a game, nothing more. Now he was serious, and wondered if his credit would be sufficient. It would be a pity if past misdeeds returned to haunt him now.

The others naturally fell back when Val began to edge his way to the center of the group. His wealth and the faint chance of a ducal title had certain advantages.

"Miss Oliphant, I trust I am not too late to capture a dance with the fairest damsel present this evening."

Not proof against the devilish gleam in Val's dark eyes, Miss Oliphant fluttered her lashes and murmured something Val assumed was agreement.

She offered her card. When he signed it, he checked the opposition, noting it was formidable but not impossible. Feeling more assured, he retired from the Beauty, deciding it was time to pique her interest in him—and in his experience nothing piqued a Beauty like having a gentleman retire to a distance.

It was then that he spotted his aunt and her protégé, Miss Thorpe, ensconced in the corner of the ball room. Surprisingly, there were as many men clustered about that young woman as there were around Miss Oliphant—precisely why that should be the case was beyond Val. As he drew closer, he had a clear view of Miss Thorpe's blue-and-silver tissue gown, noting that the neckline of the gown bordered on scandalous. Precisely what one might expect from an adventuress, he thought with derision.

Again, the others made way for one considered the acme of Society.

"Dear Aunt," he said politely, bowing over her hand with his usual polish. Then he looked Miss Thorpe in the eyes and said, "How interesting to see you here, Miss Thorpe. Not at home tending your twins?"

"I am responsible for them, but cannot claim them for my own, as you well know," Phoebe said with surprising aplomb and a level look at his lordship.

The dratted man—he was utter perfection. Garbed in a coat of midnight blue over a white waistcoat and dove gray breeches with white stockings and patent shoes, he was all elegance. His perfection was derived from the exquisite simplicity of a cravat that she suspected outshone every other in the room.

He raised a quizzing glass to stare at Phoebe with all the

hauteur of his standing in Society, then lowered it, tapping the glass against his chin. His expression was not encouraging.

"Surprised to see you here, nevvy," Lady Latham said.

"I am not surprised to find you here, however. Since Miss Thorpe arrived at your home, you seem to defy all expectations." Lord Latham smiled tolerantly at his sometimes difficult aunt, then transferred his gaze to Phoebe. "I would request a dance, Miss Thorpe," he said without any warmth of expression.

She consulted the card she still held and shook her head. "I fear they are all taken. I am devastated, my lord." It was patently untrue, and he undoubtedly knew it.

Against all that was proper, he calmly took the little folded bit of pink pasteboard from her hand and perused it, using his quizzing glass. He smiled, a particularly unsettling smile.

"I believe you overlooked this one, a waltz."

"Actually I had not thought to join in the waltz this evening," Phoebe said while lowering her gaze to the dull gold buttons on his lordship's waistcoat. She had been caught out in her prevarication. Would he sense her reluctance to partner him in a waltz and be gracious enough to permit her little ruse to pass?

"But you must, my dear girl," he purred. "Everyone will wonder if we do not dance. Our names have been linked and we must pretend to be polite." He gestured lazily with his quizzing glass, the gold rim glittering in the light of the hundreds of candles overhead.

"I should think it would be far better if we not only did not dance, but scarce spoke to one another," she said sharply, her gaze flashing up to challenge him. "You must know that I am not at all pleased with you, nor what you have accused me of doing."

The very idea of a woman being displeased with him before he had lost interest in her was a novel one. Val was determined that he would entice Miss Thorpe into at least an interest in him. Maybe he would even make her fall in love with him. He was not usually a heartless man and kept his attentions aboveboard. But Phoebe was a challenge. Surely the rules were different for a cozening female?

Phoebe's partner for the first dance appeared to claim her hand. Never had she been so grateful to walk way from any man.

She had left Lord Latham standing by his aunt. He wore a puzzled expression on his handsome face, one that made Phoebe long to chuckle in spite of the effect he had on her. Her hand fairly itched to connect with his face in a resounding slap, and she longed to tell his lordship precisely what she thought of a man who had had so little contact with his cousin. It was most interesting that his cousin thought so little of Lord Latham that not once had he mentioned him, let alone make him guardian of the twins—one of whom resembled the handsome Corinthian in a kindred way.

The succession of dances became a blur in her mind. In a way, it was rather heady stuff. Here she was, little Phoebe Thorpe, of the Little-Moreton-Under-the-Marsh Thorpes, having an incredible evening mixing with the cream of Society. The gentlemen might not all be handsome, but most were acceptably polished. Some of the women were dreadfully gowned, yet all were somehow looking quite special in their silks and satins and yards of lace.

She might wish that either Lady Elsworth opened a few windows or that the attendees of the ball were more frequent bathers, but it was easy to overcome that by sniffing the posy sent her, the sender still unknown.

"Miss Thorpe . . . I believe we are to have the next dance?" Lord Andrews said.

Phoebe smiled, thinking that Lord Andrews reminded her of a great bear, a very large version of a stuffed German-made toy bought for Anthony by his adoring mama.

"I cannot recall seeing your name on my card."

Lord Andrews smiled at her, then turned an awesomely fierce gaze on the young man who *had* signed his name on Phoebe's card. The young fellow, just down from Oxford, bowed and beat a hasty retreat.

"Just so. However, since I see your would-be partner disappearing into the next room, may I claim this dance as mine?" Lord Andrews beamed a lazy smile on Phoebe that quite delighted her.

"Absurd man," Phoebe murmured. "That was a naughty thing for you to do. The poor chap may not ever recover."

"Just as well," his lordship said calmly. "Should not have tried to rise above himself. Cannot think what was in his mind to try to dance with the rage of the evening."

"What utter nonsense," Phoebe said, accepting his arm. She smiled automatically at Lord Andrews while taking note of Lord Latham performing the minuet with the delicate Beauty, Miss Eustacia Oliphant.

"Beautiful young woman, Miss Oliphant," Lord Andrews commented when he observed the direction of Phoebe's gaze.

She refused to allow his comment to put her to the blush. "It would appear that Lord Latham holds her much in his esteem. He certainly gazes at her with regard."

When Lord Andrews again drew near Phoebe in the pattern of the dance, he smiled at her and said, "Val mentioned something about finding himself a proper wife. I would only hope that the rumors about you two do not cause a problem for him."

"You cannot be serious," Phoebe said quietly, glancing at the other couple. Miss Oliphant had to be the most insipid woman at the ball. While lovely, she certainly appeared to be lacking in conversation; she looked terrified to even open her mouth. "There must be more to gossip about than speculation as to our relationship—real or imagined."

"Well, as to that, the resemblance between the twins and you and Val is such that even Sally Jersey is having a spot of bother trying to convince others that there is no connection between you—other than Val's aunt, of course."

Phoebe digested this tidbit of information while executing a series of dips and whirls. A sensation of disquiet grew with every turn.

"Tell me," Lord Andrews commanded nicely, "how is it that you live with Lady Latham?"

Rather liking the genial giant of a man, Phoebe answered promptly, "I wrote to her requesting her advice on a matter of business involving the children. Her answer was to invite the twins and me to London. Actually, she wished to see them, for they are her grandniece and nephew, and she'd not seen them before." Feeling surprisingly at ease, Phoebe added, "I am no direct relation, yet she treats me as well as a daughter of the house. She may intimidate, but she is a dear lady." Phoebe cast a fond glance in her ladyship's direction.

"I hope that your confidence is not misplaced," Lord Andrews said softly, with a look at Lord Latham. "Val told me something about your inheriting her fortune."

"What a lot of nonsense," Phoebe said, a trifle louder than she normally would have spoken while in the midst of a dance. Several heads turned, one of them belonging to Lord Latham. It was as though an icy draft swept through the room, chilling her to the bone. In a softer voice she added, "Her ladyship mentioned a trifle she wishes to bestow on me, nothing more."

Fortunately, dancers came between them and Phoebe began to thaw. She gave Lord Andrews a puzzled look. When she had a chance, she said, "I sought advice, not money, from his aunt, regardless of whatever maggoty notion Lord Latham has in his head. I truly care about the children and seek only the best for them."

The dance concluded. Phoebe curtsied to Lord Andrews, thinking the gentleman was remarkably light on his feet for one so large.

On the far side of the room, Val escorted Miss Oliphant to where her mother sat with the chaperons. He placed a kiss in the air somewhere above the beautiful and decidedly reticent Miss Oliphant's hand, then complimented her mother on her daughter's many charms. He did wish the chit would overcome her terror of him to say a few words. However, that was not a request he might make of her parent.

His reception from Mrs. Oliphant was less than pleasing. She bestowed a glacial smile on him, drew her precious chick to her side, then dismissed Val with a "Good evening, my lord." A title brought respect, if nothing else.

Val checked the little card he had tucked in his watch pocket. On it he had jotted down the names of the women he had asked to dance and the number of that dance. He frowned at Ferdy when that gentleman approached.

"Treading rather dangerous waters, are you not, my friend?" Val's look was dagger sharp.

"Meant to do a bit of detective work for you," Ferdy said, not a whit unnerved by Val's scowl.

"And precisely what did you learn while performing a minuet with Miss Phoebe Thorpe?"

"Well, her black curls are silky soft and smell like lilacs. And those blue eyes do flash when she is annoyed—although they radiate joy when she talks about the twins. Dashed pretty girl," Ferdy mused.

"Is that all you have to report?" Val said, most disgusted with this drivel.

"I should like to know what it was that prompted her to write your aunt. Has Butterworth found out anything yet as to the identity of the solicitor?"

"Early days, my friend," Val said quietly. "But I trust my faithful and loyal secretary shall uncover the necessary information as soon as possible. Then we will better know how to deal with Phoebe Thorpe. That she is a cozening schemer, I've little doubt. It is not her black curls that entrance me, it is what goes on beneath them. Miss Thorpe is a very clever young woman. I would put nothing past her."

His estimation of the dark beauty was confirmed when he sought her out for their waltz. It was clear that she had mulled over what Ferdy had said and reached a negative conclusion. Val had to admit that it was unsettling to dance with a woman who neither flirted with nor flattered him.

"You dance the waltz with charm and grace," Val said in an effort to soothe the air between them.

"As do you, sir. I would guess you have had a great deal of practice. I make note that there are envious looks coming my way, although I confess I cannot think why," she added, annoyed with his polish and wishing he would simply tell her what he intended to do. "You have an excess of manners, sir," she concluded.

There was a snap to her words that was reflected in her aloofness. *She* did not seek to draw closer to him as most women were wont to do. Drat Ferdy for alarming Miss Thorpe. Of course, his own confrontation with her on Bond Street had not helped one whit.

When the dance ended, he restored her to his aunt. He watched Miss Thorpe glide off with her next partner, then bowed to his aunt and said, "I wish to consult with the twins' solicitor. I would make certain that my cousin's children are well provided for in his will. Or do you know the details involving the estate?"

"No," she admitted. "But Mr. Popham would."

Val excused himself, then approached Ferdy with a look of triumph gleaming in his eyes.

"What goes, my friend?" the large gentleman said in an undertone.

"Mr. Popham," Val replied, "the solicitor. Just wormed the name out of my aunt. Butterworth will know his direction. All I need to do is seek him out and learn the truth. I shall vanquish Miss Phoebe Thorpe and her flashing blue eyes. The chit says far too much and none of it pleasing." Val glanced at Phoebe.

Yet Val felt an odd twinge within as he surveyed her dancing figure. The attraction to her he reluctantly admitted must not be allowed to grow. Out of sight, out of mind was the best solution. She was as good as gone.

Chapter 6

Phoebe left Lady Latham's carriage and walked purposefully toward the entrance of the fascinating Ackermann's Repository of Art. When Lady Latham had shown Phoebe a Berlin work pattern for a canvas-work embroidery, the vivid colors of the roses appealed greatly to Phoebe's senses. She wished to work one for herself.

She paused before one of the shop windows to admire a display of fashionable textiles and trimmings. Would she ever have a home of her own to decorate as she pleased? She kept Anthony's home, but it was not quite the same as a place of one's own. Turning, she caught sight of a familiar face. Lord Latham's carriage was trapped in a snarl of traffic. For a few moments, Phoebe had a clear view of the man, elegant as ever and precise to a pin in his dress.

Intent upon extricating his phaeton from the tangle of carriages and drays that had converged upon the Strand intersection, he did not see Phoebe.

Then, amazingly, one by one the vehicles parted and all returned to normal. Phoebe watched his smart phaeton disappear up the way and wondered what it was that brought him to this part of the city. He looked to be headed toward Threadneedle Street, where she knew a number of solicitors kept offices. Mr. Popham had his office there and the very thought of the man brought a shiver of apprehension to Phoebe. What an utter toad he was.

She entered the delightful shop, setting aside the disturbing sight of Lord Latham, and concentrated on more pleasant things.

"The new Berlin needlepoint designs are extremely popular, miss," the clerk said while he delved into a drawer. "Especially the roses." He brought forth a number of charming rose designs, each neatly drawn on squared paper. "Each pattern is hand-colored," the young man explained. Previously all the patterns had been in black and white, though drawn on a finely ruled grid. How lovely to have the design in color!

Phoebe had the happy task of selecting the pattern, proper canvas, and the gaily colored wools, adding several new needles to her pile. The needlepoint would help to occupy a good many quiet hours once she and the twins had returned to the country.

When she left the shop some time later, she crossed the walk to enter the carriage that had returned for her at the appointed time, pausing again to look about her. There was no sight of Lord Latham. Somehow she had expected that dratted man to pop up and denounce her for using his aunt's carriage.

Smiling at this bit of whimsy, the smile rapidly faded as she settled back on the cushions to contemplate what must be done about *that man*, as she referred to his lordship.

What a pity he had taken it into his head that she was scheming to inherit Lady Latham's fortune. All during her drive to Lady Latham's house, Phoebe tried to devise ways and means of convincing him that she was innocent of any designs on his aunt's fortune. She came up with no solution.

"Good day, Mr. Popham," Val said politely to the solicitor. At first sight, Popham seemed like most of the legal men Val had met—pompous and given to talking in "whereas's" and "henceforth's."

"I received your message and have assembled all documents pertinent to the matter, my lord," Popham said with a brevity of words that Val appreciated. "Here—you may review the will, for as a cousin of the late fifth Viscount Waring you will have a certain interest in the new peer and maintenance of his estate."

The will was a matter of public record, but it suited Val to discuss the details with Mr. Popham.

The solicitor leaned back in his chair and remained totally silent while Val studied the document in his hand. Mr.

Popham rubbed his chin with one hand and fiddled with a quill with the other, watching Val intently as he read.

It was a simple affair, quite straightforward. When Val had completed that reading, Mr. Popham handed him a second sheet of paper. The writing was less precise but still legible. Val perused the page, then raised his gaze to meet that of the solicitor.

"This is the provision for the guardianship of his children when he realized that he would not survive," Val said. "Interesting document. It is unclear to me whether Miss Thorpe must marry to retain control of the children."

"I agree," Popham replied, pushing another sheet of paper across his desk. "I wrote Miss Thorpe suggesting that it appeared her cousin's husband intended for her to marry in order to provide a proper home for the children." He tapped the reply with one finger. "She flatly rejected the idea of marriage to anyone at that time." He exchanged a hooded look with Val as he continued, "Your aunt made it quite clear that she would not tolerate such a restriction, but allowed that if Miss Thorpe married, it would solve the matter nicely. The question is *when* will Miss Thorpe marry and *who* will be her choice if she does? You can understand that it cannot be just anyone."

"I appreciate your opinion on this matter," Val said, leaning back in his chair and beginning to think that Mr. Popham was a particularly fine example of the legal breed.

"Indeed, my lord," Popham said with a nice deference. "Were she to wed just anyone, it might be possible for an unscrupulous man to inveigle funds from the Waring estate for nefarious purposes!"

"Quite so," Val mused. He pondered the matter for a few minutes, during which the solicitor gave him respectful attention. "It might be possible to convince Miss Thorpe to wed a suitable man. I believe, however, the thing to do is to convince her to give up control of the children. It is unseemly for a maiden lady to have sole control over them, would you not agree?" About his suspicions regarding Phoebe Thorpe and his aunt's fortune he said nothing. One matter at a time.

"Had your cousin made you a co-guardian, there would be no problem at all. Since he did not have that sense, you must do as you see fit, sir." Mr. Popham gathered all the papers and stuffed them back into a folder. Placing that on his desk, he rose, and nodded politely to Val before walking at his side to the door.

"Thank you for your time, Mr. Popham. This has been a most illuminating call," Val said as he left the office.

The other man merely murmured polite words in parting. Val strode past the junior clerks and out of the building.

All the way to his aunt's home on Mount Street, he mulled over the information he had been given. While possibly ambiguous in wording, the implication of the will was clear to any *man* of sense. Who in his right mind would leave the destiny of his offspring, one of whom was the sixth Viscount Waring, in the hands of a young woman! An unmarried woman, at that. It would have been serious enough had she been a widow of no means. But for Miss Thorpe to have the custody of the twins was unthinkable.

Why, when Val looked into her luminous blue eyes, he was certain that at times he detected laughter and amusement in their depths. He appreciated a good joke, but he was *not* accustomed to having a woman secretly laugh at him. It was a deuced uncomfortable feeling. He kept wanting to ask her what she found so blasted amusing—and had to admit to himself that he feared her reply.

The worst of the matter was that he privately found Miss Phoebe Thorpe a very lovely young woman. When Ferdy had mentioned those black curls as being soft and silky, Val had known two absurd desires. One—he wanted to punch his friend in the nose for knowing such an intimate detail, and two—Val wanted to thread his own fingers through those charming curls. As to her blue eyes, well, he knew how they could flash in anger, and he had observed how the blue turned to ice when he had challenged her about the twins.

How would her eyes look when a man made love to her? What shades of blue would they become then? Soft gentian? Perhaps periwinkle? Maybe the cerulean of a summer's sky?

He was jolted from his musings by a near-crash with a dray. The driver raised his fist at Val, shouting curses that were unintelligible, most fortunately for those walking along the street.

Val turned his attention to his driving, thinking that this had to be the first time he had been so preoccupied that he had almost had an accident. Chalk another sin up to the delectable Miss Thorpe. He would simply have to dismiss her from his mind except when in the safety of his library or club. Clearly, that woman was dangerous.

"See how lovely the design will be, ma'am? All the colors set forth and so very pretty, too," Phoebe said with satisfaction as she showed her purchase to her ladyship.

"If my hands were better I would work one myself. Very pretty, Phoebe." Lady Latham traced the lines of a fat pink rose, then a lavender pansy. "It inspires one."

Phoebe agreed. She popped a tiny biscuit into her mouth, then raised her teacup and nearly choked when Smedley announced Lord Latham. She swallowed hastily, then turned to look at the man who seemed to wish her ill. She set her teacup on a nearby table with a decidedly shaky hand.

"Good day, ladies." Val strolled across the room, made his bow to his aunt, then looked at Phoebe, who by now had recovered. "I see you are about to embark on a piece of needlework, Miss Thorpe," he said smoothly, walking over to survey the design of delicate pink roses, lavender pansies, and blue periwinkles surrounded by greenery and ribands.

"I went to Ackermann's this morning to purchase the pattern and yarns. I saw you then, my lord," she said, daring to bring up what had intrigued her. It seemed odd he should chance to be in that part of the city when he had a secretary to do his bidding. She would not have given his lordship high marks for consideration of the lesser orders.

"I paid an interesting call," he said, darting a look at his aunt. "One that was most informative. I took your advice, Aunt, and went to see Mr. Popham."

A feeling of dread crept over Phoebe. She did not like the direction of the conversation in the least.

"It seems that according to one interpretation of my cousin's will, Miss Thorpe ought to be married to have custody of the children." Val avoided looking at Phoebe Thorpe, but he did wonder if it was her dagger-sharp look that made his back prickle.

"I was with your cousin those last hours of his life. He wished for me to care for the children, as I had been doing since they were born," Phoebe declared.

"What? My cousin, Viscount Waring, did not have a nurse, a nanny, or some such person to care for his twins? I cannot believe he was so paltry a man." Val stared at Miss Thorpe, waiting for her to explode. It took but seconds for her to narrow her eyes and snap back a scathing reply. Lord, she was magnificent when she was angry.

"Camilla was ever in delicate health. After the birth of the twins, she needed extra care. The nurse spent most of her time with Camilla. I cared for Anthony and Doro with the help of a nursery maid." Phoebe rose to confront Val and added, "I love the twins dearly. I cannot find it in my heart to believe that you would take them from me. I have had them from the moment of their birth," she said. "They are like my own. You could not be so cruel."

Val found that direct blue gaze downright uncomfortable. He felt the worst sort of villain, and it was not a sensation with which he was the least bit familiar. Phoebe Thorpe looked as though she might cheerfully toss him in the Thames. And that was another thing that was different about her. Most women would have thrown themselves in his arms, begging and pleading with tear-drenched eyes and swooning away in a dramatic effort to change his mind. The beautiful Miss Thorpe merely studied him with narrow-eyed contempt. Suddenly Val needed to redeem himself with her. He rose to meet her challenge.

"Perhaps there is another solution?" he suggested.

The glimmer of hope in her expressive eyes was nearly his undoing. What was the matter with him? He usually could ignore the expectant looks in women's eyes, no matter how beautiful they might be. It most likely was his imagination. He had observed that his imagination had been most active of late.

"But I think Phoebe *ought* to marry," Lady Latham announced in her high, fluting voice.

Val watched an amused expression replace Phoebe's

anxious one and suddenly realized that the notion of making Phoebe Thorpe happy was vastly appealing. It certainly had greater allure than incurring her wrath. He wondered if the delicate and lovely Miss Oliphant ever raged in anger or danced with delight. He suspected that Phoebe did both.

"Well, as to that, dear ma'am, I have no one in view," she said with an entrancing chuckle. "Do you have a candidate for me? He would have to like the twins and the country, for I fear they adore their pets. Poor Anthony has been longing for a puppy and I must refuse him. Doro—most fortunately—is satisfied with feeding ducks and buying flowers from the child across the street."

"Someone who likes the twins and pets, not to mention the country. There ought to be a number of fellows who fill that bill." Val sat down by his aunt once Phoebe had returned to her chair. Facing Phoebe Thorpe in a tension-filled drawing room was distinctly unsettling.

"Have you solved the matter of Miss Oliphant?" Lady Latham inquired, interrupting Val's ruminations concerning the gentlemen of his acquaintance.

"What? Oh, her. Well, I believe her mother is of mixed emotions. She admires my title and fortune, but is not quite certain that I am the one for Eustacia," Val said, with a wry look at his aunt.

"We had best set the tongues to rest before either of us embark on a matrimonial search," Phoebe declared in a practical way. "I have no desire to rush into marriage, thank you very much. The gentleman I seek must have a few more qualifications than those mentioned. And I find it most upsetting to go about with the knowledge that others think me less than I am. For you know"—and she gave Val an exceedingly direct look—"I am neither your mistress nor a cozening female about to cheat your aunt of her fortune. I find it very distressing to be thought either."

Val could not believe his ears. That a delicately bred female should say such words to a man was beyond thinking. Never mind that he himself had accused her of one crime and that Society believed the other.

"Plain speaking, indeed," Lady Latham said with a sharp glance at her nephew. "What say you to that?"

"We had best find Miss Thorpe a husband, then all the

gossip will cease and the harpies can jolly well find someone else to tear to bits and scraps."

"Camilla would be quite amused were she to know I must marry to raise the twins. She was forever after me to settle on a husband." She exchanged a knowing look with Lady Latham that made Val curious.

"Was there a suitable applicant for your hand?" he said, with a casual manner that he hoped concealed his interest in her reply.

"Never say she knew about Aldous Clark," Lady Latham suddenly inserted.

"I fear she did," Miss Thorpe said with a rueful grin that made him wonder what there was about the man to cause that expression.

"And she attempted to direct your interest to someone more eligible, I suppose," Lady Latham said, apparently enjoying this turn of conversation.

"Of course," Phoebe replied with a twinkle in her fine eyes. "There was the squire, you see. He was widowed with six hopeful children and a fine large manor house that needed tending as well. There must have been yards of draperies to be mended, never mind the piles of torn sheets and linens. And if I rejected him—which I admit I did—there was an aged peer who really needed a nurse more than a wife, but a wife is cheaper, you know. I fear I also turned down his offer of respectability. So, kind sir," she said to Val, "if I am single, it is not for want of applicants. It is for want of something else entirely."

"They both seemed reasonable to me. What is it you want, pray tell?" Val leaned forward, surprised at his own curiosity.

"Why, I would at least have a fondness for the man. I think it must be dreadful to go through your married life barely tolerating one another. There is a great deal involved, I believe," she said reflectively.

Val concealed a grin behind a hastily raised hand. He cleared his throat, and avoided looking at his aunt lest she guess his thoughts, which were not at all proper at this moment. He could not nudge from his mind the vision of Phoebe Thorpe in a marriage bed, delightfully sans clothing and arms outstretched in welcome to her husband. He almost envied the chap. Of course, he would have to put up with those eyes that seemed to see far too much.

"Well," Val said, daring a glance at his aunt, "I think it highly improper for the sixth Viscount Waring to be reared by a woman alone. He needs to be taught the responsibilities of his position."

"I believe that Phoebe had someone doing just that, did you not, dear girl? Aldous Clark, I think you said."

"True," Phoebe said with too much brevity to suit Val.

"You are not married to him," Val pointed out, discovering again a fierce curiosity to know more about the man.

"I believe that, given a proper motive, he would tutor Anthony to readiness for Eton." Again there was that exchange of glances between the two women.

Val recalled Mr. Popham's expressed concern that a man would marry Phoebe Thorpe to obtain access to the Waring fortune. "Well, you can forget this Aldous Clark—unless you would be willing to have me check him out?"

"Oh, no," Phoebe said hastily. "We do not have an understanding—precisely." Her blush at these words deepened Val's curiosity.

"If that is the case, we must settle on someone else, for time is flying past," Lady Latham said, her manner and tone decisive. "Val, why do you not bring several young men here—or introduce them to dearest Phoebe at balls and the like. Find a suitable gentleman, with at least a modest fortune, and I suspect he had best be someone of whom Phoebe can be fond. Is that agreeable, dear girl?" she said to her guest.

"Without a doubt," Phoebe said, while nearly smothering her nose in a posy. "But I shan't wed just to please you, sirrah." She glared at Val over the bloom.

"I shall do what I am able," Val said, at sea again, because he had recalled how unusual it was for him to be so neglected by a lovely young woman. Not that he wanted Phoebe Thorpe. Heaven forbid! But he liked women in general. He enjoyed flirting and romantic entanglements. It was the earnest girl facing him whom he found daunting.

Phoebe rose from her chair, forcing Val to rise as well in polite response. She walked to the window, then turned to face him. "I still feel the matter of the twins is none of your affair, my lord. Had my cousin's husband thought you a fitting guardian for the children, surely he would have designated you as such in his final will. Perhaps he felt you were not fit to hold that role? I have heard a few whispers about your rakish mode of living. . . ." Her words trailed off as Val advanced on her.

He did not mean to appear menacing nor the least angry, but it was dashed difficult when Phoebe Thorpe accused him of living a rakish life. At least, he amended, she wondered if he had. That she nurtured doubts about his appropriate qualifications as a guardian bothered him.

"I assure you that at present I am courting a young woman of impeccable virtue and taste. If my life had been so dreadful, I doubt her dragon of a mother would permit me to see her," Val said in biting tones.

"You did say that your title and fortune placed you in better standing with her and her mother," Phoebe said, pointing out the hole in his logic.

Deciding that if he remained he might well smother Phoebe with the handiest pillow, Val murmured something about an appointment, bowed over his aunt's hand, then met Phoebe Thorpe's candid gaze.

"I will do what I can to find a proper suitor for your hand. I must point out in advance that it will be someone who is not in need of my nephew's fortune." With that he left the room and marched out to his freedom.

Phoebe walked over to sit by Lady Latham and burst into laughter. "I am sorry, my lady, but he is the veriest clothhead and as contrary as may be."

Her ladyship chuckled and said, "I wonder how long it will be before he learns what Eustacia Oliphant is really like."

"How much does he know about her?" Phoebe said, while dabbing her eyes with a handkerchief.,

"Absolutely nothing, other than she has glorious hair—under which there are scarcely two thoughts to rub together. She is graceful and sought after and she simpers at him in the manner he expects."

"How like a man—to select a lifelong mate on the color of hair or a simpering manner." Phoebe leaned back against the sofa and said, "Where do we go this evening, providing you feel up to leaving the house? I am not at all certain you should not be abed instead of traipsing about London."

"Pish tush, my dear," her ladyship said with a wave of her hand. "I am having the time of my life."

Phoebe rose to go to her room, then paused by the door. "And what was that nonsense about Aldous Clark? I thought we had consigned him to the ranks of the unacceptable?"

"Never let any man believe there is no one in your life," her ladyship said. "Competition is what a man thrives on—until he is wed."

"Then what?" asked an intrigued Phoebe.

"Why, then it is best to allow him to believe he is not only the sole man in your life, but also that all others were just mere nothings with which to pass the time."

"That seems a trifle hard on the others," Phoebe pointed out.

"What is more important—a contented husband or a past swain with the ability to cause trouble?"

"I see what you mean." Phoebe said thoughtfully. "At any rate, if your nephew thinks for one moment that I will marry just to appease some notion of propriety he has, let him jump in the Thames."

"I'd wager you would be willing to give him a push."

"Indeed I would," Phoebe said with a smile. But on her way up the staircase, she wondered about her reaction to Valentine Latham. She found him too disturbing for her own peace. Certainly Aldous Clark had not affected her in this way. She also worried about the gossip regarding Lord Latham and herself. She did not wish to cause scandal, for it truly could affect her guardianship of the twins. Oh well, whatever the coming days brought, it seemed her time in London would scarce be dull.

When Phoebe and Lady Latham left for the theater, the evening was a fine one, and Phoebe sniffed the spring air with appreciation.

"Rain before morning," her ladyship muttered while settling in the carriage. "I can feel it in my bones."

"You ought to have soaked your hands in my potion to

soothe your pain. I wish you would not feel it necessary to see me out and about. Your nephew thinks it scandalous."

"I know," her ladyship said with a crafty smile. "I adore scandalizing Valentine. For a man known as a Corinthian, he shocks quite easily at times."

"That would mean he has standards of propriety, ma'am," Phoebe said doubtfully.

"Of course he does, with his elderly relatives who have pots of money," Lady Latham said with asperity.

"Do you?" Phoebe asked. "Have pots of money, that is. I would never ask, but your nephew believes I am out to cozen a fortune from you. Is there a fortune to be cozened, as it were?"

"True. My late husband invested wisely and when he died, his unentailed estate was the envy of his brother, the duke. But then he died as well, so I do not have to worry about his trying to snabble it away from me."

"Goodness. Is that the way of things? Is everyone seeking to gain wealth by whatever means they can?"

"All but you, I suspect. And Val. He is frightfully wealthy in his own right, and does not need to marry for money. But that is not the case with most men. Be careful of the others. If you would care to have me vet them, I would be pleased to stand mother to you," her ladyship said in an offhand way.

"I am honored, my lady," Phoebe said with a tender look. She lapsed into quiet reflection as they entered the theater and climbed the stairs to the box Lady Latham had reserved.

They had settled in their chairs, and were discussing the play, when Ferdy Andrews peered around the door.

"May I join you? I find the prospect of two beautiful women too good to pass by."

"Indeed you may," her ladyship said with a fond shake of her head. "Utter rubbish, of course, but such lovely rubbish."

Phoebe, firmly believing that what she saw depended upon what she looked for, settled back to enjoy the evening.

"Have you seen Val today?" Ferdy said when Lady Latham was otherwise occupied.

"He did stop by the house this afternoon," Phoebe admitted.

"You smile. What is he up to now?" Ferdy bestowed an amused look at the young woman who interested him.

"He is convinced I ought to marry."

"Has he a candidate for your hand?" Ferdy sat up straight in the chair, an uncomfortable feat for one his size. He looked at Phoebe with obvious curiosity.

"No, but I strongly suspect that he will find one," Phoebe said with a glimmer of a smile. "I gave him strict specifications. I must like the man I marry, you see."

"What a novel idea," Ferdy replied. "I wonder who it will be?"

"As do I," Phoebe admitted with an uneasy look across the theater to where she had spotted Lord Latham seated with the Oliphants in their box.

Chapter 7

Val glanced across the crowded theater, then looked more sharply. At first he couldn't believe his eyes. Then his second look confirmed his suspicion. It *was* Miss Phoebe Thorpe in the box with his aunt and Ferdy. Her black curls gleamed in the lights, even at this distance. The silly thing she wore on her head concealed very little of her glorious hair.

He failed to see what could possibly entertain her so that she laughed with such apparent delight. Ferdy had never acted the jester before as far as Val knew. Her gown was another one of those scandalous creations. Really, the neckline dipped lower than propriety allowed and the expanse of creamy skin it exposed was outrageous, Val thought, completely ignoring the low-necked gowns worn by most of the female theatergoers who had any pretensions to fashion. The delicate rose color seemed to blend with her skin, so that at this distance, one wondered where the gown began and the skin left off. Only the scattering of seed pearls and sequins along the neckline helped ameliorate the impression of rose-tinted skin.

"Is something amiss, Lord Latham?" Mrs. Oliphant inquired acidly.

"I spotted Lord Andrews and my aunt across the way," Val said with an annoyed glance at the large woman at his left. She had coyly informed him that her first name was Hepsibah, which she said meant "a delight to God's eye." Val thought that while the good Lord might delight in her, he was most assuredly the only one, for the woman was a crashing bore.

He turned his attention to the young woman on his other side, the delicate and lovely Eustacia Oliphant. He was determined to worm a few more bits of conversation from her this evening. The thought that he might have to go through the remainder of his life with a silent but beautiful woman at his side was unsettling.

"Do you look forward to the comedy, Miss Oliphant?" Val said in an attempt to draw out the Beauty.

"Yes, thank you," she replied. She smiled demurely and fluttered her lashes as most young women seemed to do when admired. She became silent again.

"Your aunt seems in good spirits this evening," Mrs. Oliphant said when the silence stretched on.

"Ferdy has a way with her. She enjoys his company."

"And does Miss Thorpe also enjoy his company?" Mrs. Oliphant said with a faint insinuation in her tone.

"She appears to be amused at this moment, ma'am," Val replied with an irritated side glance at the overpowering woman. How she could be the mother of the dainty beauty at his other side was beyond him.

"I do not understand how your aunt can continue to accommodate Miss Thorpe, with all the shadows on her name. I must say, Lady Latham is more generous than I could be—under the circumstances." The lady gave a virtuous nod of her head and sniffed in disdain. Val drew back and gave the woman a considering look, then said, "And what might those be, ma'am?"

"Well, that is . . . I have heard . . ." Mrs. Oliphant rapidly blinked her eyes, obviously not having expected Val to confront her with that question. As she shook her head clearly searching for a word to extricate herself from her *faux pas*, she resembled a confused hen, the illusion only heightened by the absurd puff of feathers perched atop, that quivered with her every motion.

"I may have my differences with Miss Thorpe, but as long as she is sheltered by my aunt, I would take a dim view of someone destroying her name," Val said, aware he sounded rather aggressive for one unrelated to the girl. Yet he had assumed the position as head of the family in this matter and as such intended to protect the family name.

For once Miss Oliphant spoke up. "She is very pretty. I understand she has twins?"

"Only in her care," Val replied, disliking having to defend the very woman he was trying to oust from his aunt's protection.

"How unusual," Miss Oliphant said pensively. "I thought children were normally given to responsible relatives, like an aunt and uncle. Surely a man should take charge of them?" She batted her lashes at him again, looking as though she was blinking dust from her eyes.

Since this was precisely Val's own argument, he was in no position to dispute the matter. "Point taken," he agreed quietly.

"She must be a managing female," Mrs. Oliphant inserted. "Those are the worst sort. Your aunt must know there is a great deal of talk around London regarding the details of the young woman's past."

"Miss Thorpe seems most capable," Val said, wondering when this dreadful conversation would cease. He was saved from additional comments by the commencement of the play. Never had he been so glad to see an actor stroll across the boards.

Sitting comfortably in the opposite box, Phoebe found the comedy delightful. For a while it took her mind from the troubles that beset her. It was quite enough to be responsible for the care of the twins without worrying about the machinations of the odious Corinthian who watched her so complacently from across the theater. She had found the information regarding his consultation with Mr. Popham rather alarming. That the two men she feared most were joining forces disturbed her. However, she did wonder if Lord Latham was serious about finding her a husband. Could marriage truly be necessary to enable her to keep the twins?

When the first act concluded, Ferdy offered to find them cooling beverages, and both women gratefully accepted.

Once alone, Lady Latham turned to Phoebe and said in a considering way, "And what do you think of Lord Andrews, my dear?"

"He can be amusing," Phoebe replied with caution. "I suppose my reservations are merely nonsense."

"You suspect his intentions because he is a friend of Val's, I suppose. And rightly so," Lady Latham concluded.

"You think Lord Andrews was sent to spy on

us . . . me?" Phoebe said indignantly. "How perfectly dreadful."

"Perhaps not to spy, only watch? But, how do you feel about the man now that you know him better?"

"Nothing," Phoebe said. She compressed her lips and shared an irritated look with her ladyship.

"Well, if Val truly intends to find you a husband, he will have his hands full. Perhaps he will begin to understand what fond mamas endure when trying to launch a daughter?" The older woman gave an amused laugh, then patted Phoebe on the arm. "He has been staring over here more than he ought, you know. Miss Oliphant will think there is more to his interest than seeing you wed . . . or whatever he has told them. For if I know anything at all about Hepsibah Oliphant, she will try to worm all she can about you from poor Val. For once, he has my sympathy."

"Miss Oliphant does not appear to be a good match for Lord Latham," Phoebe observed.

"She is naught but sugar. The first sign of trouble and she will melt away. He needs someone made of sterner stuff, who can withstand anything that comes along."

"But she is very pretty," Phoebe reminded.

"Pretty is as pretty does. It is what's inside that matters in the long run. Looks can fade, as he might see if he would but consider her mother. Hepsibah was a reigning beauty in her day. Amazing, is it not?" she added when Phoebe hastily concealed a gasp behind a gloved hand.

"Goodness," Phoebe murmured, risking another look at Mrs. Oliphant. It was difficult to imagine her as a beauty.

The door opened and Ferdy returned with a tray of beverages: lemonade for the ladies and wine for himself.

Within minutes the second act began, and Phoebe forced herself to concentrate on the silly plot until the hilarious conclusion.

They left early, not remaining to see the farce. Phoebe was concerned about Lady Latham and the lateness of the hour. That their early departure might also serve to avoid any meeting with Lord Latham also occurred to her.

Lord Andrews bowed over Phoebe's hand as he assisted

her into the Latham carriage. "It will be interesting to see what the coming days bring," he murmured.

"You are aware of Lord Latham's intentions?" Phoebe said with a sinking heart. How many of his cronies had he told about his plans?

"Val confides in me on occasion. However, he generally keeps his thoughts pretty much to himself," Lord Andrews said, before closing the carriage door.

Somewhat assured, Phoebe bid the large gentleman good night, then settled next to Lady Latham in the carriage.

"I think you can cross Ferdy Andrews off any list you might make," Lady Latham declared after they set off down the street. "I sense a lack of regard there," she said, before lapsing into a silence that continued until they reached the house on Mount Street.

After Smedley had removed their cloaks, Phoebe gently assisted her ladyship up the stairs.

"I have no intention of keeping a list, ma'am," Phoebe said in parting. "I find the entire matter a trifle bizarre."

"Then I will," her ladyship mumbled, a crafty look crossing her face. "I cannot wait to see who Val thinks is acceptable marriage material for you."

The following afternoon, Lord Latham arrived at Lady Latham's town house with two gentlemen in tow. He introduced them to Phoebe, then prodded them all into a polite conversation.

Phoebe could not make up her mind whether to be insulted or infuriated. The two gentlemen were dull as dishwater—indeed, she wondered if their wits had gone begging. The lanky Mr. Pippen-Jones towered over them and had no chin at all, whereas Mr. Connington was nearly bald and extremely plump to boot. Were these the first of the candidates for Phoebe's hand? She decided they must be from the bottom of his list. They simply could not be at the top!

In an attempt to confound Lord Latham, Phoebe was more than polite; she set out to dazzle them. She urged delicacies and tea on them, sent bright smiles their way, and praised what she might when Lord Latham pointed out their interests.

"Mr. Pippen-Jones raises beagles," Lord Latham said, obviously trying to find something of mutual interest.

"Anthony adores dogs and beagles in particular," Phoebe said enthusiastically, hoping she managed to look profoundly impressed. "Such clever little beasts," she concluded.

Mr. Pippen-Jones beamed his approval of such an intelligent boy, although he cast a confused look at Phoebe for her remark about clever beasts.

Not to be outdone, Mr. Connington informed Phoebe that he bred racehorses. "Finest of stock, don'tsha know," he boomed.

Phoebe politely murmured words of encouragement while he nattered on about his animals as horse lovers are prone to do. Within minutes she had learned more about raising horses than she'd ever dreamed of knowing.

The two men munched and sipped their way through a light tea and conversation, surreptitiously studying her face and figure with obvious interest. When it came time to depart, they rose, earning a fervently thankful smile from Phoebe.

"I thought the lad would do better than that," Lady Latham said when they had left, indignant at her nephew's selections.

"Perhaps his choice is limited?" Phoebe said with a wry glance at her ladyship. "I believe I have earned a respite, my lady. I will spend time with the children, if you please." Slipping from the room with her ladyship's blessing, she sped up the stairs.

At the top of the house she found the twins playing peacefully. Anthony sat astride a rocking horse unearthed from the attic, declaring he was practicing for the day he acquired a pony. It was clear that day could not come soon enough for him. Phoebe wished they might locate a docile mount for him, but doubted they could find one in the city.

Doro perched with her favorite doll in the window seat, looking out at the street from time to time. When she saw Phoebe, she slid from the chair and crossed the room to tug at one of her aunt's hands.

"Aunt Phoebe, I see Pansy, the flower girl. She looks so

cold. May I give her my old pelisse?" Doro pleaded. "She's small and so thin."

Aware that she had not spent as much time with the twins as she had when they lived in the country, Phoebe quickly agreed and the two spent an agreeable half hour searching through the clothes press in Doro's room for a dress and a pelisse that would be suitable.

Once the garments were found, Doro persisted in dragging Phoebe down the two flights of stairs and out the front door. What anyone might think of her being ungloved and without a bonnet on her head, Phoebe didn't consider. She was totally absorbed with Doro's wish to help an unfortunate child.

After Doro had given the clothes to little Pansy—who seemed frightfully small for her age—Phoebe said, "Your mama will permit you to keep these, will she not?" Phoebe suspected there might be a desire to sell the garments rather than allow the girl to wear them.

"I hope to see you with them on," Doro said earnestly.

Pansy allowed as how she would do her best. Doro trotted back to Lady Latham's house, well pleased with her afternoon efforts.

Anthony had followed Phoebe and Doro down the stairs and waited for them just inside the door.

"I should very much like to go to the park again. The rain has stopped," he reminded his aunt.

"Capital idea. After the company we had this afternoon I feel a need for a breath of fresh air." She was heartily glad the two suitors had left—although the aroma of the stables and kennels yet seemed to linger about the entry.

In a short time, the three had dressed properly, left the house, and were on their way to Hyde Park at a brisk walk.

"Our maid, Molly, said some gentlemen came to see you today," Doro reported. "Were they nice? Molly says you must find a husband. What does that mean?" Doro asked, studying Phoebe with that clear gaze that can so disconcert an adult.

"It appears that some people believe I should marry. I promise you that if it becomes necessary, I will pick someone who likes you as well as he likes me."

"Maybe I could have a pony," Anthony said, then ran on to investigate a puppy that wandered about by itself.

"I would like to be in the country again," Doro observed. "I think it would be good for Pansy, too."

"Indeed, love. There are a great many children in London who would be better off living in the country. I doubt their parents could move, however."

Phoebe did not have the heart to explain to Doro the sort of lives lived by most of the people who sent their children out to work the streets: unheated rooms with little food, most likely a mother who frequented the gin shop and a father who was even worse. Phoebe had attended two lectures given by a woman devoted to the cause of the poor. There was so little a young woman might do to help, especially one like Phoebe who had limited resources. But, she had decided that she would try to help little Pansy.

This resolve tucked in the back of her mind, she watched the children run and play. Her heart overflowed with love for her two dears. It pained her to admit that they did most likely deserve a father. But how could she be sure a husband would love them as he should? Many gentlemen looked upon children as no more than a necessary nuisance to ensure the succession. Children not only were to be never seen—much less heard—they were to be forgotten whenever possible. And few men would welcome a ready-made family.

"Oh, look, Aunt Phoebe," Doro said with an awed voice, "that is the most beautifullest lady I have ever seen." The little girl tugged at Phoebe's hand and stared across the park at a vision in pink and white. The young woman in the elegant carriage drawn by a pair of grays was indeed breathtaking. With a sinking heart Phoebe recognized Miss Eustacia Oliphant.

"Yes, love. That is your cousin driving her. I believe he intends to marry her."

"Looks as though she'd scream if she saw a frog," Anthony observed. "You would never be such a ninny," he said to his cousin in a gruff little voice, as though trying to conceal his partiality.

"Not many ladies are fond of froggies," Phoebe said in all fairness. "She is very lovely."

Then a plume from the exquisite bonnet adorning the blond curls blew away and Anthony dashed after it. He captured his prize before it touched the ground, and held the fragile feather as gently as though it were one of his precious frogs. Before Phoebe could stop him, he had run after the carriage, calling out to Lord Latham to stop.

Since carriage traffic was in its usual snarl, their pace was necessarily stately. Anthony caught up to them with ease.

Phoebe swiftly grabbed Doro's hand and followed. She reached the carriage just as Anthony, bowing slightly, proffered the pink plume to the seated couple, saying, "If you please, Cousin Val, the plume blew away from the lady's bonnet."

Val gave a nod to his tiger, who hopped down, took the feather in his gloved hand and gave it to Miss Oliphant.

Miss Oliphant was clearly in a dilemma, Phoebe realized. With her head turned away from Lord Latham, he could not see the look of distaste on Eustacia's pretty face as she viewed the plume. It had actually been in the hands of first, a dirty little boy, and secondly, a tiger who attended the horses!

"Thank you," she finally said with frigid politeness.

"Good lad," Lord Latham said. "That was a fine piece of running there. You ought to do well when you are at Eton; might even make the football team in time."

Anthony beamed with pleasure. "Thank you, sir," he said in his piping little-boy voice.

Phoebe, knowing her manners had gone begging, took a calming breath and said, "Good afternoon, Miss Oliphant, Lord Latham. Nice weather, is it not? Miss Oliphant, may I present Dorothea Latham and Viscount Waring? How nice of Anthony to return your plume to you. Why, it never had a chance to touch the ground and become soiled." Aware that she verged on babbling, she paused, then concluded quietly, "He is a very thoughtful boy."

Phoebe smiled at Miss Oliphant, and recognized that the young woman in pink was struggling to cope with the admittedly odd situation. Before her stood a boy the very image of the man at her side—the man she had every intention of marrying. The little girl looked remarkably like

Miss Phoebe Thorpe, and these two children were known to be twins.

"How . . . how nice of him."

It must have cost Eustacia a good bit to utter those polite words, Phoebe thought. The beautiful Miss Oliphant had not one drop of compassion within her for a child. Phoebe wondered precisely what the young woman *did* have within her, for she looked like an empty shell—an exquisite shell, to be sure, but an empty one.

"Those are bang-up horses, Cousin Val," Anthony said with all the longing of a little boy who would adore a drive in the splendid carriage, but dare not ask outright.

"We must be on our way, but I promise to take you for a turn in the park as soon as may be," Lord Latham said, before tooling the carriage off into the traffic at as good a clip as possible.

Phoebe wondered if he had become uncomfortable at the silence from his intended bride. Certainly she was not one for conversation.

"Lovely day for a walk," a voice boomed from behind her.

Phoebe whirled about to find Lord Andrews standing not far away, looking rather hesitant. "Goodness, sir, but you startled me out of six years growth."

"Hardly that," he said with his wide and amiable grin. "I have it on good authority that such an event would put you back in the schoolroom."

Phoebe laughed and allowed the large gentleman to join them in their saunter through the environs of Hyde Park on the sunny spring day.

As they strolled along the Serpentine, she related the encounter with Lord Latham and Miss Oliphant. Lord Andrews laughed his hearty, booming laugh to Anthony's delight. Doro gave Lord Andrews a curious look and tugged at his gloved hand to gain his attention.

"Do you have a carriage, sir?" she said. "We never drive in a carriage, 'cept," she added in an effort to be scrupulously honest, "when we came to visit Great-aunt Latham."

Before Phoebe could scold her, Lord Andrews bent down to look Doro in the eye. "I do have a nice carriage. I would deem it a great pleasure if you and your brother, and of course your cousin, would take a drive with me on the morrow."

Both children gave Phoebe such a look that she had no option. "We would be charmed, sir. But," she added with a reproving and almost flirtatious look, "that was not fair of you."

"Whoever said fairness was necessary? Not Val, I'll wager." He exchanged a wry look with her that put Phoebe quite in charity with the genial gentleman.

"Lord Latham introduced me to two men this afternoon—Mr. Pippen-Jones and Mr. Connington. Do you know them?"

Lord Andrews gave Phoebe a startled look, then chuckled. "Beginning at the bottom of the barrel, I perceive."

"Precisely what I thought," Phoebe said, not even trying to conceal her ire.

"He told me that he thought you were not fit to have charge of the twins," Lord Andrews said quietly some time later, when they had left the Serpentine and strolled back toward the Standhope Gate. "I cannot believe he is serious. Else he has not watched you with the children. You far surpass any nanny I have seen, and a good many mothers, come to think on it. I doubt my sister has ever taken her tots for a walk in the park."

Anthony, who had caught the last of this, said, "We go for walks most days when the weather's nice. I quite like walking, for I can chase squirrels and hunt for frogs when I please. Although," he added diplomatically, "a carriage must be very nice."

"Anthony's passion of the moment is frogs, you see," Phoebe said with a laugh. She gazed up at Lord Andrews, surprising a peculiar expression in his eyes. She made no remark about it, but merely turned to offer her hand to Doro, who looked as though she was about to wander away.

"And you tolerate frogs? Amazing woman," Lord Andrews said with a grin.

"Cousin Phoebe is the bestest lady in the world," Anthony announced grandly.

"You know, lad, I believe it." Lord Andrews bowed to them, then left them with a murmured assurance that he would not forget the drive in the park on the morrow, setting a time before he strode off in the opposite direction.

"Anthony, you put me to the blush," Phoebe chided gently. "Such extravagant praise! Goodness."

"Well, we are going for a drive tomorrow," Anthony said as though that made it all perfectly clear.

Phoebe chatted with the two children, but could never have said about what. Lord Andrews's words haunted her, sticking in her mind with the tenacity of day-old porridge. Not fit to have charge of the children? Whatever did Lord Latham intend should Phoebe continue to turn her nose up at the gentlemen that he paraded before her?

Regardless, she would not yield to the likes of those men. More dull, dreary specimens she could not imagine. No. Never. She would spirit the children away from London and secrete them on the Waring estate with instructions that Lord Latham be shot—in the leg—should he dare to follow.

She was so incensed by the time they reached the house on Mount Street that when she saw Lord Latham was awaiting them before the door, she was hard pressed not to attack him then and there.

"Good day, Miss Thorpe."

"Sir, I have never in my life been quite so angry." She made to pass him and enter the house and found to her utter frustration that he ignored her words, most likely deciding a woman would never take umbrage at him. He simply placed a gentle hand beneath her elbow and ushered her inside with a knowing nod to Smedley.

"Tea, I believe, or some restorative. Miss Thorpe has had a less then pleasant walk, I fear."

While Smedley bustled off to the rear of the house and the nursemaid gathered the children to whisk them up to their rooms for early supper, Phoebe found herself guided along to the morning room. It was empty this time of day.

"Now what did Ferdy say to overset you? I caught a glimpse of him with you in the park. I know he is a bear of a man, and not always possessing the polish most women admire, but he has a very good heart and is the best of friends."

Phoebe stared up at the handsome and infuriating man

now facing her and wished she knew of some way to make a permanent impression on his mind. Never before in her life had she longed to do violence to anyone. She did now.

"I thought you would be having tea with Miss Oliphant," Phoebe said at last.

"You are reluctant to tattle on Ferdy. Very well. I admire loyalty in a woman," he said with a gentle smile that curled the toes of Phoebe's Morocco slippers. "Miss Oliphant declared it unbelievable that you and I are merely polite acquaintances, related by marriage through those twins. I believe she imagines a much closer connection."

"Miss Oliphant has a shocking mind," Phoebe snapped, sorely tired.

He reached out to stroke her cheek, then tilted up her face. That gentle smile had reached his eyes this time and Phoebe felt some of her anger melting away. Those dark eyes held intimate mysteries, inviting a girl to wish for anything—well, almost anything.

Then she recalled Lord Andrews's words. Lord Latham had declared that she was not fit to have care of the twins! She had been longing to do violence to him from that moment on. And what did he intend now? A bit of rakish persuasion so he might say her behavior proved his point.

"I think you might call me Val, considering what the world and his wife thinks about us," he teased.

The only problem with his remark was that Phoebe had endured far too much to accept his words as teasing at this point. She drew herself up and swung her hand. The resounding slap was most satisfying. He not only looked astounded—perhaps no woman had rejected him so strongly before—he looked affronted.

"I think it time we understand each other, sir—*Lord Latham*, that is. I am not for dalliance, no matter what you think of me. Or others, for that matter. Why, Aldous Clark is a saint compared to you. A saint, sirrah!" With that statement, she marched out of the room past a puzzled Smedley and up the stairs.

Val stood with his hand to his cheek, sharing a rueful look with his aunt's sympathetic butler. "I believe the lady misunderstood me."

"They frequently do things like that, sir," Smedley

replied, then left his lordship to a glass of claret in the silence of the morning room.

Val walked slowly to the window and stared blindly out up the sky. He had been about to kiss Phoebe Thorpe. Why? He considered her an improper companion for his aunt, unfit to care for the twins. Yet he desired her, indeed he did.

Chapter 8

Rosbert, I want to know everything there is to know about this Aldous Clark person," Val said while pacing about his bedroom. This was one area he could be certain all words spoken remained in strict confidence. There was always the possibility of some servant overhearing bits and scraps of a conversation and repeating them, to Val's detriment. "He obviously means something to Miss Thorpe. I want to know *what* that might be. My aunt said something about Mr. Clark having tutored my nephew. He must live close to Beeches, if that is the case."

"Indeed, sir. If this Mr. Clark tutored your nephew, it would seem logical that he might be the local vicar or curate. That is often the situation in rural localities as I understand these things. You wish me to go at once?" Rosbert stood at attention by a table upon which a stack of papers and narrow storage boxes vied for space.

"A vicar? Well, it would account for her description of the man as a saint. Once in a while they actually are." Val rummaged through a small stack of papers, then extracted a map of sorts from the pile. "I have been going through all the correspondence with my cousin from past years—what little there is of it. This is a map that ought to guide you to the estate. Mind you, it is not the easiest place to find. However, if you go to the village and locate the vicar—or whoever Mr. Clark is—you will not need to hunt out the estate." Val handed the map to his valet, reflecting that that was such a deceptive term for a man of so many talents.

Rosbert studied the map for some moments while Val resumed his pacing back and forth, pausing to look at the stack of papers now and then.

"On the other hand, Rosbert," Val said reflectively, "I

think it might be an excellent idea were you to examine the estate—just cursory, not in depth. I would like to know its general condition. Who knows how closely Popham watches over it? We both know that stewards can falsify reports. And you might be able to learn something useful about Miss Thorpe while nosing about. You could say I sent you to look for a book I loaned my cousin some years ago and now wish to claim. Any plausible excuse that comes to mind when there will do. I have utmost trust in your judgment, old fellow."

Rosbert allowed a smile of regard to soften his normally impassive face. He carefully tucked the map into a pocket inside his coat. "I shall do my best, milord."

"I am determined to protect my aunt," Val declared with a glint in his eyes, "no matter what the cost. The very fact that Phoebe Thorpe came to London to reside with my elderly aunt, who shortly thereafter declares she is willing her fortune to Miss Thorpe is highly suspicious."

After picking up the sum of money allotted for his journey, Rosbert set out at a brisk pace to make final arrangements. He would take the gig, a speedy little vehicle that would permit him to travel where he wished without much notice. Since the gig was a common vehicle, being much used in the country, it would arouse no comment. And, although the trip was not a secret, the less attention paid to him, the better.

Once Rosbert had been sent on his way, Val strolled along to St. James's and White's where he hoped to find Ferdy. As luck would have it, Ferdy was about to depart just as Val ran lightly up the front steps.

"Going somewhere?" Val said, stopping on the top step thus barring Ferdy's way.

"I had planned to, before you blocked my path. Care to join me? I thought I'd see what's on at Tatt's, then observe who is in the park, and possibly stop by your dear aunt's house on Mount Street."

"Of course," Val agreed promptly. This was better than he had hoped, for while going to Tattersall's he could speak to Ferdy without interruptions.

Although the distance was not very great from St. James's Street along Piccadilly to where Tattersall's was located just beyond Hyde Park corner near the turnpike, no fashionable gentleman would walk such a distance. This was particularly true of polished Corinthians, of which group Val and Ferdy were shining examples.

Ferdy's groom brought his curricle along to the front of the club, transferred the reins to Ferdy, then hopped up on the small seat behind. Val quickly joined his friend and they were off, Ferdy neatly turning the corner onto Piccadilly with considerable panache.

Traffic being somewhat lighter than usual, Val felt free to bring up the topic on his mind. "Have you by chance seen Miss Thorpe lately?"

"Saw her at the theater . . . that what you mean?" Ferdy replied while skirting around a slow-moving dray.

"Not in the park?" Val countered. He did not wish to discuss Ferdy's behavior while at the theater. That would hold until another time.

"Yes, well, I did encounter her yesterday. I believe it was after little Anthony had returned that pink plume to your Miss Oliphant." He gave Val a quick glance, brows raised in inquiry.

"She is not *my* Miss Oliphant at this point. So you chanced to speak with Phoebe then. Hmm," Val murmured. He pondered this information, then said, "Were any comments made, by chance?"

"She evinced only slight curiosity about Miss Oliphant. And what do you mean, she's not *your* Miss Oliphant. Everyone expects you to make an announcement before long. You have never danced attendance on any woman for this long before. The banns are as good as read."

"Good grief. A fellow dances with a girl a few times, escorts her to the theater once or twice and they are leg-shackled forever."

"Especially if she has a dragon for a mama," Ferdy added with a wide grin.

"Are you implying that Mrs. Oliphant is a dragon?" Val said, then continued, "No, do not answer that, for she is."

"I wonder if the fair Eustacia takes after her mother?" Ferdy exchanged a look with Val, who barely repressed a shudder at the thought.

"You are certain you said nothing Miss Thorpe might

take exception to while in the park?" Val said, reverting to his original question. He wanted to know what it was that had infuriated Phoebe before their encounter yesterday.

"Nothing that crosses my mind now," Ferdy replied easily. He guided his pair of chestnuts up to the entrance to Tattersall's, then handed the reins to the young groom who had jumped down and run up to catch them.

Val, no wiser as to what had angered Phoebe, left the curricle, strolling along at Ferdy's side into the interior of the establishment that catered to those who wished to sell and buy horses. The odor of horse and leather permeated the air. Cigar smoke drifted across the room. The din was muted and general. Val waited to speak until they reached the less-crowded area of the Ring, where the sale horses were paraded about so one might inspect them. Ferdy paused, quite obviously looking about for something.

"What do you have in mind? Surely you do not wish to replace the chestnuts?" Val said in a voice tinged with horror.

"Actually, I heard that Portreve is selling his son's pony. I've seen the animal and it's a good one. Thought I might pick it up for your young relative. Anthony must miss his country pony—if he has one. To my knowledge, women are seldom as eager to put a chap on a pony as a man would be. The lad has no doubt missed a good deal by not having a father about for things such as that." Ferdy's face gave no inkling as to what his own thoughts were in regard to children or their rearing.

Val said nothing immediately, merely considered his friend's remarks while they wove their way through the throng of gentlemen. While he might not want Miss Thorpe for himself, he discovered he didn't wish Ferdy to have her either. With a faint frown, he said, "I believe it would be improper for you—not being related and all that—to buy the pony. As Anthony's relative, it is quite acceptable for me to do so. I shall outbid you, otherwise," he concluded with a half smile that did not reach his eyes.

"Indeed?" Ferdy said with a narrow look at his longtime friend.

"Quite so," Val said. "Ought to have thought of it myself. Can't think why I didn't." But it did occur to him that buying his cousin a pony might serve to lessen Phoebe's obvious aversion to him. Shrewd planning required that she be disarmed, and how better to do it than with a gift for the boy, who after all *was* Val's relation. There was nothing wrong with a gift to his own cousin.

"A pony? For me?" Anthony exclaimed when Phoebe explained the gift to him sometime later, after she had summoned the children out to the mews.

Val thought it fortuitous that no one else had been interested in the pony; he had picked it up for a song. It was a dandy little pony with nice manners and a pretty dark brown coat, speckled here and there with white splotches. The lad was clearly enchanted. What Phoebe Thorpe thought about the pony, much less the giver, was unclear.

"Thank you Cousin Val," Anthony said with a nice show of good manners. "A pony is a first-rate present." He dropped his polite mien and eagerly inspected his new pony, who stood placidly outside his stall, munching thoughtfully on a carrot provided by the groom.

"I bought all the gear—saddle, tack, all that—so he may take a ride in the park whenever you allow," Val said to Phoebe in a quiet aside.

"I appreciate your gift, for I know how he has longed for a pony. And I also appreciate your discretion—purchasing the pony for him without fanfare. I will most likely permit him out with a groom on the morrow." There was a strained silence on her part following this brief statement. Then, with hands composed before her, she gave him a very direct look and added, "I must apologize for my behavior yesterday. I have no excuse other than I had been sorely tried. I am not normally given to striking people."

"Apology accepted, Miss Thorpe," Val said smoothly, relieved to be on a better footing with her. "Is there anything I might do to improve matters?" Val gave her a bland smile, confronting that direct scrutiny with equal force.

"I suppose it would be beneath the dignity of a noted Corinthian to go into the park when Anthony has his first lesson?" she said with a small chuckle.

Val could not imagine what his top-lofty associates might venture to say, and discovered to his surprise that he was more desirous of pleasing Phoebe Thorpe than his friends. "What time would you wish me to be here?" He was rewarded with a lovely smile.

"Morning . . . perhaps ten of the clock? The park is far from crowded at that hour and should he take a tumble, his dignity will suffer far less if he is not observed."

"That is very thoughtful of you, Miss Thorpe. Little boys—and I well remember this—do take tumbles and dread being seen when doing so. I will be here, barring a disaster, in which case I would notify you immediately."

Phoebe took a calming breath and bid the gentleman good day. She spent a bit longer with Anthony and his new pony—named Prince, they had been told—then persuaded the lad to return to the warmth of the house. "Mrs. Norris has baked some treacle tarts I think you might enjoy."

"Treacle tarts?" he said with wide-eyed delight. "Oh, jolly good show, Cousin Phoebe."

Phoebe blessed the idea she'd had of having Mrs. Norris, Lady Latham's housekeeper, prepare the treats for the children. It eased Phoebe's conscience a little for deserting them again to spend the evening away from home.

The little party held up in the refurbished nursery was a gay one. Doro claimed the now-rejected rocking horse.

"I wish to learn to ride, too, Aunt Phoebe. When may I have a pony?" she demanded earnestly.

"You may ride mine, if you like," Anthony offered generously.

"In good time," Phoebe said, trying to appease the little girl. "I suspect when we return to the country there will be ever so many things we will be able to do. I quite long to go." She poured Doro another cup of nursery tea—which was served with a generous amount of milk and sugar—and offered a second treacle tart, a delight that was rapidly consumed.

In truth, she wondered if she might not be better off returning to Beeches now. Lady Latham insisted they all remain until summer, but Phoebe felt her heart might be in better condition were she to take the twins and leave now.

She felt confused, all of a whirl in her mind. While listening to the twins' chatter, which centered on the amazing and wonderful pony, she mulled over her problem.

Mostly it was her feelings for Lord Latham. Mr. Clark had kissed her hand once when she had been picking roses and had offered him a bud. She had received a hasty peck on the cheek from the squire's son while still at Moreton-Under-the-Marsh. But nothing had affected her quite so much as being near the dratted Corinthian.

It was all quite so confusing. She would wager that the splendid Corinthian actually detested her. He had accused her of attempting to cozen a fortune from his aunt, which was patently untrue. And he had questioned her story about the birth of the twins. She was quite sure that he would push marriage on her as a condition for keeping them, and since he stood as head of Anthony's family, she supposed he legally had some say in the matter. Phoebe was sorry that she had left the papers regarding their history at Beeches that would easily prove their parentage to his loftly lordship. Of course, the twins' birth and baptism were recorded at the church. Phoebe had stood as godmother to them. Their godfathers, for two were required, were George's friends.

She left the twins to their play while the nursery maid kept watch, and wended down to her room. Here she studied the reflection in her looking glass.

"Silly widgeon," she scolded herself. "The man is a Corinthian, a polished member of the *ton*. He has had females doting on his every smile, his looks, from the time he was an infant, I've no doubt. He has that certain charm that draws you even when you do not wish to be drawn. Oh, bother the man!"

The rumors floating about Town had not truly affected her as yet, most likely because of Lady Latham's support. It troubled her that the man who so attracted her could think ill of her. And it troubled her even more that anyone could believe she might be party to a liaison that produced the twins. She wasn't that sort of girl. She walked over to the chair by her window and spent some minutes in reflecting on her situation.

"Why did he buy the pony?" she wondered. Then she shrugged her shoulders and rose from her chair, resolved to put the elegant gentleman from her mind. The only way she might avoid him was to leave London, and now she found she wished to see what might happen next.

The following morning in the heart of Mayfair, Val entered the austere drawing room in the Oliphants' London residence at an unusually early hour. He had been summoned by the young lady whose hand he sought, and he took this as an encouraging sign. He had dressed carefully and driven over in his curricle so as to present himself without the scent of the stables about him.

His reception had been oddly chilly, but then London butlers were seldom forthcoming. He looked about him, noting the scarcity of furnishings, the almost Spartan look to the room, indeed all that he had seen of the house. Then Eustacia entered and he gave her a keen look.

"Lord Latham," Eustacia Oliphant said in her little voice, which Val had heard so seldom. "I am glad you could come so soon. You are such a busy person, I was not sure when I might see you. And I did wish to see you soon."

Her mother had sailed in behind her, settling down on the austere sofa and clearing her throat, although she said nothing.

"I would always make time for a beautiful lady," Val said, bowing low over her extended hand. "Is there something I might do for you?"

"This is most painful for me, but it is something I must say." Eustacia twisted a ring on her little finger and glanced at her mother as though for prompting.

"And that is?" Val said, suddenly suspecting that something had gone wrong in his courtship of the lovely Eustacia.

"When we went for our drive in the park and your, ah, cousin caught my pink plume, I noticed something. He is very like you, sir. Very like, indeed. And the little girl resembles Miss Thorpe amazingly." She darted a nervous look at her mother. "I have resisted the gossip about them, feeling that an honorable man would do the right thing and marry the woman who had borne his twins. Since you had not and you are reputed to be an honorable man, I held judgment. I cannot any longer. Or do you deny they are yours?" She clutched her hands before her, anxiously awaiting his reply. Her simple blue muslin dress was a perfect foil for her blond beauty, but her soft blue eyes now held curiosity and contempt.

"They are not my children," Val said with rising ire. "They were born to my cousin and his wife, who was a cousin to Miss Thorpe."

"Truly?" Skepticism rang in her voice. It was clear to Val that she was too polite to challenge his statement, but that she didn't believe him. Again she looked to her mother, who had heretofore remained blessedly silent.

"My lord, it is much to ask of an innocent girl that she ignore so blatant a resemblance," Mrs. Oliphant said.

Val stiffened, all senses offended. "I had hoped to pay my addresses to you in due course, but I would never consider an alliance with a woman who had no faith in me."

Val bowed correctly to her and her mother. Then, without another word of argument or explanation, he strode from the room, leaving a very uncertain young lady standing in the center of that stark drawing room, looking as though she suspected she had greatly erred.

Fury and disgust warred within Val as he drove back toward his home. He had originally planned to go to his club, but now he could not bear to mingle with friends, chatting about social nothings. It would be ideal to head for Gentleman Jackson's for a round or two, but Val decided he needed action in a different direction.

Then he recalled that it was time to meet Anthony in the park and he grimaced. Anyone who saw him would likely draw the same conclusions as Miss Oliphant. "Well, they can jolly well take their filthy minds and do as they please. I shan't allow some tattle-monger to dictate my life," Val declared and wheeled his curricle into the park at a spanking pace.

The groom led Anthony along a path often used by children over the years. The lad showed a remarkable aptitude and what promised to be an excellent seat given time and practice. Val drew alongside the path, then watched for some time before stepping down and walking over to where Prince and Anthony awaited his verdict.

"I am very impressed, indeed I am," Val said. He repressed a smile of amusement when Anthony let out an enormous sigh of relief.

They discussed the pony's good points—which, according to the lad, were numerous, indeed. Then Val offered a few suggestions that he recalled having been given when he first learned to ride. Anthony listened and did as told, to Val's enjoyment. Before long it was time for Anthony to return to Mount Street. Val promised to see him later.

He was a good lad, worthy of being a Latham, and certainly Viscount Waring. Good bottom, Val thought. Then he espied several gentlemen whom he deemed just the ticket for his purpose and drove over to where they were discussing a recent Newmarket race.

"Come with me, you three. I would like for you to meet an interesting lady."

"Does that mean she is platter-faced and rich, or a lovely and poor relative?" Albert Doulton asked with a grimace.

"Most likely the latter," James Hervey said with a grin for his old friend.

"Are you up to something, old chum?" George, Lord Ackhurst, said with a considering look at Val.

"Actually, I would like you to meet my aunt and her guest, and enjoy an excellent spot of tea. My aunt does tea very well, if you must know." Since all three gentlemen were amenable to this idea, within a short time they were marching up the stairs to his aunt's drawing room.

"Dear Aunt, forgive me for barging in like this on you—and with a parade of gentlemen, besides—but I thought you might welcome a bit of male company," Val said, his customary twinkle restored to his eyes now that he was involved in a bit of nonsense.

The gentlemen displayed their excellent manners and settled in comfortably to relish Lady Latham's notion of tea. They had all taken tea at various homes and displayed the studied elegance of the true Corinthian. But their eyes widened in surprise at the display set forth by her ladyship's excellent housekeeper. Seated before the tea table, Phoebe smiled as she gracefully poured tea, and offered dainty sandwiches and other tasty bits of food from the ample array set forth.

"You are looking exceeding demure today," Val murmured while leaning over the tea table.

"Are these gentlemen here for my inspection, my lord?" she said sweetly, with a sudden flash of her blue eyes. She rose to face him.

Stung that she had so quickly grasped his motive for bringing his friends over to the house, Val gave her a disgruntled look, then hastily masked it with a bland expression.

"Thought I would introduce you to my friends. One can never have too many acquaintances when on the town. They, in turn, can introduce you to others. Perhaps then you may find the man you will accept as a husband." Val had the distinct pleasure of seeing Phoebe Thorpe startled.

"I think it is *quite* unnecessary that you take it upon yourself to do this. However, if I do meet someone who can match Aldous Clark in character and quality of mind, I will be happy to consider him," she said in a low, syrupy voice. "You are quite determined marriage is necessary?"

"Yes," he bluntly replied.

The other gentlemen chatted with Lady Latham, Mrs. Bottomley, and Miss Pringle, who had arrived shortly after Val and friends, and who were clearly enchanted with the entire group. The men consumed quantities of everything, polishing off two trays of food, in spite of that splendidly elegant manner they so studiously cultivated.

All were ignored by Phoebe and Val, who were locked in a very quiet contest close to the tea table.

"I suspect you want me gone," Phoebe said blandly. "Why do you not suggest that to your aunt? She insists I remain until summer—although with the time passing so rapidly, perhaps it will not be so very faraway after all."

"I agree with Mr. Popham. If you are to care for the twins, they should have a man to look after their interests as well. Consider that pony. The boy should have been riding long before this. Why, I had my first lessons before I was three. A man would know this. You may do well enough with the little girl, but a boy needs a man to emulate—for guidance."

"Oh," Phoebe said sweetly, "you intend to take the lad to the opera, perhaps? And the green room afterward? Or to the race track? White's? Gentleman Jackson's, perchance?" She smiled—rather unkindly, Val thought. "It has been my observation that most children are left to their nanny and rarely does a father pay the slightest attention to the boys until they at least reach the age of eleven or so. Anthony has a few years until then. I should say that I may take all the time in the world to select a suitable mate, sirrah."

With that pithy remark, she returned to her seat at the tea table and poured another cup of fragrant bohea tea, and with an unreadable expression, handed it up to Val. "Enjoy your tea, Lord Latham."

His friends certainly had enjoyed their tea, clattering down the stairs behind him when they left with all the bonhomie of distinguished Corinthians.

Not one of them had made an impression on Phoebe Thorpe—for the simple reason that she would have none of them. Did she really want a saint? Val wondered.

"Good of you to invite us along, Latham," Albert Doulton said, before striding off toward his town house.

The others agreed and disappeared with equal speed. Val was left to drive himself home, pondering the mysteries of a woman's mind.

The following days progressed slowly. Val kept away from the social whirl, unwilling to expose himself to possible knowing looks regarding Miss Oliphant's defection. She would instantly turn to another gentleman—just whom, Val did not care in the least. He admitted his pride was slightly wounded, his heart untouched. Would it ever be?

Deciding it too deep a subject for him at the moment, Val headed for the opera and a view of the new opera dancer Ferdy had praised. She was lovely, but he found he had no interest in pursuing her, which—had he thought about it—was decidedly odd.

Rosbert returned late in the afternoon, five days after he had left for the country. He carried a neat packet of notes, the map, and wore a peculiar expression that Val could not begin to interpret.

"Well, out with it, man. I gather you uncovered something of interest?" Val invited his valet to sit down, an unprecedented action, and repeated, "Well?"

"I had not the least trouble in locating Aldous Clark. The gentleman has served as curate in the village for several years. He has been a close friend to Miss Thorpe. And according to the tavern keeper and the village gossip I encountered at the local shop, all thought that were he in a position to do so, he would ask her to marry him."

"Oh," Val said quietly. "I don't suppose he looks like a Latham, either?" Val had never heard of any baseborn children in his family, but that did not mean they didn't exist.

"Not unless you have a redheaded, freckle-faced relative somewhere. However I did learn something of interest about him."

"First tell me of the estate," Val inserted, curious to see how Popham had administered the place.

"It appears well enough to me, milord. Everyone thereabouts speaks highly of the bailiff and the place looks prosperous."

"And Miss Thorpe?" Val queried, thinking that Rosbert had been sent on a wild goose chase.

"She is much loved by all and considered an excellent guardian—and godmother—to the children. Mr. Clark showed me their baptismal records and there is no doubt but what they are your legitimate cousins."

"To return to Mr. Clark. You said you learned something of interest about him?"

"Aldous Clark has been declared heir to the Earl of Airlie, sir. Seems the previous heir was killed in a freak accident. Mr. Clark had not the slightest notion that he was next in line to inherit. Not only will he have a title and wealth, but he will claim the courtesy title of Viscount Clark immediately."

"Why that scheming jade," Val murmured in reluctant acknowledgment of Phoebe's cleverness.

Chapter 9

"She must have known somehow," Val exclaimed, aware of a most curious stab in his heart at this knowledge. Surely this would be proof positive that Miss Phoebe Thorpe was not what she claimed to be. Was that not what he wished, in order to protect his aunt from a cozening female? He pushed aside the peculiar twinge and turned to study his valet.

"As to that, milord, I could not say but I doubt it. I am of the impression that the news was fairly recent." Rosbert stood, face impassive, waiting for additional instructions.

"You say that Miss Thorpe is much loved by the local people?" That did not fit into his mental picture of a scheming hussy. But then, Miss Phoebe of the shining black curls and sparkling blue eyes did not fit his image of a cozening female in the least.

"Indeed, sir. Likened her to an angel, coming as she did to care for Lady Waring, then devoting herself to the twins with never a thought as to her own future."

"That," Val charged, "was because she had other expectations. Just wait until my aunt hears this!" But a seed of doubt had been sown in his opinion of Miss Thorpe.

"Well, milord, I would move with caution, if I might be so bold as to offer a word of advice. I sense something is not quite what you may think it is."

The two men had been together too many years for Val to dismiss this suggestion lightly.

The valet cleared his throat and said, "They also claimed she is an excellent housekeeper and oversaw the maintenance of the house with great diligence."

"Aha! Spent a packet redoing the place, I'll wager. I well know how women like to redo a house, changing everything in the place to the latest novelty in decoration." Val paused in his ambulation about his room to give Rosbert a triumphant look.

"As to that, I believe it is well-known that Miss Thorpe is accomplished in mending curtains and turning sheets, milord," Rosbert said with a hint of a smile. "'Tis said she is a skilled needlewoman and even sewed the children's clothing when they were babes, indeed, until they came up to London."

Val frowned at this demonstration of housewifely talents. "Well, I shall be highly interested to see her reaction when she discovers that I know her intentions."

Normally Rosbert would never have inquired, but it was plain to see he itched to know what it was his employer thought. "And they are?" he prompted softly.

"I suspect that Miss Phoebe Thorpe decided to snabble herself a fortune so she would be in an excellent position to marry the heir to the Earl of Airlie, the new Viscount Clark."

Rosbert frowned as though he did not agree with his employer, but was too prudent to say anything to the contrary.

"'Tis a fine day. I believe I shall stroll on over to my aunt's place to see if the stupendous news has reached our villainess, Miss Thorpe," Val said, ignoring that distressing twinge in his heart. His breakfast of steak and eggs must have disagreed with him—most unusual.

With those words, he allowed Rosbert to assist him into a new corbeau coat that went extremely well with his dove gray pantaloons. Val inspected his new waistcoat made of white merino, discreetly embroidered in wine and gold, and thought it sufficiently restrained to be allowable for a Corinthian. His cravat exuded an air of reserve, tied in a simple arrangement. He always felt better able to confront a foe were he properly dressed and groomed. And he felt that Miss Phoebe Thorpe was the most dangerous foe he would ever face.

So, all neatly in place and looking fine as fivepence, Val sauntered out of the door. As he strolled, he considered what he had learned. He could not be pleased that Aldous Clark had made such advancement in life. Sounded like a rabbity sort of chap with that carroty hair. However, his title certainly made him an eligible husband for Phoebe. As Viscount Clark, he had acquired a tidy income with greater prospects to come. Val stifled his inner dismay at this thought and turned to his new conclusion—which he admitted lacked a certain something.

Smedley led him up to the drawing room with starched dignity, announcing Val with more than the customary hauteur.

"Val, dearest, how good to see you. Have you come to learn of Anthony's progress on his pony? Dorothea is all eagerness to learn to ride as well." Lady Latham smiled at her nephew with the fondness of a doting relative.

Val listened as Miss Phoebe Thorpe expounded on the little boy's improvement, while carefully observing her face. He hunted for signs of change, hints that she knew what he now knew. Either she was extremely clever, or word of Mr. Clark's elevation into the peerage had not reached her yet.

"Do you correspond with anyone at Beeches?" he inquired during a lull in the conversation.

The young woman blushed a delicate rose and shook her head. She traced the design on her handkerchief and failed to look up at Val, both suspicious actions in his eye.

"Then you have had no word from anyone there as to . . ."—Val searched for the proper term and found none—"anything?"

She flashed him a bewildered look. "I fear that the housekeeper is not much for writing, although she does know her letters and can read. All the staff in the house are able to read," she said with quiet pride.

"There is no one with whom you correspond?" Val said in an attempt to draw her out, reach the truth he suspected.

"Have you heard something? Has anything happened at Beeches? or to anyone there? Oh, do tell me!" Phoebe leaned forward, extending her hand in entreaty.

"Well, I chanced to learn that one of the inhabitants of the village, the local curate as matter of fact, has had a change of circumstances." Val watched the girl with keen eyes, surprised at her seemingly genuine bewilderment.

"Aldous Clark? How odd. He has been much neglected by his relatives, if I may be so bold as to criticize such a grand family as his. He is related to the Earl of Airlie, and I suppose ought to be grateful for being given this petty post, but really, one would think the earl might have come over more handsomely. A curate barely earns enough to keep bread on his table."

"And not enough to set up a family?"

"Indeed. Paltry wages for a man of God, sir."

Her rosy blush set seal on Val's suspicions about Miss Thorpe. He wondered a trifle at his reluctance to charge her with an infamous scheme, and decided that those earnest blue eyes had made him soft in the head.

"Do you not wish to know what the change in circumstance is?" Val said, still watching her like a cat about to pounce on its quarry.

"Indeed, sir, if you would be so kind?" Her face remained still, but those fine blue eyes gleamed with hope. Val observed the tip of her tongue nervously touch her lower lip and knew the oddest stirring within him.

"I heard that with the unexpected death of a distant cousin, Mr. Clark is now become heir to the Earl of Airlie, and assumes the courtesy title of Viscount Clark."

The news was received with all the reaction Val might have wished. At first she paled, then she turned to Lady Latham and exchanged a significant look before crying, "This is above all wonderful! I am truly pleased for him, for he has an elegant mind and will be a worthy successor to the title. I know he will do honor to the family name, for he is a wise man and most kind."

"Extravagant praise, indeed for a *single* gentleman," Val said, leaning back in his chair to study Miss Thorpe. "You must know him well."

"As to that," she drew herself up to give Val a cool look, "I do know him moderately well. He was so kind as to give Tony lessons, you know."

"So he was at Beeches often? Enjoyed a cup of tea now and again, that sort of thing?" Val queried lightly, tilting his head to one side, while fixing Miss Thorpe with his piercing gaze.

She gave him a hostile glare and said, "True. There is nothing improper about a curate taking tea with the village spinster and their mutual friends. I would never entertain a gentleman in private, I assure you, Lord Latham."

Val ignored the bit about her being a spinster for the moment and leaped ahead, saying, "You must have pitied the chap—a fine gentleman with such little subsistence. I trust he had a decent meal from time to time."

"Whenever I chanced to invite the neighbors over for supper, he was included, yes." She gave him a sharp look, then continued, "Why are you asking these questions? I detect a direction in them that I find most peculiar."

Val decided not to charge her directly. He wished to discuss the matter with his aunt, sensing that perhaps he might do better if the charming and lovely Phoebe Thorpe was not present when he leveled his allegations.

"Not in the least, Miss Thorpe. I am pleased to note that you have such sympathy for a lowly curate. Many a young woman would have an eye to the main chance and ignore one so unfortunate." Val gave her what he hoped was an approving smile, and was about to continue when Smedley paused at the entrance to the room to announce Lord Andrews.

"How lovely to see you again, Lord Andrews," Lady Latham said, with a curious look at the new visitor.

"I wanted to see how young Tony fared with the pony. Doing well, is he?" Ferdy ambled across the room, made a credible bow to her ladyship, then had the temerity to sit on the sofa next to Miss Thorpe, much too close for Val's sense of propriety.

"Oh, indeed," Miss Thorpe exclaimed with obvious delight and a beaming smile for Ferdy.

"Phoebe has indicated that Tony is continuing to do well. I have had the pleasure of watching him. He has an excellent seat and promises to be a first-rate rider," Val said in a quiet drawl, drawing the attention of both those on the sofa in his direction.

Ferdy fixed his gaze on Val, fully aware that his friend asserted his family status to call Miss Thorpe by her first name. Val smiled at him.

Ferdy returned his gaze to the lovely Miss Thorpe, ignoring his old friend who sat some distance away. "I shall make an effort to view this paragon of beginners. Does he ride tomorrow, weather permitting?"

Before Phoebe could answer, Val smoothly inserted, "He usually rides at ten of a morning. I shall be pleased to show you his advancement if you like. I ride over now and again to see how my cousin comes along."

"Tony has not said a word about it, *my lord*," Phoebe said with another glare at Val. She had emphasized the last two words, putting Val in his place as it were.

With a lift of his brows, Val smiled, then said, "My dear Phoebe, gentlemen do not always inform the ladies what they are about."

"I can believe that," Phoebe riposted.

Lady Latham leaned back in her chair, her eyes glittering with amusement. "Should I summon Anthony? He might wish to greet Lord Andrews and tell him about the pony."

Val cleared his throat and gave Ferdy such a look that even that large gentleman could not mistake the intent.

"I fear I must be going, ma'am," Ferdy said, obedient to the unspoken threat.

"I wish to speak to you privately, Aunt, but will return at a time you specify," Val said casually, as though he intended on discussing some trivial thing.

"Anytime this afternoon. We go to the Fotheringales' musicale this evening."

The gentlemen rose and made their farewells, then sauntered down the stairs to where Smedley awaited them.

Once outside, Ferdy stopped to demand, "And what was that all about, pray tell?"

"Nothing terribly important. Phoebe does not know that I bought the pony after you first thought of it."

Ferdy grinned hugely, a sly grin, Val thought. "And you want to impress this woman you feel is an imposter, a cozening female out to con your aunt from her fortune?"

"You needn't laugh, old fellow. I have my reasons. Come, let us see what is afoot on Bond Street."

With that change of topic, the two ambled off in the direction of said street, while deep in discussion of the latest society scandal that involved one of their select group.

Later, after leaving Ferdy, Val returned to Mount Street and sought audience with his aunt. She was found in the morning room.

"Now what is it that you do not wish Phoebe to overhear?" his aunt demanded.

"I did not say that," Val said with a frown.

"But you meant it. Now, explain, if you please."

Feeling like a boy called on the carpet, Val sat next to his aunt when she beckoned him, and attempted to begin.

"You find it difficult? Does it by chance have anything to do with Aldous Clark?"

"How did you guess? I did not know you had taken to mind reading," Val said with a glance at his aunt, then lapsed into silence as he considered his words.

"I am waiting. At my age one has less patience, you know," she said, by way of apology.

"It strikes me as distinctly odd that Phoebe would write you about her worries, then come to live with you as though she had no expectations, when this Aldous Clark obviously means something to her and she must have known he was in the direct line to inherit the title."

"I invited her, if you will recall," her ladyship pointed out.

"True," Val admitted. "But if she were to take advantage of this stay with you to become close to you, even replacing me as your beneficiary, would it not place her in a better position to catch a fine husband? An heir to an earl, as it were?" Val gave his aunt an earnest look, one that openly revealed his concern for her.

Her ladyship considered this proposal for several minutes. Then she looked at Val and said, "I feel that Phoebe is good and honest, the kindest young woman I have yet to meet. What you suggest is pure stuff and nonsense."

"She can be kind and good to you, and still have the fortune in the back of her mind. Marrying the heir to an earldom is a powerful incentive, ma'am." Val leaned forward to place a comforting hand over her somewhat withered one.

"I still do not believe it for a minute. I know you mean this for my best interest, but I refuse to confront her with this conjecture. It would hurt her terribly to be so misjudged. I do not believe that she is capable of such deception."

"Even after what I have said?"

Lady Latham sat straighter and gave Val a studied look, one as piercing as his own. "I do wonder why you are so determined to drive her away from here. And also this, how do you know that Aldous Clark expected to inherit? What age was the previous heir? If an age with Mr. Clark, now a viscount, would he not believe that this cousin would provide his own heirs to the succession?"

Val was silent at this, for his aunt had a point he could not refute. "I can see your mind is as sharp as ever. I must find an answer to those items."

"Sharper, for I am not deluding myself," she said to Val's puzzlement. "Stop and ask yourself why you are so set on discrediting Phoebe. If I did not know better, I should say you are piqued that she does not fawn over you."

"I mean to protect you," he said by way of explanation. "You know that I care not a scrap for your fortune."

"I know," his aunt said fondly. "That is why I made you my heir. You are the one person in this world who would look in on me because of your concern, not because you wanted my money. Sometimes money is an unpleasant duty."

Val laughed at her complaint, yet was much touched at her earnestly spoken words. "And yet you would will your fortune to her?"

"Indeed I shall. She is like my own daughter."

Both heads turned at a gentle rap at the door. On command, Phoebe entered, then paused when she saw Val seated with his aunt.

"Oh, excuse me, I will come back later."

Val found he could not accuse her of duplicity. The words stuck in his throat, no matter how he wanted to charge her with concealing the truth and wanting a fortune so as to capture the new viscount as a husband. He had to admit it was a pretty outrageous scheme.

The sight of Phoebe dressed in a simple white muslin trimmed with blue ribands affected him rather oddly. She looked so innocent and very young. What had she given up to go to her cousin's and take charge of those infants who were not her own? Did she realize how her action would affect her future? That it would change her prospects for marriage? Had she simply accepted the quiet years immured at Beeches as her due, caring for the twins as though her own as she had said? Somehow he did not believe that she would have thought of dipping into the estate coffers to line her pocket. She had not sought the help of Aldous Clark to that end, either. Of a sudden, Val was confused, a state in which he rarely ever found himself.

Why did he want to find her a villainess? What were these odd stirrings he felt of late?

Perhaps it would be best were he to bide his time and see how she behaved. He would have to find out if any communication existed between Clark and Phoebe. And he wished to know more about Clark's deceased cousin.

"I was just leaving," Val said quietly. He almost chuckled when he heard his aunt's sigh. She apparently was relieved that Val had chosen not to create a scene. He glanced at the needlework in Phoebe's hands and gave it a pointed look. "Trouble?"

"Indeed, yes," she said with a smile, rustling across the room to stand by his aunt's chair. "I seek her ladyship's expert opinion on the pattern. I am unsure about a particular shade of rose, you see." Then she blushed.

"I suggest you look in the mirror, for you are a pretty shade of pink at the moment," Val teased.

"Oh, fie on you, Val, to tease a girl so," Lady Latham scolded. "Show me your yarns, my child, and let me see your problem. Do we see you this evening at the Fotheringales'?" she asked Val as he paused to watch the pair.

He stayed at the doorway and gave her a considering look. At her tiny nod, he said, "I will be there, Aunt. Would you wish me to pick you up?"

"Come for dinner first and we may go together."

Val left the house, convinced that his wily aunt was determined to have him spend time with Phoebe so as to better know her charms and character. He was willing to study the girl. He could be wrong in his assessment. He had never been wrong about a woman before, but he supposed there could be a first time.

* * *

When he reached his home he found Butterworth in the library, going over accounts.

"I would like you to find out all you can about the Earl of Airlie and his family, particularly his new heir, Viscount Clark, formerly Mr. Aldous Clark."

"I will do my best, my lord." The secretary left the desk to pull out several volumes on the peerage and its history. Taking the books with him, he retreated to his own small study on the upper floor of the house.

Once alone, Val stared into the low flames of the fire burning in the library grate. He settled into a chair to think, but fell asleep before he could reach a conclusion regarding Miss Phoebe of the shining black curls and the flashing blue eyes. He woke some time later to the gentle nudging of his good friend.

"Afternoon snooze?" Ferdy said. "Old age creeping up on you." He sank into his favorite chair and looked pointedly at the tray of wine off to one side.

"Quite so," Val said, amused at the thought. He rose, poured out fine claret for Ferdy and himself, then resumed his seat. "Dare I ask what brings you to my house?"

"Oh, nothing in particular. Just happened to be at loose ends for the moment." He settled back and chatted about generalities.

It was not long after that that Butterworth returned, tapping gently on the door before poking his head around. Upon seeing Ferdy, he would have retreated. "Sorry, I thought you were alone, milord."

"Come in, for I sense you have met with success?"

"As to that, my cousin is secretary to the Earl of Airlie and I have kept his correspondence over the years. The books provided the basic information, but the letters offered family details you might find illuminating."

Val, first excusing himself to Ferdy, perused the page of information with his usual keen attention to details. He smiled when he read the concluding paragraph.

"What's amusing about a family history?" Ferdy inquired.

"The dowager countess is a redheaded dragon, it seems. I gather she is an old harridan whose red hair may have faded, but not her temper." He set the paper down and thanked Butterworth for his excellent service.

When they were again alone, Val said casually, "Do you go to the Fotheringales' musicale tonight? They usually have rather good entertainment. Understand there is to be an outstanding soprano this evening."

"Cannot abide that caterwauling," Ferdy said with a shake of his head. "I'm off to White's. Join me?"

"I have an engagement this evening—dinner with my aunt."

Ferdy paused by the door, an arrested expression on his face. "And Miss Phoebe Thorpe, as well?"

"Indeed. You know, she most likely has had little by way of entertainment, stuck in the country as she has been. Poor girl needs to have a change."

"And besides, you will be able to better keep an eye on her if you are at her side," Ferdy said with a sage nod. He made his farewell, then ambled off toward White's with a speculative look on his face. Did Val realize how contrary he was behaving to his normal existence? From the moment he had laid eyes on Phoebe Thorpe, he had acted most peculiarly.

It was not like the Val he had known all these years to be so accusing—especially of a young and lovely woman—without more proof. His behavior was irrational, which made Ferdy suspicious of Val's motives. Did Val realize what prompted him to act so? This thought brought Ferdy back to his original confusion.

The large and amiable gentleman shrugged and hailed a hackney. "White's," he ordered and was off.

"I want you dressed your prettiest this evening, my dear," Lady Latham said, studying Phoebe over the pile of needlework.

"Why so, ma'am? I had thought to wear my blue and silver." Phoebe's mind had been in a whirl from the moment that Lord Latham told her about Aldous Clark. What would his change in circumstances do to their relationship—such as it was? There had been hints of a desire for marriage, but with no prospects, they had small chance for a future. Mr. Clark had offered to teach Tony, even though young. But the boy was extraordinarily bright and soon knew his letters.

And now Aldous Clark was not only heir to a great title and even greater fortune—for the family had never produced a spendthrift—but he would hold a courtesy title, that of viscount. Phoebe was thrilled for him. He was a very deserving man, so devoted to the needs, both spiritual and physical, of his parish.

But would he cast Phoebe aside for someone with more polish, better connections, and wealth to equal his own expectations? Someone who did not have the burden of caring for a pair of orphaned twins?

"Well," Lady Latham said briskly, bringing Phoebe back to the present with a sudden thump, "dinner will come soon enough. My nephew joins us. I would not have him think you own but one gown. Why do you not wear the rose sarcenet this evening?"

"Yes, ma'am," Phoebe said with the ghost of a smile. What with her mental wanderings, it was a wonder that her ladyship did not take Phoebe to task for absentmindedness.

At dinner Phoebe was conscious of frequent glances from Lord Latham. He seemed to watch her far more often than necessary, yet he included his aunt in all conversation. In fact he seemed to sparkle with wit and charm, while Phoebe felt almost voiceless.

In the carriage he sat opposite her and his aunt, and kept up a stream of pleasant talk, never excluding Phoebe by referring to people she did not know or events she'd not heard about. She was confused, not but what he was normally polite to his aunt, but the sarcasm that often lurked beneath his speech was absent. And he seemed to have given up that nonsensical bit about Phoebe trying to cozen his aunt of her fortune. Where he had dreamed that up, she couldn't imagine. Perhaps his aunt must have set him straight, which must account for his improved manners.

As usual, the Fotheringale home exuded charm and grace, ablaze with hundreds of candles and adorned with abundant fresh flowers. Phoebe handed her cloak to a maid while admiring the many lovely floral arrangements.

"Planning to execute that in wools?" Lord Latham said close to her ear.

"That would be an achievement," Phoebe said with a laugh. "I fear I rely on those colored charts for now, the ones I found at Ackermann's. Perhaps someday I may be so bold as to attempt to sketch one of my own designs."

"I feel sure it would be lovely," Lord Latham said, curving his hand under her elbow to guide her along to the drawing room where the music was to be performed.

Phoebe had known his touch before and was forced to admit that he affected her as Aldous Clark had never managed to do. While Mr. Clark was most pleasant and she truly enjoyed his company, Lord Latham made her tremble with longing to be in his arms—and *that* had to be the silliest thing in the world.

The soprano had a pleasing voice and sang charming songs in French and German. Even if Phoebe didn't understand the words, the music was glorious. She had yearned for this sort of pleasure while deep in the country. Not that she would ever give up the twins to another, but there had been moments when she had wished for more.

When the pause came, while the soprano refreshed herself and the group gathered at the Fotheringales' also sought something to sustain them, Lord Latham excused himself. Over the rim of her glass of lemonade, Phoebe watched him cross the room to seek out an older redhaired woman. Her face lit up when Val spoke to her and Phoebe wondered if there was a woman in London who did not fall to his charm.

"One of the Earl of Airlie's sisters, Lady Mary Portman. Married quite well, I believe," Lady Latham said quietly to Phoebe.

"Your nephew seems to have a salubrious effect on women—they fairly glow with pleasure when he talks with them," Phoebe said and wondered why she felt irritated.

"Been that way since he was in short coats. I believe you are the first woman he has ever crossed words with—to my knowledge, at least."

"'Tis plain he never crossed words with Lady Mary," Phoebe said, then turned her back on the sight.

Across the room, Val laughed at a remark from the witty and lovely Lady Mary and said, "Why is it that the most original women are always married?"

"Because they are the only ones you feel comfortable with, my dear," she said with a flirtatious smile. "You ought to find one of your own."

"That reminds me that you have had a change in the family—I was sorry to learn of your cousin's death. Do you know Aldous Clark well?"

"Not at all. He accepted that dreary post in the country somewhere, one of Papa's livings, I believe."

"It would be a kindness were one of the family to invite him to London, to find his feet in society, as it were. You would not want him to make an unsuitable alliance, would you?" Val exchanged a meaningful look with Lady Mary that brought a thoughtful expression to her face.

"I see what you mean. Perhaps I could send down an invitation. I would like to see him again after all these years." She exchanged another look with Val.

"I thought you might see it that way," Val said, bowing low over her hand.

Chapter 10

I was unaware that you were acquainted with Lady Mary," Lady Latham said when Val rejoined them.

"Somehow I doubt if there is an attractive woman to be found in London that I have not met, dear Aunt. They seem to find me no matter what," her nephew replied with a twinkle shining in his dark eyes.

"They find you and not the other way around? What nonsense that is," Lady Latham said with a look that was undoubtedly intended to be reproving but actually indicated fond censure. "You are entirely too sure of yourself, my dear," she scolded gently.

Phoebe watched the scene with oddly mixed emotions. It was most likely true that Lord Latham was the target for a good many women. Handsome, wealthy, and titled, he possessed all the attributes that any woman wished. That Phoebe found him otherwise would shock all those who sought his attention. She made a rueful *moue* at the thought that while he was all those wonderful things, he was also the most aggravating man alive. Phoebe simply wished he would go away and leave her alone.

Lord Latham had made it quite clear that he believed her capable of cozening his aunt into leaving her fortune to Phoebe. And he had also made it plain that he felt Phoebe to be an inadequate guardian to the children, one of whom was now Viscount Waring. She disagreed, of course. But the notion that he somehow might push her to marry in order to keep the children in her care positively haunted her. She strongly suspected that his presence at their side was merely to keep an eye on Phoebe. Did he perchance think she might find a husband who would prove unsuitable? The thought brought a wistful smile to her lips.

She was roused from her musings by the curious sight of Miss Eustacia Oliphant staring at Lord Latham as though he were a particularly fine plum cake and she a starved waif. Why would the Beauty look so longingly at a man who was reputed to be hers?

"Miss Oliphant is trying to capture your attention, Val," Lady Latham said in a quiet aside.

"Is she, now? Odd, I cannot seem to see her." Val looked about them in seeming confusion. "Oh, over there, on the far side of the room, dressed in that pink gown."

The words were acceptable, but Phoebe hoped that no one ever spoke of her with such icy disdain.

When he turned to face Lady Latham, she raised her brows in inquiry. "What now?"

"Why, I was requested to call upon the young woman and found that she questioned my relationship to the twins and Miss Thorpe. It seems that she believed me innocent of misdeed until she chanced to see Miss Thorpe and the children in the park. When I explained the relationship to her, it seems that Miss Oliphant chose to believe otherwise." His words were softly spoken, but his voice again sent a chill down Phoebe's spine.

"Foolish twit," Lady Latham murmured, but she wore a curious look that gave Phoebe pause. Phoebe knew the lady well enough to be certain that she was not the slightest bit unhappy at her nephew's news . . . so why that look?

They returned to their seats and Lord Latham draped a shawl over his aunt's shoulders with kind regard. Then he eased himself on the chair at Phoebe's side.

She slanted a surprised look at him, before turning her gaze to the front of the room where the soprano was expected momentarily. "Petty behavior, sir?" she whispered, outraged that he should seek to pretend an interest in herself just to show his scorn for Miss Oliphant.

"Actually," he said quietly, "I wished to impart a bit of information to you about Viscount Clark."

"What?" Since this was totally unexpected, Phoebe gave him a startled look, searching his dark eyes for a hint of teasing. She found nothing other than a disturbing gleam that she could not interpret.

"It seems your country neighbor will soon be coming to

London. His cousin plans to invite him for the rest of the Season. I feel sure he will wish to renew his acquaintance with Lady Mary and the rest of his family." He smiled at Phoebe, then added, "With the possible exception of the Dowager Countess Airlie, who is reputed to be a veritable dragon."

"I suspect you have been mousing around to learn so much about him," Phoebe said with rising indignation.

"I felt it my duty to investigate him—because he had tutored Anthony, you know."

"Some tutoring—teaching him his letters," she whispered back with a fulminating glare. "I cannot for the life of me think what these women see in you, my lord. You are the most arrogant, overbearing, interfering man I've had the misfortune to met."

"And you have met so many," he purred in return.

Phoebe was prevented from outright brangling by the simple means of the soprano returning to stand by the pianoforte in the front of the room. Good manners forbade any whispered argument during such melodious entertainment.

She so simmered and seethed with resentment that she scarce paid attention to the lovely music. That Lord Latham should have the temerity to mouse about in regards to Aldous Clark's background was the outside of enough. His high-and-mighty lordship had gone too far.

The problem was that Phoebe's hands were tied. Were she an heiress—truly an heiress, and not something Lady Latham teased her nephew about—she might ignore the danger he represented. As it was, she knew only too well—and this was borne in on her daily—Lord Latham, combined with Mr. Popham, could take the twins away from her. Indeed, they most likely could find a way to prevent her from ever seeing her darlings again.

So distressed was she, that a tear of anger and frustration edged its way from the corner of her eye. She bravely concentrated on the soprano, when she longed for a good cry. And she also would have liked to crown his lordship with a brick, were one handy.

Why could he not be fat and ugly, with a wart on the side of his nose and a nasty habit of clearing his throat? Or lank as a reed with spectacles down his nose and thinning hair and have a squeaky sort of voice? Instead he was as handsome as may be, with a delicious voice that sent shivers through her at times, and dark eyes that fascinated her clear into sixes and sevens. Elegant clothes and proper manners enhanced his looks, but he possessed that something that attracted women like hummingbirds to nectar. She reluctantly admitted that he managed to turn her into a bundle of frazzled nerves when he chanced to fix his attention on her. Fortunately that was not often. She smiled rather grimly at the understanding that any civility from him must be suspect.

When the musical performance concluded, Phoebe rose and turned to assist her ladyship with her shawl and reticule. Lord Latham also helped, then draped Phoebe's warm shawl over her shoulders with a lingering touch. Or was he merely taking an opportunity to disconcert her?

The redheaded woman he had spoken with earlier approached them with a purposeful air. "Lady Latham, it is good to see you out and about again. It has been far too long," Lady Mary said with a lovely show of manners.

She was impossible to dislike, Phoebe decided, for she seemed the ideal woman, all grace and charm.

"Thanks to my grandniece and nephew's guardian, Miss Phoebe Thorpe. She is responsible for my better health, you see. All her potions are magical." Lady Latham beamed a smile of approval on Phoebe that warmed that young woman's heart.

Phoebe made a disclaiming murmur, aware of Lord Latham's considering stare.

"I was sorry to learn of your cousin's death at such a young age, my dear," Lady Latham said to the younger woman. "And no possibility of an heir in that line?"

"Two girls, but no heir, I fear," Lady Mary said with a significant glance at Lord Latham.

"Phoebe is acquainted with your cousin, Aldous, Lord Clark," he said in return. "He taught my young cousin his letters and was quite friendly with my young relatives. And Phoebe as well, stopping over for tea and the occasional dinner."

His words seemed innocent enough, but Phoebe had the

uncomfortable notion that he was subtly communicating something to Lady Mary. Then Phoebe decided she must be imagining things. There could be no possible reason for him to caution Lady Mary about herself, even though to her ears it sounded as though he gave a hint of impropriety in their behavior.

"Lord Clark was all that is proper, my lady," Phoebe said with a quiet voice that managed to be heard above the chattering around them.

"I look forward to seeing him again. I imagine you do as well?" Lady Mary said, with an alert expression on her face while she watched Phoebe.

"As to that, it remains to be seen," Phoebe replied. "I would hope that he might call upon us when—and if—he comes to London. He is very attached to his parish, you know."

"Indeed," a thoughtful Lady Mary said. "Well, I shall have to point out that as the new heir, he has also acquired new responsibilities as well. Someone else can be appointed to take his place. As our new viscount, he will need to learn many things for his future life." Her smile seemed genuine and the look she gave Phoebe was almost commiserating. "There is so much involved."

There was not a thing she said that Phoebe could fault. Every word was undoubtedly true. But somewhere in those words lay a hidden warning.

All the way home Phoebe remained locked in her private thoughts, wondering what lurked behind those words from Lady Mary. The murmurs of the other two in the carriage slipped past her ears.

Once at the house on Mount Street, Lord Latham set a time to visit his aunt on the morrow, added something about watching Anthony ride in the morning, then left.

Phoebe trailed up the stairs, murmured an absent good night to her ladyship, then wandered along to her own room. Once inside, she sank down upon the slipper chair by the fireside to mull over the situation.

Then it dawned on her. Once she put Lord Latham's chat with Lady Mary together with her ladyship's words, the unspoken warning became clear. Lady Mary was kindly cautioning Phoebe not to expect that rural friendship to continue now that Aldous had acquired the inheritance and title. The worst of it was that most likely Lady Mary had the right of it. Phoebe and Aldous might care for each other, but the situation had changed considerably. He now must look much higher for a wife.

Unhappy and annoyed with the interfering Lord Latham, Phoebe went to bed, dreaming of thwarting his obnoxious lordship in some way.

The following morning saw Val at his aunt's house at an early hour. He had decided to present his idea to her first thing, before she became involved with her daily activities.

"Val, I am scarcely out of my bed," she complained. "What is so important that we must confer at this hour?"

"Do you suppose we might manage a cup of coffee while we chat? What I wish to present is something that requires a bit of consideration."

She obligingly rang for coffee and also requested scones, for she knew how he enjoyed her cook's delicacies.

They chatted about trivial matters until served, then Val sat back on his chair and studied his aunt. "You do realize the children cannot remain with you in London."

"Why?" she demanded with a disgruntled look at him, stirring the milk into her coffee with loud clinking of the spoon.

"Children ought to be in the country, having sunshine and good air." Val parroted what he had heard parents say as to why their children remained in the country.

She bent her head to study her coffee cup. When she looked up at him again, he was surprised to see a deep sadness in her eyes. "I suppose you have the right of it. Although I do enjoy having them here. They are delightful children and not the least trouble."

"But you would wish what is best for them, am I not correct?" he urged.

"What do you consider best?" she asked mildly, her gaze bird-sharp as she peered at him.

"I propose to send them out to Latham Hall. Goodness knows there is staff enough to take care of them royally. All I need find is a nanny to take charge. They will be well-cared for and looked after there," Val said in quiet deliberation. He had given his proposal a great deal of thought. He wanted to separate the children from Miss Thorpe. He truly felt it would be in their best interest. Anthony would need training to assume his rightful position in the *ton* and Miss Thorpe was not the one to accomplish this. That there were tutors who could, he preferred to ignore.

Out in the hallway, Doro had paused to listen as she had been told not to do. She had been intent upon hiding from Anthony. The conversation in the next room alarmed her, and so she attended to her cousin's words with care. Further frightened by what she heard, she began to tiptoe down the stairs.

"There is another angle to this, and I feel certain you will agree with me," he continued. "As long as Miss Thorpe remains as guardian to the children, devoting her life to their care as she has done for over five years now, she will remain unwed. She must be all of twenty-two now. I know you are fond of the young woman. Do you not think she deserves a chance for some happiness?"

"With Aldous Clark, perhaps?" Lady Latham said, her eyes narrowing at the thought.

"As to that, I could not say," Val said with a shrug of his well-tailored shoulders. "There may have been a mild attachment when they were village residents, but Clark's circumstances have changed now. He has money and position to consider." Val thought he had made a telling point. He had caught the start his aunt had made when he set forth his logic. Her gaze had darted about in puzzled speculation while she turned over his rationale in her mind.

"You feel that Phoebe could not become a suitable countess? She has acquitted herself admirably while with me." Lady Latham drew herself up and gave Val one of those piercing looks that he hated to receive. They made him feel the veriest schoolboy.

"That is not my opinion, I merely hazard speculation as to what Lord Clark will do. Have you not observed how acquiring sudden money and position can change people?"

He could see his aunt was much struck by his words. She became pensive, sipping her cooling coffee while all the time her mind was undoubtedly hunting for a way to keep Miss Phoebe Thorpe at her side.

"There is another possibility," he offered. "If you feel it necessary to see Miss Thorpe properly wed, you could have her stay with you for a short time, try to find her a suitable match. Goodness knows I've had no success. While I feel certain you ought not make her your heiress, you might settle a small sum on her to assist in the scheme." He had figured that once Phoebe Thorpe found she would no longer stand to inherit the fortune, she would be on her way to greener pastures.

"Sell her off, you mean?" came the sharp retort.

Val shrugged again. "It is what is done, dear Aunt."

"I will think about what you propose. You are aware that you do not have the authority to insist upon this—no more than I do. Phoebe was made legal guardian, and until a judge decides she is unfit, she will remain in that capacity." Lady Latham gave a firm nod to emphasize her point.

"Do you honestly believe that any judge would rule in her favor?"

"Judge Scott might, for he has been shown to be considerate of a woman's plight. He even granted one sorely tried young woman a divorce."

"Miss Thorpe is not seeking a divorce from a cruel husband. She is a cozening female who seeks a fortune from you, and the main chance in handling the Waring fortune."

But even as he spoke, Val found doubts surfacing within him. He was beginning to wonder about the inheritance of his aunt's fortune. Had his aunt actually put it on paper? Or was it an idle threat to make him jump. He wouldn't put it past her. And as to dipping into the Waring coffers, that appeared unlikely, given Phoebe's vaunted ability to mend and sew for the children. He considered the rose sarcenet she had worn last evening. While it was not the product of a village mantuamaker, some of the other garments she wore had a simple air about them, clinging faithfully to her charming figure.

She also disliked him, a most novel reaction from any woman. He found his feelings toward her uncertain. That doubts about his conclusions had surfaced bothered him more than a little. Could he be wrong? Never, he argued. Yet he knew an odd frustration that his emotions were so wavering.

He studied the designs on the Turkey carpet of the morning room while he mulled over these finer points. The silence grew, with only the closing of the front door to disturb the peace.

"I will let you know what I decide to do," Lady Latham said at long last.

"It will be interesting to meet Lord Clark once he arrives at Lady Mary's."

"I suppose you put her up to inviting him?" Lady Latham said with a shrewd look at her nephew.

"You must admit what she said is correct. The new viscount has much to learn to take his rightful position in Society. Much will depend on how well he takes advice."

"When did you become such a pompous ass? I vow that you are worse with every passing year," she grumbled.

"You," Val leveled a haughty look at his dragon of an aunt, "have not had the lady you selected to grace your home and hearth charge you with gross impropriety—fathering twins and bringing their mother to reside with an aunt. It has been damned annoying to endure all those simpers and giggles, the nudges and looks from people who are no better than what they believe I am guilty of having done."

"There is nothing like seeing the mighty brought low," Lady Latham observed. "I wish that you could find a wife you might care for just a little."

"What a nonsensical idea, dear Aunt. Hardly the thing," he said, before finishing off his coffee.

"But infinitely more enjoyable, I should think," she shot back.

"I intend to see Popham about the matter, whether or not you agree with me," Val concluded, while rising from his chair. "You must agree it's for the best."

"I wish you would not," she said wistfully.

Val paused in his steps. He could not remember when he had heard that note in her voice. "Perhaps you might reconsider this inheritance business?" he said, with a little hope she might actually see sense.

"My will shall remain unchanged, except for a minor point or two," she declared in surprisingly firm tones.

"Then I must proceed as I believe best," Val said, bowing over her hand with mingled affection for the old dragon and exasperation with her obtuseness.

"I suppose you will," her ladyship said, leaning back in her chair as though tired. "What a horrid way to begin a day. I believe I will go back to bed and begin all over again."

"Do you plan to go out this evening?" he paused to inquire.

"Phoebe wants to take the children for an outing this afternoon, I believe to the Tower of London. She will no doubt be tired when they return. I think it will be best if we remain at home."

"Then I need not worry about you," Val said, walking toward the door, suddenly in a haste to be off.

"If you worried about me, you would leave Phoebe Thorpe alone. I like her and I do not wish her name bandied about London—which it will be if you proceed."

"That will be no more than it is at present, dear Aunt. I am trying to fix matters."

With that parting shot, he left the house on Mount Street and went around to the mews, where he found Anthony about to set forth for the park. The lad sat straight on his little pony, showing promise for the years to come.

"Good morning, Cousin Val," Anthony sang out happily, giving his polished relative an admiring and grateful look.

"Shall we be off?" Val said, vaulting onto the back of his own Valiant, which had waited for him while he visited his aunt. Ferdy had twitted him about the name he gave his chestnut, but Val knew the name was more than a play on words. The horse had lived up to this name in every instance. Val would not have parted with the animal for anything.

The morning ride through the mists of a London morning was invigorating. Val watched with a critical gaze while Anthony was put through his paces by his aunt's groom. He could not fault the man in the least; he did an excellent job. When Anthony went to Latham Hall he could learn, little by little, to take the jumps and other requisites for a rider. The park was a poor substitute for a proper training area.

"Good show, lad," Val said in ringing approval.

Anthony reddened with pleasure, then cried, "Here

comes Lord Andrews. See what I can do, sir?" And Anthony was off at a trot, anxious to display what he had learned to the other gentleman, who seemed to have an interest in his progress.

"Early morning, eh?" Ferdy said to Val.

"I'll refrain from saying the obvious bit about the bird and the worm, but, yes—I have accomplished a little so far this morning."

"Lad is doing well, I'd say," Ferdy said with a nod toward Anthony.

"Lesson over for today," Val decreed after a glance at his pocket watch. "Appointment," he murmured to Ferdy.

"Ah, the lovely new dancer at the opera, I suppose?" Ferdy said with a grin.

"Not in the least. I thought her a bit overblown, myself. Haven't had time for the opera lately."

"You ain't your old self, Val," Ferdy complained while they jogged along behind Anthony for a time, before turning off to Val's mews. "Haven't kicked up a dust in ages. In fact, you are becoming downright staid," he chided.

"Perhaps the new self will be an improvement," Val said with an amused look at his friend. "I've an appointment, so I need to change. Come up?"

"No. Will I see you later?"

"White's if you like," Val suggested. They set a time, then Val hurried into his home and up to his room, where Rosbert quickly assisted him into proper dress.

Val pulled on his leather gloves, then left the house, and went to see Mr. Popham.

The gentleman was quite obliging in the matter of arranging for the custody to be transferred. "I will begin the paperwork immediately. As you say, most any judge would grant you custody without question."

"Most?" Val pounced on the word, knowing that it held the clue to his success.

"Judge Scott sometimes takes a different stance than we expect." Mr. Popham shuffled the papers from the Waring folder together while giving Val a frank look.

"Then try to see that the case is not brought before Judge Scott." Val rose, then paused on his way out. "I need not reiterate that I wish this proceeding kept as quiet as possible. I would be greatly displeased were word to seep out that this is underway."

Mr. Popham gave Val his steady regard, then said, "I quite understand, my lord. Naturally, all be in strictest confidence."

"My greatest concern is the welfare of Viscount Waring and his sister. I believe the children will be best off in the country and Miss Thorpe relieved of their burden."

Val left the office feeling dissatisfied, although he ought to have been pleased. Surely this would be in the children's best interest. He tried to shut out the recollection of their fond devotion to Miss Thorpe. Children forget easily, he persuaded himself. They would soon attach themselves to a pleasant nanny. All he had to do was to find the right person.

He was about to return to his home, when he was prompted to stop by his aunt's house and inform her how well Anthony was doing in his riding lessons—a point in his favor and for their removal to Latham Hall.

A young lad came running up to catch his reins until a groom could come around to take his horse. Smedley ushered him up to the drawing room with stiff propriety, causing Val to wonder what he'd done to displease the old fellow. Smedley had to be the oddest butler in London, taking strange dislikes at the merest whim.

"Well, and how are you now, good Aunt?" Val said, bowing over her ladyship's hand with his usual grace.

"Not as good as I might be," she snapped back with asperity.

Val ignored this thrust and said, "I observed Anthony during his lesson and the lad shows remarkable aptitude. He seems to be a fine boy."

"Worthy of the Latham name? You can thank Phoebe for that, you know. She has had charge of them from the moment they were born. Taking the children from her would be like tearing them from their mother," she scolded him.

"I am trying to think of the best for *all* concerned," Val reminded, wishing his aunt did not make him feel like a criminal. He truly did wish the best for all, even Phoebe of the shining black curls and dazzling blue eyes—and highly kissable mouth.

He turned his head, as sounds of rustling skirts and whispers that sounded most upset came from the hallway. He glanced at his aunt, raising his brows in inquiry.

"They are most likely playing a game. The children love to scamper up and down the staircase, often playing hide-and-go-seek. I repeat, Valentine, I shall miss those children if they must leave me. I may just take my fortune and will it to distressed parlor maids."

"If I thought you really meant that, I would see Mr. Popham again."

"And forget this business about the twins?"

"Not likely. I would have you declared certifiably in need of care."

"I believe you would, at that. Never mind my dratted fortune. I may just go out and spend the lot."

"That would put a bit of change in circulation," Val said with a lazy smile.

The rustling of skirts came closer and suddenly Phoebe burst into the room, wringing her hands, tears glittering in her eyes as she looked from one to the other.

"What it is, dear girl?" Lady Latham cried in alarm.

"Doro is gone! We have looked everywhere and cannot find her. They played hide-and-seek . . . and she's gone!" Phoebe turned to Val and held out her hands. "Please, I . . . I need you."

Chapter 11

"That is, to assist me," she amended, clearly flustered.

Val had risen when Phoebe entered the room so precipitately, and now stepped forward to take her by her shoulders. "Explain, please."

Phoebe raised worried eyes to meet his questioning ones. "I was with her all morning until it was time for Anthony to return from the park. I decided to have Cook make a little treat for the twins, so left Doro playing in the nursery. When I returned, she was gone!"

"The nursery maid?" Val said urgently.

"She had stepped out of the room for a time to bring up their clean clothes from the laundry. We have left one or both of the children in the room for a short time before with never any trouble." Phoebe turned from Val to look at Lady Latham with an anguished face.

"And she is not hiding in one of her favorite places?" Lady Latham said, rising from her chair to join the two. "You know how those two scamps adore playing hide-and-seek."

"We have searched the house from top to bottom."

"But she must be here. Where would a five-year-old girl think to go?" Val looked to his aunt, then back at Phoebe.

"I cannot imagine where she would go, she has not been out and about very much, what with Anthony and his colds and all." Phoebe closed her eyes, then said, "If anything has happened to her . . . "

"I shall speak to Smedley." Lady Latham hurried from the room, her words drifting back to the two.

"If one hair on her head is harmed, I shall never forgive myself, never," Phoebe declared in a broken voice.

Val instinctively drew her close to him, cradling her in

his arms, and stroking the silken black curls with a gentle hand. She was so slim, so vulnerable in her distress.

"We will find her, never fear," he said in a firm, though quiet, way. "If necessary I will call on Bow Street to assist in the hunt."

"Do you think someone kidnapped her? The Waring estate is extremely rich," Phoebe said, turning in his arms to gaze up at him with trusting blue eyes. Oddly enough, she reminded him of a kitten he'd once had. It had been injured and looked at him in much the same manner when he'd attempted to tend the hurt.

Val drew her close to him again, vowing, "We shall leave no stone unturned in the matter. She will be found, and soon, I promise." He patted her on her back.

She buried her face against his shoulder and again Val experienced the most peculiar feelings. Although he had accused Phoebe of dire deeds, he found he relished holding her, comforting her in his arms. Conflicting emotions raged within him. Could anyone as sweet and seemingly good as Phoebe actually be out to snabble a fortune from his aunt? Yet, with Doro gone missing, it more or less proved his point that Phoebe Thorpe was an unfit guardian for the twins. Oddly enough, he felt no elation at that particular knowledge. It did show the necessity to send the children off to the country where they would be safer.

And yet, any child could go missing. It did not mean that Phoebe was necessarily unfit as guardian. He recalled her tender and loving care he had observed when around them. He was most confused. On the one hand, he sought to protect his aunt and the twins, and on the other, he found himself drawn to Phoebe. He did not wish to be attracted to her. She was not what he had in mind for a wife. Then he wondered what had brought that word to mind. What a dilemma.

Her slim body was soft and gently curved, and nestled against him with a pleasing sensation. He tilted her face up so that she would look at him and he could see her expression. Gazing into those tear-drenched blue eyes, Val experienced a strange twisting in his heart.

What was it that Sally Jersey had said, that she adored a vulnerable rake? Val would not describe himself as a rake, but at the moment he felt exceedingly vulnerable. When Phoebe had cried out that she needed him, it had gone straight to his core. He could not recall anyone ever telling him that they actually needed him for comfort or assistance, especially in such a dramatic circumstance.

Val placed a light kiss on her lips, then set her away from him. The temptation to deepen that kiss was too powerful. There were more urgent matters that required attention. He drew her along with him to the hallway.

"Come, we will see if my aunt has learned anything from Smedley. Then we will question all of the servants one by one. I can take the men, you the maids and such."

Phoebe gave him a dazed look, following along with him as though he had not just kissed her and sent her heart cartwheeling. What a baffling man—to scold her, charge her with neglect and scheming, then turn about and kiss her. It had been the merest touch of his lips, but Phoebe felt as though their imprint would remain a long time.

Smedley could tell them nothing, to his obvious grief. He explained that it was normal for him to leave the door unguarded at times while he went about his duties. Anyone might have slipped in or out during those moments.

The footman whose duty it was to stand by the door while Smedley was away could not be found at first. Phoebe feared he had kidnapped Doro. Then he popped around the corner, explaining that Norris, the housekeeper, had sent him on an errand.

The following half hour was frenzied with questioning everyone on staff, quizzing them for the slightest detail that might be of help.

They met with Lady Latham in the morning room to hold a council of sorts. "The mews," Phoebe said, now that the questioning had come to a fruitless end. "She said something about wanting to learn to ride Anthony's pony. Could she be there, I wonder?"

"It is possible. Come," Val demanded, tugging her behind him, with a glance at his aunt to reassure her that he would do his best. The older woman gripped her hands in worry; tears glistened in her eyes. If Val had doubted her attachment to the twins, that doubt was squelched completely at her display of anguish.

Phoebe grabbed a cloak as they passed through the entry, then ran along at Val's side until they reached the mews. The pony stood placidly in his stall, as did the four horses that his aunt kept for her carriages. At the far end of the mews those carriages stood. Exchanging a speaking glance, Val and Phoebe ran to the first one.

"You take the landau and I'll inspect the town carriage," Val snapped out, while beginning to search the elegant vehicle.

Phoebe found no trace of Doro in the landau. As open as it was, it offered quick access. "Nothing here," she called out to Lord Latham. She looked about the stable area, examining the mounds of hay, glanced at the tack hanging on the walls, then walked to one side of the area.

"The grooms sleep up above here. You do not suppose that she might go up there?" She studied the narrow door at the top of the short flight of steps.

Lord Latham joined her at the foot of the stairs. "You have gone over the house from attic to basement. I will look up here, while you try to think of any other place we might search." He ran lightly up the steps, scratched on the door, then entered.

Phoebe paced back and forth, wondering what had prompted Doro to slip off. Where could the child be hiding? And why? She refused to believe the girl had been kidnapped. No one could possibly have entered the house without someone seeing him. Could he?

"Cousin Phoebe," a piping voice cried and Phoebe whirled about at the cry. Anthony ran around the corner of the mews and headed directly for her. "Doro is not in any of her hiding places. I looked."

"Thank you, Anthony," Phoebe said, while patting him on the shoulder in an effort to comfort him. The twins were inseparable and Anthony would feel keenly even the momentary loss of his twin. Knowing that Doro was the more adventuresome of the twins, Phoebe was not too surprised to learn that the girl had discovered a new place to hide—wherever it might be.

Just then Lord Latham came clattering down the steps followed by the groom who gave Anthony his riding lessons. "Not a thing up there," his lordship informed Phoebe, glancing to where Anthony leaned against her.

"Little one gone missing, has she?" the groom said in a sympathetic tone.

"We are at our wits end to think where she might be," Phoebe said, still looking about her to see if anything might trigger her mind to a possible clue.

"Perhaps she will come out of hiding when she is hungry," Lord Latham said, hope clear in his voice. "The children are about due for their midday meal, are they not?" He recalled the rather stodgy dinners served about this time of day when he was a lad. "Hunger ought to bring her to us."

"I do hope so," Phoebe said fervently. She was not quite so certain of this as Lord Latham, for Doro was quite clever at cadging a bit of food from the kitchen without detection. She seemed to have a way of quietly slipping in and out, leaving no one the wiser.

"I wonder if she has left the house?" Phoebe said suddenly, thinking Doro was quite capable of doing just that.

"Where would she go?" Lord Latham queried. "I cannot believe a child of five would take off across London on her own."

"The flower girl does," Anthony pointed out. "Doro said she lives a long ways from here and never gets lost coming or going."

Phoebe exchanged a startled look with Val, then glanced at the groom.

"You do not suppose . . ." Phoebe said before turning to go to the front of the house.

The groom stayed behind, instructed to look everywhere he could think a child might hide. Lord Latham strode along behind Phoebe, who was by now running.

"She is not there," Phoebe cried when they had rounded the corner.

"Who is not there?" Val demanded, perplexed as to Phoebe's intent.

"The little flower girl. I suspect she is older than Doro, but is tiny for her age. Doro was captivated by her and insisted upon giving her some clothes in addition to buying flowers every day. Doro was always looking out of the window, keeping an eye on the girl."

"If she isn't here, how could she help us?" Val said, still puzzled.

"Perhaps she failed to come this morning. Doro might have taken it into her head to find her," Phoebe mused.

"She was there when I went for my ride," Anthony piped up while tugging on Phoebe's skirts. "I showed her my pony and she admired him very much. She called him a 'right 'un.'"

"Oh dear," Phoebe murmured, horrified at all the possibilities that flooded her inventive mind. "She could not possibly have sold all her flowers. I doubt she ever does, even with Doro's daily contribution."

"So you think . . ." Val said, then stopped at Phoebe's warning look and a glance to where Anthony stood frowning at the empty street.

"Why do we not return to the house," Phoebe said. "I suspect we may need to call in Bow Street after all." She took Anthony by the hand and marched ahead into the house.

Val followed along, scarcely noticing when Ferdy loped up to join him.

"Something amiss? You look frightful." Ferdy gave Val a nudge when he failed to reply.

"Dorothea has gone missing. Not been seen for hours. Indeed, since Anthony went for his riding lesson in the park. Phoebe thinks the little flower girl, who is usually across the street, may offer a clue."

"Kidnapping?" Ferdy sounded as horrified as he looked.

"Phoebe suspects not, but that Doro went to find the girl, who must have sought out a better location. Come along, we shall need everyone we can muster."

"Why the flower girl?" Phoebe cried to Lady Latham, who looked equally puzzled.

"Doro is a tenderhearted creature. She worried about that girl, told me about her concerns—no proper clothes—and I dismissed her words as childish ramblings. I ought to have paid more attention to what she said," Lady Latham said with a frown.

"We all should have paid attention to her, poor child,"

Phoebe hastened to say, patting the older woman on her hands.

"Well, we had best seek out Bow Street—after I have a look around at the area," Val said. At Phoebe's questioning glance, he added, "Just to see if perchance Doro walked along with her while the flower girl sought a better corner."

Unable to think of anything better, Phoebe nodded, then sat back to comfort Anthony and Lady Latham.

The last glimpse Val had of Phoebe was the sight of her black curls bent over the boy, cuddling him to her in consolation. Val could not recall his mother doing such a thing during his childhood, and for a moment he envied the lad. Then he remembered the missing girl and Phoebe's lack of attention there.

"Dashed peculiar thing to happen." Ferdy hurried along at Val's side, their long legs eating up the distance quickly. "Was the child unhappy? They are inclined to run off if they are, you know."

"I was unaware you were so knowledgable about infantry," Val shot back. He paused to check each corner, then plunged on, with Ferdy easily keeping pace with him.

"My sisters, you know," Ferdy said just as they reached the next corner. "Each of them has a brood of chicks and what they cannot think to do is unbelievable."

"Indeed, I was given to think that I was the most recalcitrant child in the world. It is comforting to know there are others at least equal to me in naughtiness," Val said reflectively.

"Your mother left you to a nanny like mine did, I suppose," Ferdy mused. "Most women do, you know. Miss Thorpe's unusual. She may not be their real mother, just took over like one. Actually, she's better than some mothers."

Val threw his friend an annoyed glance. "And how did you become so conversant about Miss Thorpe?"

"Asked questions. Amazing what you learn that way," Ferdy shot back, amusement lighting his eyes when he surveyed his friend's ire.

At Oxford Street they drew another blank. There were flower girls and beggars and costermongers with their wares. There was no little five-year-old girl with black curls and blue eyes.

Val hailed a hackney. "Bow Street, and hurry." He and Ferdy climbed into the vehicle after snapping out the request.

The jarvey, apparently startled at the urgency of Val's demand, took off in a quick trot that threw the men against the squabs.

At the Bow Street office, Val explained their problem and the possible connection with the missing flower girl.

"Do you have an idea of just how many flower girls there be in London, milord?" the man at the desk said. "There be more than I can count, I tells you."

"You are the detectives, you tell me where the one that usually stands on the corner from my aunt's house on Mount Street goes at the end of her day." Val gave the man a description of the clothing Doro wore and a sketch that Phoebe had done of the child not long before.

When he and Ferdy left the office, Val was obviously disgruntled.

"Not very encouraging, is he?" Ferdy said in commiseration.

"I should like to return to that corner and explore the area a bit more. Perhaps there might be a clue we overlooked before."

Understanding his friend's need to do something, and his reluctance to merely sit around and wait, Ferdy nodded, and they set off again.

Val stood off to one side for a bit, watching to see who passed the area. Then he politely began to stop people, asking if they had seen a child matching Doro's description. All knew the little flower girl, and some remarked that they often bought her flowers, out of pity, mostly.

"Not a one has seen your little cousin," Ferdy observed after a time. "Looks to come on rain. Why not go inside, see if the ladies have thought of anything else," he urged.

"I hate to give up. I do not place a great deal of confidence in those fellows at Bow Street, I can tell you that. What this country needs is a first-rate patrol of the city, not those ineffectual Charleys with the magistrates who are easily bribed . . . if they can be found."

Ferdy shook his head. "People fear policing, you know. Rather put up with the criminals than have some official poking his nose into their business."

Val paused before his aunt's home and glanced about the quiet street. "Phoebe remarked that what you see depends mainly on what you look for, and I am wondering if we look for the wrong thing."

"You think Doro's disappearance may have nothing to do with the flower girl?" Ferdy cast his gaze along the street. "Look at this place, the epitome of respectability. Who would think that anything like a kidnapping might happen here."

"I still believe she has not been kidnapped," Val insisted.

Ferdy gave Val a dubious look, then followed him into the house.

Phoebe had heard the door open and rushed out to the landing, peering over to see who might have come. When she saw Val and Ferdy, she hurried down the stairs to confront them. "Did you learn anything, see anyone?"

"We gave the information to the man at Bow Street and he promised to do what he could. As he said, there are an amazing number of flower girls in London." Val hated to dampen her hopes. He wished he could have come through the door with Doro in his arms, just to see Phoebe's lovely face light up with joy again.

"They must all obtain their flowers from the same area," she said. "I wonder if each one has her own territory, so to speak? Do you suppose that if we find out where that might be, we could ask around?" Her eyes pleaded with Val to do something.

"That would most likely be Covent Garden, Phoebe. You cannot possibly go there."

"But you could, could you not?" She did not question his statement for, although not a Londoner, even she had heard of that notorious area of the city.

At the look of dawning hope in her eyes, Val couldn't say no. "Yes, we can go. Allow us a bit of food and we shall be off."

"Food," she echoed vaguely, as though it were an alien substance. "Oh, yes, of course, food. I shall see what Mrs. Norris can offer us by way of a meal." She hurried off in the direction of the kitchen and was back within minutes. "If you will follow me, a hot meal will be on the table immediately."

They were joined by an anxious Lady Latham and sat down to a hearty soup followed by other substantial food.

Phoebe looked at the offerings and a ghost of a smile lingered on her face as she turned to Val and said, "Apparently Mrs. Norris thinks we require extra sustenance while worried. I only hope that Doro is having a meal."

Val noted the worry in her voice and attempted to cheer her up with tales of lost children restored.

By nightfall, they decided that Bow Street would have to do the searching. A ramble through Covent Garden had been harrowing, to say the least, and quite fruitless. As was often the case, the citizens of that section became silent when questioned by the Quality. They would not tell on one another if there was any danger of punishment involved.

"I didn't see the Tower today," Anthony observed sadly. "Doro wanted to see it, too. I wish she would come home again. I miss her very much."

Phoebe exchanged looks with Val and put a comforting arm about the little boy. "We do too, love. We do, too."

The following day produced no Doro.

When Val entered his aunt's house, to join them for dinner, he met Phoebe's worried gaze with great difficulty. "I stopped by Bow Street and all they would tell me is that they are looking for the child." Val did not dare add that he had been told of a gang of white slavers who trafficked in little girls. Not even Phoebe would hold up under that news.

"If we were in the country, I might consider that the Gypsies had stolen her," Lady Latham said. "There aren't Gypsies in the city." Unspoken was the threat of other horrible possibilities.

Phoebe stared at Lady Latham, then turned to Val, her eyes huge. "You do not consider that some ill may have befallen her?"

"No, no," Val said, hoping he sounded more reassuring than he felt. "I have no doubt but what she is safe with that flower girl, most likely sipping a bowl of broth right this minute."

Phoebe gave him a searching look before returning to the food on her plate, little of which was being consumed. She mostly pushed her meat about, poked at the potatoes, and nibbled at the other delectable foods Mrs. Norris had kept in readiness for the concerned family.

Across London, in the heart of the Covent Garden district, Doro huddled under the thin but fairly clean blanket used to keep the chill at bay in the unheated rooms. When Pansy the flower girl's mother returned from the bake shop, she carried a tureen of soup. With no stove in the room, Mrs. Hawkins, like much of London, sought out the baker's stove to heat a bit of supper for her family. The chipped tureen was set in the center of the table with a flourish. Then Pansy's little brother produced a loaf of bread that had a suspicious gray tinge to it, as though chalk had been added to the flour to extend that expensive commodity.

"This not be the meal you be accustomed to, milady, but it be hot," Mrs. Hawkins declared, planting her fists on her hips. Mrs. Hawkins did laundry each day, spending long hours over wash water and lye soap. Her hands were red and rough, but clean.

Tin bowls were plunked on the table and steaming broth ladled into them. Chunks of bread were torn from the loaf and handed to each person. There were six in all at the table. In addition to Doro and Pansy, there was little brother Tom, elder sister Meg, and the parents, both of whom looked ancient indeed to Doro.

The room was as clean as could be with little soap, less hot water—Mrs. Hawkins used every precious bit for her laundry—and not much in the way of a broom. Doro surveyed those around her, noting the patched clothing, pinched faces, and the haunted expressions to be found on the poor and those without hope.

Her soup was thin and somewhat tasteless, as though far more water than chicken bones had gone into the pot. Slivers of meat lurked here and there. It was not like the fine chicken soup that came up from Cook. Doro wished she might offer her friends that sort of soup. Perhaps then they might not look so sad.

"I 'opes we don't get no trouble from takin' her in," Mr. Hawkins said with a jerk of his thumb at Doro.

"They were goin' to send 'er away to a 'orrid place," Pansy explained in the broad dialect of the London slums.

Mr. Hawkins gave a harsh laugh. "I 'spect it would be a 'eap better than this."

"My Cousin Val said we are to go to the country faraway from Cousin Phoebe. I love Cousin Phoebe. I do not wish to go far away from her," Doro explained.

"Well, lovey, I 'spect you 'ad best talk them 'round your way. We can't keep you 'ere for long," Mr. Hawkins declared firmly. " 'Ave our heads, they will, keeping Quality away from 'er 'ome and fam'ly."

"One more day?" Doro pleaded.

The Hawkins exchanged looks, then nodded. "One more day." Within minutes the soup had disappeared and the family prepared for the night to come. All slept in the same room on pallets that were spread here and there on the hard floor. Doro shared a space with Pansy and Meg, and thought of her soft bed at Aunt Latham's.

"No news," Phoebe reported when Val joined them the following morning. "I trust the men will find her soon. I shudder to think of what she is living through."

"Children will view it differently than we, my dear," Val said, guiding Phoebe to a high-backed chair and urging her to sit down.

"I hope so," she glumly concluded.

The hours dragged past, with the house oddly silent, as though everyone waited for the slightest indication that the little girl had been found. Phoebe and Val took a carriage drive, going around the city where they thought flower girls might be seen.

"They all look depressingly alike," Phoebe said at long last. "I fear this was a waste of time. Perhaps if we return home—" Her words ceased abruptly and she clutched Val's arm with an iron grip. "There she is. Both of them."

Val immediately brought the carriage to the side of the street. They barely ceased motion when Phoebe scrambled down, running the rest of the way with absolutely no regard for dignity or decorum. "Doro!" she cried, stumbling a bit, for it was difficult to see with tears in her eyes. She knelt on the dirty walkway with not the least regard for her fine pelisse.

"Cousin Phoebe," Doro cried in return, wrapping her little arms tightly about her adored relative. "You will not let him take me away, will you? I will *not* go." She nestled close to Phoebe, glaring at Val with hostile eyes.

"No, darling, I will never let him take you away from me. Everything will be all right. You'll see."

Val surveyed the pair, then turned to the flower girl, who watched with a wary gaze. She was poised to run.

"You took care of her?" Val inquired gently. "We shall have to see what can be done for you." He dug into his pocket and pulled out more coins than Pansy saw in months. He gave her the lot, then crouched down to her level and said, "Take these to your mother. Mind you, be careful, for money is easy to steal." He asked a number of questions, then gave her his card, concluding with a suggestion that her father call at his home. His secretary would offer additional help if wanted.

Doro chattered all the way to the house on Mount Street, full of her adventures with Pansy, and informing both Val and Phoebe about the grim life led by that family.

When they drew up to the front door, Phoebe asked the burning question, "Why did you run away?"

"Because he"—and she pointed at Val—"said he was going to send Anthony and me away and we wouldn't see you anymore. I want to stay with Cousin Phoebe," she said with a dark look at Val.

"What made you think such a thing, dearest?" Phoebe said, while drawing the child into the house with her.

"I heard him. I was going to hide so Anthony would have to find me. Then I heard him"—and she glared at Val again—"say we could not live with you anymore. I do not like you, Cousin Val." She shook her finger at Val, then turned to greet Lady Latham and Anthony, telling them about her excursion as though it was a great adventure.

"You intend to take them away from me by one means or

another," Phoebe said quietly, her accusing look cutting right to Val's heart.

"You must admit that this little episode does not speak well for your care," Val said.

"But she ran away because of what *you* said!" Phoebe cried indignantly.

Before Val might answer her, there was a sharp rap at the front door. They all became silent as Smedley bustled to answer the impatient sound. As one they watched a tall red-headed man enter the room. He went straight to Phoebe and grasped her hand, bowing low over it.

"Lord Clark, what a surprise."

Chapter 12

I trust I have not come at an inconvenient time. I wished to see Miss Thorpe and the children." Lord Clark stood uncertainly, casting a questioning look at Phoebe, then Val.

"We are pleased to see you," Phoebe said warmly.

Val surveyed the stranger with a somewhat narrowed gaze. So this was Aldous Clark, the erstwhile curate who had captured Phoebe's interest, if not her heart. He wasn't a bad-looking chap, if you cared for flaming red hair and the pale skin so often found in redheads. Multitudes of freckles were not so terrible, either, if you did not mind them. He had kind gray eyes—a point in his favor—and perhaps with a few bountiful meals that lanky frame might fill out a trifle. Of course he would be much improved by a visit to a first-rate tailor.

It did not occur to Val that it was quite unlike him to be so critical of another man, particularly one who had done him no harm, picking him to pieces. Normally Val was the most charitable of people, demanding much of himself but inclined to be lenient toward others.

"I am so happy for you, Lord Clark," Phoebe said with a pretty blush and delighted smile. "It is so seldom that a worthy person reaps just rewards." She disengaged her hands from his with seeming reluctance.

Val took a step forward, thinking the fellow had blasted cheek to be so bold as to hold her hands for longer than polite. Some curate he must have been.

"'This is the one I esteem: He who is humble and contrite in spirit,'" Aldous quoted from Isaiah. "Actually, it was a great surprise. I mean, my cousin was in excellent health with two little girls and every possibility he would produce a boy in good time. I had not even considered the likelihood of such a happening."

"Nonetheless, I am delighted for you," Phoebe said, her cheeks pink with pleasure. The strain of the past hours faded some in the happiness of seeing her old friend and would-be beau.

"I have a pony, Lord Clark," Anthony piped up, tired of being ignored, especially when he wished to share such important news with his old friend.

"And I had a 'venture," Doro inserted, not to be left out.

Phoebe exchanged a guarded look with Val, then turned to her friend. "Doro thought she might be sent to the country without me and ran away. We were so frightened." Phoebe knelt beside the child and said, "Promise me that if you are ever angry or upset that you will talk with me first before doing anything so hasty. I am glad you found a friend to care for you. Next time it might not turn out that way."

"Their room was cold and the soup was not very good and my bed was hard," Doro confessed. "I will not do that again." She went willingly with the nurse maid for a promised bath and hot meal. Phoebe watched from the bottom of the stairs until they disappeared from sight.

Val turned to Lord Clark and murmured, "One cannot help but wonder what she *will* do."

"She is a very inventive child. Both are bright beyond their years, I believe. Anthony has the makings for a first-rate student some day—a quick intelligence and an inquiring mind," Lord Clark responded with a friendly smile.

Val was oddly pleased at this praise for his young relations, even from Lord Clark.

"You can thank Miss Thorpe for their cheerful dispositions," Lord Clark said with an intent look at Val. "Life for orphans is not always good; so often they are shunted from one uncaring relative to another. She has given them a feeling of family. Without her loving care, they would be quite different children."

Val gave Clark a thoughtful look, then returned his gaze to where Phoebe stood with Anthony leaning against her in obvious affection. Her hands lovingly curved about his head, then patted his shoulder in soothing motions, reassuring him.

Could he be wrong? Val wondered. Was it possible for a spinster, a very young spinster, to rear children and do it well? He dismissed the consideration that governesses were spinsters; they were paid and few were truly caring. The same could be said of a nanny. His own nanny had managed to seduce him at a tender age. It had altered his perspective on life and the female gender considerably. He would have to rethink his feelings about Phoebe. Heaven knew they were muddled enough.

"Come, let us retire to the drawing room," Lady Latham urged tactfully. "I must hear more about Lord Clark's experiences since acquiring his title. Do you stay with your cousin, Lady Mary? Her husband Mr. Portman is such a pleasant gentleman."

Lady Latham led the way up the stairs, Lord Clark at her side, chatting about Lady Mary and the Airlie family and quizzing him about any of his connections that she might know.

"She does not miss very much, does she?" Val said to Phoebe, who gave him a startled look in return.

"Well, I expect she is curious. I must confess, I have learned more about Aldous, that is, Lord Clark's background these past minutes than in our conversations at home."

"Then what did you talk about? Surely not the weather," Val asked with a hint of irritation creeping into his voice. What could a vibrant young woman like Phoebe find of interest in such a dull dog as Clark?

"We discussed books," Phoebe said, pausing to send Anthony to the nursery with a maid. Once she had watched him head up the stairs, she turned her attention to Val again and with a cool reserve continued. "I fear our topics of discussion would bore you. Buried in the country, the doings and gossip of the *ton* are as remote as the moon. Nor do we have an abundance of entertainment, other than what we make for ourselves. It is a simple life, sir, but a comfortable one."

She gave Val a defiant look, then marched past him into the drawing room where she joined Lady Latham on the sofa. She seated herself with a sedate air, brushing down her blue muslin skirts in a demure manner and turned her total concentration on Lord Clark. Which must be immensely flattering to the man, Val mused. She spared not so much as a flicker of a glance for him as he crossed the room to stand by the fireplace, propping himself against the mantel so he could watch everyone without seeming to.

Val wondered where she had acquired the notion that he had to be constantly amused and cared nothing for books. He overlooked the actuality that he had done nothing to enlighten her regarding his many interests.

He considered anew the restricted life she had led these past five years or more. Books, homespun entertainment, social calls on the local ladies, church, and tending the children was not his idea of what a young, unmarried woman should know. That sort of thing more properly was assigned to a wife. And yet she fought him on placing the twins where they would be well-cared for so that she might find a life of her own.

Well, Val thought, he would have to change all that. It was borne in on him that she was not the cozening female he'd thought her, he had been quite wrong about that. And he allowed that she had done a fine job with the children. She deserved a family of her own. He renewed his determination to help her find a husband, a proper mate. Since Lord Clark would undoubtedly look much higher for a wife—and Lady Mary would be sure to point out the financial and social advantages of such a direction—Phoebe could not look to him for marriage.

The problem was to find the right gentleman for her husband. Ferdy certainly seemed to admire her, but he was a confirmed bachelor. Val decided the best thing he could do would be to collect another assortment of men and more or less parade them before Phoebe. He would allow her to make her own choice from his selection. Not considering himself the least self-righteous, he made a mental list of likely prospects while Lady Latham urged Lord Clark to join them at the theater that evening.

"Oh, please do," Phoebe added quietly. "It is one of the plays that we discussed, if you recall. I should like to see how Mr. Kean portrays Hamlet on the stage."

"Indeed, Lord Clark," Val inserted, making himself heard for the first time in the conversation, "it will be a pleasant introduction to the delights of London."

Lord Clark gave Val a quick, assessing look before nodding his agreement to the scheme. "Lady Mary said something about the theater this evening. I feel certain she would not mind if I seek the company of an old and dear friend. But, of course, I must confer with my hostess first."

Val resented Lord Clark's familiarity. The fellow was far too presumptuous in his claim of an *old* and *dear* friend. Feeling at odds with the world, he left the house shortly after Lord Clark made his proper farewell.

Phoebe stood by the window, watching the two men disappear down the street.

"Val was not himself today. I wonder what bothers him," Lady Latham said, casting a glance at Phoebe before turning to rearrange a bouquet of tulips on a side table.

"Somehow I doubt that he has abandoned his intention of taking the children to the country—to his estate. There are times, dear ma'am, when I find your nephew excessively aggravating—perhaps a little frightening, as well. What a pity that Doro happened to overhear his plans. And yet you know he blames her escapade on me. He feels it is my fault that she ran away." Phoebe exchanged a vexed look with Lady Latham before excusing herself to prepare for the evening.

In truth, Phoebe wanted nothing more than to reassure herself that Doro was indeed safe and sound. Then she intended to mull over the enormous change for Aldous Clark and its implications.

"Promise me that you'll not run away again, no matter what," Phoebe quietly demanded of Doro when she found her in the nursery. "Come to me first. I believe I could straighten things out for you, if you let me try. Have we not done splendidly so far?"

"I do not think Lord Latham likes us," Doro observed.

"What a daft thing to say," Anthony cried. "He's a bang-up gentleman and I like him," he said, before stalking off to play with a set of soldiers that his lordship had brought as a gift.

Phoebe reassured Doro, then retired to her room to

change for the evening and the promised reflections on Aldous Clark, not to mention a few thoughts regarding Lord Latham.

After hanging her blue muslin in her wardrobe, she stared at her reflection in the cheval glass. Embroidery enhanced her petticoat so that it looked almost like a gown. And above that virginal garment, her face seemed too ordinary, certainly not a face to compete in the marriage mart as Lord Latham seemed to think she should.

"What am I to do, pray tell?" she asked the young woman in the looking glass. "I am drawn to a man who clearly wishes me to the far ends of the earth. He has to be the most contrary man in the world. One time he accuses me of cozening her ladyship out of her fortune; another time he charges I am unfit to raise his young cousins. And today he inspected Aldous Clark for all the world like someone intending to replace a horse in his stables. I truly do not know why he should care if Aldous has any intentions in my direction. Actually, I should think it would suit his purposes extremely well."

Utterly vexed, Phoebe compressed her lips and shook her head, trying to make sense out of the behavior of one of London's premier Corinthians. "What an utterly confusing, maddening, and," she admitted, "handsome man. I will be civil to him for Lady Latham's sake, but if not for her I would wish him to perdition!"

Just as Phoebe descended to the dining room, a note arrived for Lady Latham from Lord Clark offering his apologies, explaining he would be with his cousin, Lady Mary, that evening. Lady Latham handed the note to Phoebe with no comment.

While Phoebe was disappointed, she also quite understood his dilemma and readily forgave him. One did not desert one's hostess to spend an evening with an old friend. That he had termed her an old friend had rankled, she admitted, feeling he had added years to her age.

Following an early dinner, Phoebe and Lady Latham set off for the theater, for her ladyship detested arriving amid the press of people.

"I prefer to watch them enter and settle into their chairs,"

Lady Latham confided. "I have a far better view of the gowns and jewels and who is with whom."

Phoebe watched as Aldous Clark entered a box opposite where she sat with her ladyship. Lady Mary and a man Phoebe presumed to be her husband were at his side, plus a young blond who wore a stunning white silk gown that made her look like an angel. She shimmered and sparkled, the diamante decoration on her gown twinkling in the theater lighting. All she lacked was a pair of gauze wings to complete the image.

"Lord Clark will be well occupied this evening," Lady Latham said quietly to Phoebe in a manner that was most commiserating.

"It seems that Lady Mary, as a representative of the family, has plans for her cousin." Phoebe had no bitterness, merely resignation. If that young woman's gown was any indication, her family did not lack for money.

"Lady Catherine Stanford has a fine dowry and her father, the Earl of Carington, has a lineage to equal that of Airlie. I could not deny that it would be a splendid match. Be aware that the heart rarely has anything to do with a marriage in these circles. She will marry where bid by her parents." Lady Latham turned to Phoebe and gave her a thoughtful stare. "It is a pity that you do not have your parents to assist you in finding a husband."

"Please, ma'am, all I wish for is the twins," Phoebe said, aware that she sounded overly defensive.

"Nonsense. As I said before, you deserve babes of your own." Lady Latham turned away to inspect a newly arrived couple. "Oh, dear me," she whispered, but offered no explanation.

At this point Phoebe caught Lord Clark's eye just as the door to the box opened behind her and Lord Latham entered with another gentleman at his side. She turned away from the apology she thought she detected on Aldous's face to greet the newcomers.

"I'm pleased to see there are chairs enough for us," Lord Latham said to Phoebe. "Let me present a friend of mine, Lord Winterton."

Phoebe darted a suspicious look at Lord Latham, wondering why he was being so congenial. Then she smoothed her face and nodded graciously to Lord Winterton. While quite tall, he was also somewhat corpulent and creaked a trifle when he bowed over her hand. Sporting side-whiskers and smelling strongly of eau de cologne, he did not greatly appeal to Phoebe. His bow could not match Lord Latham's in gracefulness.

He dangled his quizzing glass in his hand while he surveyed those attending the performance. "I see our newest member of the peerage is here this evening. How like Lady Mary to arrange the melding of the Stanford and Clark fortunes."

"They have barely met, sir," Phoebe protested, with another glance across the theater.

"What has that to do with it?" he asked with an air quite as lofty as Lord Latham when he nattered on about Phoebe not being suitable as guardian for the twins.

Recalling what Lady Latham had said about arranged marriages among the *ton*, Phoebe said no more. Surely Aldous would not permit the tenuous understanding they had known in the country to be swept away by his kind but imperious cousin, Lady Mary. And then again, he had never been one to put his foot down, preferring to follow rather than lead. It rather put paid to Phoebe's hopes.

"I was under the impression that the new Lord Clark was to join us. Did he send you notice of his change in plans?" Lord Latham whispered to Phoebe when his aunt quizzed Lord Winterton about his parents.

"Indeed, my lord, he did, explaining that Lady Mary had made special plans for the evening." Phoebe glanced at Latham before returning her gaze to the front of the theater—anywhere to avoid those knowing eyes.

"I suspect that Lady Mary means to guide his steps in the labyrinth of London Society," Lord Latham said with a hint of insinuation Phoebe could not miss.

Fortunately, before Phoebe could foolishly debate that point, the curtains parted and the play began. She was enthralled with the production of Hamlet, particularly with the acting of Edmund Kean in the title role. She had read the play, of course, but an entirely new dimension leaped forth at seeing the melancholy Dane come to life before her eyes with such splendid acting.

When the interval came, Phoebe felt as though she was being dragged forward in time and found she was reluctant to chatter about inconsequentials with Lord Winterton. Something she said was deemed witty by him, then Lady Latham made a remark that prompted Phoebe to retaliate with a bon mot that had both her ladyship and Lord Winterton chuckling. Lord Latham looked as though he had been sucking a sour lemon.

"Is anything amiss?" she dared to inquire.

"I believe we must have a little chat, my dear Phoebe. I shall call tomorrow to discuss the matter with you."

This exchange so puzzled her that she had a difficult time turning her attention to the performance on the stage. Why, oh why did his lofty lordship want to have a little chat with her tomorrow? and what did he intend to discuss? With Lord Latham, Phoebe felt sure it would somehow be a contrary confrontation. He surely meant to scold her.

So, to redeem herself, during the next interval, she set about entertaining the pompous Lord Winterton—to whom she rapidly took a dislike—with as much sprightly conversation and humorous remarks as she might devise. There could be no complaint of her laughing at him or failing to give him due attention.

Phoebe decided that his lordly lordship truly intended to find her a husband—as ridiculous as it might seem. Why else had he trotted out Lord Winterton and those other men as well to meet her? Did he intend to select the men he felt appropriate for her to wed? While she supposed she ought to be grateful that anyone took an interest in her future, she found she resented Lord Latham poking his nose into her affairs. And so she would tell him when they had their "chat."

"Would you mind if we left early, my dear?" Lady Latham said quietly when the play concluded.

Phoebe could see shadows of fatigue on her ladyship's face and immediately rose from her chair to arrange a shawl about her shoulders. Since Phoebe doubted she would concentrate on the farce that followed, she was only too happy to leave the theater. Her frequent glances at Aldous had revealed his devoted attention to Lady Catherine. It had not made Phoebe feel confident regarding the affection she believed Aldous knew for her. She suspected it would fade rather rapidly in exposure to the charms of polished London beauties, not to mention Lady Mary's manipulations on his behalf.

Lords Latham and Winterton bade the ladies farewell, escorting them to their carriage with correct demeanor. Phoebe suspected that the men would not return for the farce, but continue on to their club for the rest of the evening.

The following morning, Phoebe was in the morning room arranging a cluster of spring blooms for her ladyship when Lord Latham entered. He paused, watching her tuck the last of the tulips into the vase, then joined her by the window.

"Is it time to have our chat so soon?" Phoebe glanced about her for a means of refuge.

"Do not be alarmed, Phoebe," he said in that correct and lordly manner he'd adopted with her recently. "I have decided to take you in hand, so to speak. You have no parents to assist you and my dear aunt is too infirm. I wish to guide you in selecting a husband."

"I have no wish for a husband, but thank you kindly," she said, of a sudden finding the situation amusing. The man she found to be most attractive and possessing more charm than a dozen others proposed . . . to find her a husband. It was a jest she could have done without.

"Nonsense, my dear girl," he said, drawing closer to where she stood.

"May I suggest you do better in your selections than the ones you have trotted out so far? Lord Winterton is a pompous bore," she declared, deciding to burn that particular bridge behind her. "As matter of fact, I can truthfully say that not one of the men you have introduced to me entices me to leave the single state. Not Mr. Pippen-Jones, Mr. Connington, nor Albert Doulton, James Hervey or Lord Ackhurst or Lord Winterton."

"You must learn to appreciate the finer points of choosing a proper husband." He frowned at her barely suppressed grin of amusement.

Phoebe knew that if she didn't laugh she would crown

him with the vase of flowers and that might be detrimental to that luxuriant head of hair . . . not to mention what passed for his brains.

"You displayed far too much wit last evening. Wit is deemed a dangerous talent for a girl." He sounded as though he was quoting something he had read, she decided. "And for pity's sake, do not appear sensible. Men will think you a bluestocking. I know you are educated, but avoid making it obvious, for some men might find it off-putting. When you converse, shun such topics as politics and philosophy. Do not mention books you have read, unless it is a bit of poetry or some other innocent diversion." He touched her cheek lightly and added, "At least you do not use powder or cosmetics."

"Goodness, sir, what *am* I to discuss? The weather? There is little remaining that is of interest." She gave him an arch look, then turned aside to peer out of the window into the little garden to the back of the house. "Gardens, I suppose, would be an acceptable topic."

He stepped forward to touch her arm and she shook off his hand with impatience. Her amusement had faded and she found a rising anger within her.

"Tell me, have you consulted some worthy volume of advice to young ladies? Advice on how to capture a man? I have little desire to look and sound like most of the girls I have seen in London. I am not a miss from the schoolroom. And, I thank you kindly, I shall pick out my own husband, should the opportunity and occasion arise."

"I note that you do not speak of love," he said with approval. "Dr. Gregory declares love an irrelevant consideration with contemplating marriage."

Phoebe whirled about, only to find that he had inched up on her and she now was far too close to the dratted man. Nevertheless she raised her gaze to meet his, saying, "Above all I desire that elusive emotion you so coldly call love. I believe there are many facets to love, sir. Romantic love is but a part of them. Respect, admiration . . . so many things I wish. I have no liking for Dr. Gregory and his advice." She referred to the popular book written by that esteemed gentleman to his daughters many years before.

"A woman who would marry should be obedient to those

who would guide her," he said, watching her face for her reaction to his statement.

"You are impossible, sirrah. What a pity I just finished the flowers," she murmured so softly that Val barely caught the words.

"No, it is you who are impossible." He looked down at her, possessed by the strongest desire to kiss those rebellious lips. Indeed, she had taken over his thoughts to a point where he could consider little else. This would never do. It was all the more reason for him to find her a husband. Firmly taking himself in hand, he drew away from her, aware that she continued to exert a strange pull on his senses.

"This is to no avail, this chat you have insisted upon," she said from the safety of the window embrasure. "Dredge up some husband for me, then. But know this, I will not accept any man I cannot love."

"We really ought to permit the children to spend some time in the country, you know. Any man who sees you with them, particularly Dorothea, will entertain suspicions about their parentage."

She flashed Val a look that would have curled his toes at closer range. "You would introduce your supposed doxy and mother of your twins as a respectable consideration to a friend for a wife? That is what you are saying. Now *you* are being impossible. I suspect your argument is merely a ploy to take the children away from me."

As this was precisely Val's intent, he was annoyed and a little chagrined that she could have seen through his intent so easily. He was slipping.

"If Miss Oliphant disbelieved your innocence, would any of the friends and acquaintances you drum up for me do as well?" Phoebe charged, advancing on him with a menacing look in her eyes. "High-stickler that you are, who will you select for a wife if Society still wonders about the twins? Or your relationship with me?"

"Do we have a relationship, Phoebe?"

She looked confused, then retorted, "Indeed, my lord, none but as relatives to the twins."

"Good." This time he gave in to that wicked impulse that had plagued him earlier and kissed her most soundly. For a few seconds he found her soft and pliant, sweetly scented and delightfully responsive. Then she squirmed away and glared up at him, looking like an angry kitten.

Phoebe was breathless when he released her. Never would she understand this infuriating man.

"Well, so this is where you are," Lady Latham said, drifting into the room on a wave of lavender scent. She examined the lovely bouquet Phoebe had arranged, then turned to survey the pair before her, who looked as guilty as though they had just stolen the crown jewels. "What a lovely morning. Lord Clark sent a note requesting the pleasure of your company for a drive in the park this afternoon. I sent your acceptance."

"Lovely!" Phoebe declared with a defiant glare at Val.

Chapter 13

Lord Clark!" Val exclaimed. "I assume you mean Phoebe and not me. A drive in the park? Well, that is a surprise." Under his breath, so that Phoebe scarcely heard it, he added, "Lady Mary must be slipping."

Phoebe stood stock-still, unable to think, much less move. How like Lady Latham to sail into the room, totally ignore the proximity of her nephew and her guest, then come forth with an outrageous announcement.

"Indeed, ma'am," Phoebe managed to say politely. "How kind of you to anticipate my desire to drive out with Lord Clark." She glared at the presumptuous man still standing too close to her.

"I had planned to stop by later with a friend of mine," Val said with a deliberate air of injured dignity.

"As to that, you may come a trifle earlier than four of the clock. You know you are always welcome here, even though normally I do not see you from one end of the year to the other." The acid bite to her ladyship's words drew an unexpected smile from Val.

"Now, you know that is untrue. I pop in on you from time to time. True, since my young relatives arrived in London," he slanted an assessing glance at Phoebe, "I have chanced to attend you more often. I would not have Phoebe thinking I am neglectful in my duty."

"What I think scarcely matters, does it?" Phoebe said, with more than a touch of tartness in her voice.

"As guardian of the twins, your views interest me greatly, dear Phoebe. I believe that one of these days we ought to sit down and plot out their education. Naturally Anthony will attend Eton. Do let me know what you contemplate for Doro. Training at home? Or perhaps a select academy for young ladies?" He cocked a rakish eyebrow at Phoebe, and she steeled herself against that charm he oozed with unknowing expertise. Or did he?

"I am sufficiently skilled to train Doro myself," she said, aware she sounded odiously prim.

"Watercolors . . . embroidery . . . all those domestic arts?" he asked in a suspiciously lazy manner. He left Phoebe's side to stroll about the room, dangling his quizzing glass from well-manicured fingers.

Phoebe's gaze followed him, fastening on that glittering gold glass that hypnotically swung to and fro.

"Of course she could teach Doro all she needs to know about the domestic arts," Lady Latham inserted. "Not only needlework, but managing a household as well." Her ladyship toyed with her handkerchief while eyeing Val. "I do not know what sort of bee you have in your bonnet, but accept that Phoebe is most skilled in keeping a house. Indeed, most capable."

"A veritable paragon, you would say. Then you agree with me that she ought to have a house of her own to manage, children of her own to rear?" Val challenged.

"That goes without saying," her ladyship snapped back with an apologetic glance at Phoebe. "But the fact remains that she is highly suited to caring for Anthony and Doro."

Val bowed to his aunt, as though acknowledging a hit.

Phoebe saw a chance to escape this uncomfortable scene and took it. "Which reminds me that it is time for me to work with them on their reading. Good day, my lord. I trust it will be a pleasant one for you." Without waiting to be excused, she nodded to Lady Latham and whisked around the door and up the stairs as fast as she might go.

"Am I all about in the head or do you have new plans for Phoebe's future?" her ladyship said, sinking down onto a chair near the window where the sun could warm her shoulders.

"I do," he declared. "Oh, not including myself," he hastened to assure her. "But I feel an obligation to Phoebe. She has been so dutiful in her care. I intend to do my best to find her that proper husband," he said with a righteous air. Then he added reflectively, "Just fancy a brood of little black-haired, blue-eyed infants." He did not consider the remote possibility of any redheaded tots.

"She loves the twins, Val. Do not tear her apart by taking them away from her," Lady Latham cautioned.

"And what man do you know who would accept them into his household?" he pointed out for what had to be the fourth time. "With the tittle-tattle that has been whispered about London Society, no amount of disclaimer would satisfy him as to her innocence," Val insisted.

"He would know once wed," her ladyship pointed out astutely.

If Val was disconcerted by her blunt reference to what would be revealed in the marriage bed, he gave no indication of it. He paced back and forth, continuing to absently dangle his quizzing glass.

"Have you selected this paragon of men for her yet?"

"Well," Val admitted, "I have brought several to her attention, but she insists that she must care for the gentleman and found none of my choices to her liking."

"If you mean that nodcock Winterton, I can see why," Lady Latham retorted.

"There is nothing wrong with him," Val said. "However, I am at a loss to find a man who might meet her standard."

"I can think of one," her ladyship muttered, then feigned innocence when he cast her a quizzical look.

"Enough of this," Val said, after a glance at the clock that sat on the mantel. "I am due elsewhere shortly. I wonder what this invitation to a drive with Clark portends?" he said with a casual air that did not deceive her ladyship in the least.

"Time will tell. It could be that he wishes to tell Phoebe that he still nurtures a *tendré* for her." Lady Latham rose from her chair, crossing the room to join her nephew.

"Or," Val countered, pausing by the doorway to make his parting shot, "it could be that he must reveal the family's plans for his future—plans that do not include an impecunious young woman with a shadow over her reputation."

"I do not know what occurred before I entered the room, but I would have you know that Phoebe is a proper young lady, not one to be trifled with, Nephew."

"Trifle? I am not given to trifling with proper young ladies, dear Aunt," he said in a mocking tone.

"Well, I am sure Phoebe will be pleased to know it was something else," Lady Latham said, walking alongside Val to the entry. She went over to the stairs and paused before going up. "I only hope that you come to your senses before it is too late. Aldous Clark would make an excellent catch, true, but there are other men who are not blind or stupid. One of those gentlemen might just snabble Phoebe from under your nose before you know it."

Val appeared too stunned to reply. Smedley arrived with Val's hat and cane. Val absently drew on his gloves, donned his hat, accepted his cane, then left the house without saying another word.

Lady Latham chuckled as gleefully as a naughty girl while making her way to her room and a comfortable rest. Oh, her scheme was going well indeed. Now if those two would only cooperate a trifle more!

Out on Mount Street Val strolled along the walk, lost in thought. Whatever did his outrageous aunt mean by her not so subtle remarks? Surely she did not think that he nourished an affection for Phoebe! Impossible. They would be at daggers drawn all the time. That is, except when he was kissing her delectable mouth. He considered other enticements offered by marriage and had more difficulty shrugging the notion away than he could believe. It was one thing to grudgingly admit she was not a cozening female. He was not willing to concede Miss Thorpe a place in his life. It simply would not do. No, he would continue to look about with the hope he might find a suitable gentleman who paid no attention to gossip. And he would not have red hair.

Gentleman Jackson's patrons were witness to a particularly fine round of sparring when Val encountered his friend Ferdy there. Jackson himself watched, wondering, perhaps, what drove Lord Latham to practice a punishing right so diligently.

That afternoon, it was with a fluttering heart and after many anxious glances in her looking glass that Phoebe went forth to greet Aldous Clark. She had donned her prettiest pelisse of soft blue kerseymere, for the day was on the cool side. On her head, she wore her new Gypsy hat of chip straw trimmed with knots of matching blue ribands and cream silk roses. The hat tied under her chin in a saucy bow with broad bands of blue silk. In the morning room, she smoothed her gloves of York tan leather with nervous fingers while awaiting his arrival.

"You do look a treat," Anthony said with the air of one much older and wiser than his five years.

"Cousin Phoebe looks like an angel," Doro observed with the partiality of one who loves.

"Well, you do make me feel better," Phoebe began, then halted when Smedley paused at the door.

"Lord Clark is here, miss."

Stiffening her backbone for whatever was to come, Phoebe followed the butler to the entry where Aldous awaited her.

He was garbed in a fine gray coat of Bath cloth over darker gray pantaloons. His vest was a deep green and someone else had managed his cravat, for it was a miracle of a valet's skill. All in all, he looked finer than Phoebe had ever seen him.

"How well you look," she said, giving voice to her thoughts.

"And you as well. Fine feathers do make fine birds, it seems. Shall we be off?" He waved to Anthony, who peered around the corner of the morning room to see his old friend's new splendor.

Not wishing to delay this momentous drive, Phoebe hastened to the door, which Smedley whisked open for her.

Aldous handed her into his carriage with a solicitous care that Phoebe found to her liking very much. She noted that while the carriage did not boast a crest, it was a fine new one of the latest design. "I see you have a new horse and the latest in cabriolets."

"My cousin informed me that I must maintain a certain standard to uphold the family name."

There was no mistaking the wry note in his voice and Phoebe gave him a curious look. She remained silent while he negotiated the throng of traffic leading into the park. Then when they were settled, more or less, in the stream of carriages and riders that flowed along, she spoke.

"Your cousin is most admirable. In addition to being charming and lovely, she seems to have a genuine regard for her relative from the country."

Aldous slowed the horse to a walk. Fortunately there was no one close behind him to mind.

"Indeed." He fell silent for a time, seeming content to plod along rather than show off his dashing equipage. "It is good to see you again, Phoebe. I missed you when you did not return home right away."

"I have missed you as well," she said, wondering what this was leading up to and how she might fare.

"London is a different place. The people are not like our country folk," he observed.

Phoebe agreed, then said, "There have been many changes for us both of late, particularly for you."

"As to that, I am discovering that my new world is not quite what I hoped. It seems there are family demands." He paused for a time, then took a deep breath and plunged on. "The earl has informed me in no uncertain terms precisely what he expects of me. He has selected my bride-to-be, negotiated a settlement, and all but proposed to the young lady on my behalf."

The chill that settled over Phoebe's heart made her shiver in spite of the pleasant day and filtered sunshine. "Is she someone I might know?"

Aldous gave Phoebe a look of gratitude for her calm understanding, mixed with his regret for what must be. "Lady Catherine Stanhope."

"I saw her with you at the theater. She is very beautiful." Phoebe forced the words out, though she was sincere. How could she compete with beauty and a fortune, not to mention an uncle who demanded the deed be done for the family name? Aldous was not the sort to rebel.

"Perhaps when I know her better I will find we have more in common. I scarce feel I know her at present."

"That is often the way of it, I understand," Phoebe said, after clearing her throat.

"What about you, Phoebe? Do you have plans for your future?" He gave her an anxious look, then realized he was holding up traffic. Once the horse moved forward at a respectable pace, he glanced at her again. "Phoebe?"

"Indeed, sir. Yes, I have plans. There is a gentleman who has captured my interest," she said with the knowledge that this was at least true. "Whether or not something will come of it remains to be seen. I do not have an earl paving the way for me, you see," she concluded with an attempt at humor.

Before he could respond to her remark, Lords Latham and Andrews rode up to their carriage. Ferdy gave the cabriolet an admiring look.

"Smashing rig, Clark. Hullo, Miss Thorpe. Nice day," Ferdy said with his customary bumbling charm.

"Coming up in the world has an advantage or two," Lord Latham said in a jocular way.

They chatted briefly. If Lord Latham noticed the pinched look on Phoebe's face, he gave no indication. However, Ferdy frowned at her as if trying to decide what might be amiss. They soon rode off none the wiser, for neither Phoebe nor Aldous gave the slightest hint of what had transpired.

The drive through the park came to a blessed end when Aldous returned her to the house on Mount Street. He handed the reins to his groom, then escorted Phoebe to the front door of the house.

"Good-bye," Phoebe said, pausing before the door to offer her hand to Aldous. Behind him, the carriage was a visual reminder for her of the many changes that had occurred.

"I will see you again, no doubt," he said.

"Perhaps. The children are very fond of you, you know. I fancy they would enjoy a call from you." She sounded as though she was talking to a stranger, not the man who had raised such hopes within her.

"But not you?"

"That has nothing to do with it." Then she withdrew her hand from his and slipped inside the house before he could say anything more.

Back in the heart of Hyde Park, Ferdy surveyed his friend with curious eyes. It was obvious that something plagued him, had been plaguing him for some time. Ferdy decided that the lovely Miss Thorpe had a good deal to do with whatever it was that bothered Val so much.

"I gather the family has plans for Lord Clark," Val muttered. "It was plain on her face that he had told her something unpleasant."

"Surely she had no expectations of marriage once he acquired the title," Ferdy said.

"There is nothing the matter with Phoebe in the least," Val said vehemently. "As my aunt pointed out only this morning, she is a proper young lady. Aunt intends to give her a respectable dowry, so Phoebe is not without attraction there, either."

"You must have had quite a chat with your aunt," Ferdy said, prompting Val to confide in him.

"I intend to find Phoebe a decent husband who will appreciate her for her own worth."

"Well," Ferdy said with a respectful nod. "That is interesting. Any candidates for her hand so far?"

"She won't have 'em. Says she don't love them. Such folderol," Val concluded. Then he sprang forward to canter the distance of the green with Ferdy thoughtfully following behind him.

Val had not brought over a gentleman to meet Phoebe that day, nor did he the next. In a way, Phoebe was just as glad for it. After her disappointment with Aldous Clark, coming as it did following that heart-stopping kiss from Lord Latham, she did not think she could cope with anything more just now.

She settled in the morning room with her piece of fancy needlework, enjoying the change from turning sheets and mending draperies. While poking about in the depths of her workbasket, she raised a surprised gaze when Smedley announced Lord Andrews had come to see her.

"Of course I will see him. What a pleasant surprise." She deposited her needlework atop her workbasket and rose to greet her friend.

"Call me Ferdy, Miss Thorpe. I scarcely know any other name to answer by," the amiable giant said as he strolled in immediately behind the butler. He carried an enormous toy sailboat of proportions to match his own size—huge.

Phoebe eyed the boat carefully, then looked up into Ferdy's kind hazel eyes. His sandy hair flopped over his forehead in an endearingly boyish manner, and he looked for all the world like he should be off to the park with his nanny.

"That is a very large boat," she observed at last.

"I hoped I might take you and the children to the park. We could have a bit of fun."

Before Phoebe could answer him, Anthony slipped around the corner, intent on the large man who chatted with his cousin. "That is a big, big boat," he said in much the same manner as Phoebe had before.

"It looks to be a fine sailing vessel, I think. I was hoping Miss Phoebe would permit you to join me in the park so we might test it out. I need a first mate, you see."

"Could Doro come too?" Tony asked. He had half turned to face Phoebe but never took his gaze from the enticing sailboat.

"If Lord Andrews could wait for a bit, we will all gladly join him for an excursion to the park. Smedley," Phoebe said to the butler who had just happened to be near the door, "be so kind as to bring Lord Andrews some refreshment while I prepare the children to go to the park."

In a trice, Ferdy was comfortably seated in the largest chair in the room with a glass of particularly fine claret in hand. The sailboat, much admired by Smedley, reposed by the door.

Up in the nursery, Phoebe whirled about the room, instructing the maid on what the children ought to wear before dashing down to her own room to don the pretty blue pelisse and her new Gypsy hat. Just why she sought to look her best for one who was deemed without hope for a girl bent on marriage, she couldn't explain.

When they set off for the park, Phoebe could not help but admire the picture they made in the landau. Anthony had on a skeleton suit with a sailor collar, over which he wore a neat short jacket, and sat next to Lord Andrews with well-mannered demeanor. At his side, Ferdy was garbed much as most of the Corinthian gentlemen in the latest of fashion, only on Ferdy the clothes looked comfortable, not stiff. He was not one who could look pompous, no matter how hard he tried.

Opposite them, Doro perched wearing a pretty white dress with rows of ruffles and blue bows under her blue pelisse. Her little bonnet, while not as fancy as Phoebe's, looked nice on her. The thought occurred to Phoebe that to anyone chancing to see the landau, the four would appear a family on an excursion. The thought did not displease.

Once by the Serpentine, Ferdy and his little group left the landau in the hands of Ferdy's coachman, and with laughter, chattered their way to the water's edge. A groom placed a hamper filled with delicacies close by.

With an apologetic look at Phoebe, Ferdy said, "I thought the little ones might enjoy a sip of lemonade or a bite of ginger cake later. I know I will."

She compressed her lips so she didn't burst into laughter, then did so anyway. He was so large, he doubtless needed sustenance fairly often. When her chuckles subsided, she graciously nodded and sparkled a smile at him. "I think you have quite splendid ideas, sir."

He gazed at her for a few moments, studying her flushed face with intent eyes before turning to an impatient Anthony.

The boy set about the serious business of learning how to sail such an immense boat. He nibbled his lip while concentrating on Ferdy's instructions, then hunkered down along the bank of the river to do as bid.

The boat sailed along the shore as fine as anyone might wish. When a whisper of wind came up, it turned and majestically took off for the far shore.

"Oh, sir, look what happened!" Anthony danced up and down, beside himself with worry.

Phoebe recalled the dire results of Anthony's last ducking in the Serpentine and surreptitiously offered her hand to him. "Why do we not go to the other side to see if the boat lands there safely. Perhaps we might send it back to Lord Andrews?" She glanced at Ferdy to catch a look of approval in his eyes. How lovely it was not to meet mockery or the displeasure she so often saw in Lord Latham's gaze.

This hadn't occurred to the lad and he tugged Phoebe by

the hand until they reached the opposite shore, where the boat nosed in just as they reached it.

Anthony was in raptures. He carefully set the boat about, following instructions called to him by Ferdy and then sent the little craft on its away again.

"Oh, jolly good, Cousin Phoebe. Look how it goes." He pointed as the boat did its maker proud by performing flawlessly.

On the far side, Doro had reached for Ferdy's hand, tucking her little one inside his huge paw with no problem. Phoebe felt a constriction in her throat when the large man scooped Doro up high in his arms and she squealed with delight. How the children desperately longed for this sort of male company and admiration.

Doro settled comfortably in Ferdy's arms, not minding in the least while her brother sent the large sailboat across the Serpentine again. She nestled against Ferdy with all the confidence of a little girl who knows she is safe.

The toy craft made quite a number of crossings without incident before Ferdy pulled it from the water.

Anthony trotted up to him, disappointment clear on his face. "Must we stop now?" He was too polite to cry, but it was plain he had relished the treat.

"I confess I grew hungry, if you must know. I wondered if you might be willing to join me in some lemonade and ginger cakes?" Ferdy nodded to where a rug had been spread and the hamper set out for them.

Doro clapped her hands and placed a bold kiss on Ferdy's cheek. Anthony danced about, then tugged Phoebe along to where their repast awaited.

"This is the bestest day since we came to London," Anthony declared, with Doro's firm agreement.

Soon they were happily settled to a picnic of sorts, laughing and quite at ease. Phoebe felt the disappointment she had known when Aldous had informed her of his future plans fade away. Lord Andrews had to be the kindest man in all of London and if he wished to shower her and the twins with attention, she was quite willing to accept it.

Across the park, Val glanced their way, but dismissed the sight at first, most certain his old friend would never be in such a domestic scene. He decided that another woman had a pelisse and bonnet similar to Phoebe's.

Then he looked again and brought his mount to a halt. There was no mistaking the twins. Their laughter rang out to draw his attention, even if he hadn't been looking. And it was definitely Phoebe who tended to them as might a mother. And it was a mighty cozy arrangement there under the chestnut tree, with the lemonade and cakes, and all the friendly laughter. They looked like a family. This thought was so outrageous that Val felt himself close to erupting, although why, he couldn't say.

As for Ferdy—well—his old friend was behaving in a most uncharacteristic manner. He would have to do a bit of explaining.

Val urged his horse forward, unwilling to intrude, yet wishing, for some peculiar reason, that he could break up that comfortable group.

"Look, there's Cousin Val," Doro cried, jumping up to scamper toward him.

"Doro, be careful," Phoebe begged, springing up to follow her, worried that the daring girl might not be wary of Valiant. He was an impressive horse, but that might not bother such an intrepid child.

"I'll take care of her," Ferdy assured Phoebe, rising to stride after Doro, then swinging her up in his arms with ridiculous ease.

Doro squealed. Phoebe relaxed against the rug once again while Anthony also rose to hesitantly approach his cousin.

"Well, what have we here?" Val said in an attempt to sound jovial when he felt closer to anger.

"We are having a boating party," Doro announced with a wave of her hand that encompassed the hamper and rug, the large toy boat with the Serpentine behind, and which also included a pink-cheeked Phoebe demurely seated on the rug.

"So I see," Val replied, noticing how at ease his old friend seemed cradling the little girl in his arms. One would have thought he did it every day of the week. Val swung down from Valiant, then looped the reins over a low-hanging chestnut branch.

He approached the group with caution. "Ginger cakes?"

"Could I entice you to enjoy one?" Phoebe asked. "They truly are excellent." She held out a large tin of generous-sized ginger cakes, the sort Ferdy favored.

The errant thought popped into Val's head that Phoebe could entice him to do a great many things, none of which included a ginger cake. He accepted the cake with what he hoped was an appearance of pleasure.

"I learned to sail a boat, Cousin Val," Anthony said after deciding that Val seemed in a good mood. "Ferdy is a very good teacher and that is a splendid boat."

"Lord Andrews, dear," a flustered Phoebe inserted.

"I told him to call me Ferdy. The other is too much for a lad to say while learning to sail a boat. Time enough for the proper later on," Ferdy said complacently. He set Doro down now that they were some distance from the huge horse, and she immediately headed for the tin of cakes. His gaze on the children while they consumed another of the ginger cakes was most indulgent and gave Val outright chills.

Suavely concealing his disquiet, Val joined the group for a time, then remounted Valiant. Before he left them, he looked at Ferdy and said, "I expect I shall see you later? Dinner?"

Ferdy exchanged a look with Val, then nodded. "I will join you then. Usual time?"

Val nodded, then rode off with more dispatch than customary in the park.

"That was a surprise," Phoebe said while the children examined the boat and softly discussed its merits.

"I do not think my good friend was pleased with our outing," Ferdy said, looking for all the world as though he was delighted with this turn of events.

Mystified at his reaction, Phoebe murmured something about the afternoon growing late and it being time to return to the house.

Ferdy tended to the matter by scooping up the boat in one arm and Doro in the other. The landau had pulled up close by and so it was but a matter of minutes before all were comfortably seated within, the hamper and rug stowed, and they were on their way.

"You are amazingly efficient," Phoebe said, thinking that for so large a man he could move with almost alarming swiftness.

"I do have a way of accomplishing what I wish," he admitted.

Phoebe wondered what he meant by that oblique remark. She found the situation unsettling, yet intriguing, and wondered what it was that Ferdy wished.

Chapter 14

Some hours later, when a contented Ferdy sauntered into Val's study, he found his host in an irritable mood.

"Something disturbing you?" Ferdy inquired while settling himself on the large, comfortable chair he claimed as his own when calling on Val. A cozy fire snapped in the grate, pleasantly removing the chill from the room. In spite of it being a lovely day, the paneled study always wanted a fire.

Val absently poured out a cup of coffee for his friend, then took his own in hand to the chair that faced Ferdy.

"Coffee?" Ferdy gave a quizzical look at the cup of coffee Val had given him, then took a tentative sip. Steaming hot and quite fragrant, it pleased one who had been active and out of doors for hours. He sipped and waited patiently for Val to reply to his original question.

"Disturbing?" Val echoed. "Not really." He sipped his cooling brew, then cast a baleful look at Ferdy. "Had a busy day, did you?"

"Well, I began thinking about what you said regarding Miss Thorpe—her being a proper young miss and having a respectable dowry and all. I may not be in dire straits financially, but a healthy dowry does entice a chap. My sisters are always nattering on about it being past time I found me a wife. And I have found Miss Thorpe to be right charming. Do you know she never once remarked on my height or size?" Ferdy exclaimed. "She is a rarity, my friend."

"Indeed," Val replied in a somewhat repressive tone.

"She'd make a good mother," Ferdy observed ingeniously. "I must thank you for tipping me off as to what a catch she is." He sipped his coffee for a time, then went on, sounding alarmed. "You have not found some other fellow you want to introduce to her, have you? I'd take a dim view of that."

"Indeed, I suppose so," Val said dryly. "Particularly after investing in that boat."

"Beauty, ain't it," Ferdy said with obvious satisfaction. "That little lad is right quick to learn. Picked up on sailing in a trice, he did. Smart boy. I'd not mind having him about now and again when school was on holiday. He's about due for Eton, y'know. Girl is a bit of a scamp, but I figure that in the country, she would not come to a great deal of harm."

"You think you have it all sorted out, eh? By the bye, Doro still keeps an eye on that flower girl, I am told. Child returned to her spot across from the house on Mount Street the next day." Val rose from his chair to place his empty cup on the sideboard, then began pacing restlessly about the room. "There are bound to be problems in taking on another chap's children. His estate, for one thing," Val pointed out in what he thought to be a helpful way.

"I asked Miss Thorpe about that. She assured me that between Popham and the estate bailiff, the place is in good hands. Not but what the man who married Miss Thorpe would want to keep a careful eye on the management of the place. Could rent it out, I suppose. Hard on a house, but not good to leave the place empty, either. One would have to find exceptional tenants," he concluded pensively.

"You have really been giving this some thought, haven't you," Val said with rising consternation that he tried not to show. It would never do for Ferdy to become enamored of Miss Thorpe. Just why this was so, Val didn't consider at the moment. Then he wondered just how attached his friend was to that lady. "You fond of her?"

"Well, she is charming, as I said," Ferdy mused in a reflective way that set Val's teeth on edge.

"She insists she must have a deep affection for the man she weds," Val said in an attempt to dig deeper into this budding relationship. Ferdy had never shown more than a cursory interest in a woman before. This was unprecedented.

"I know." Ferdy gave Val a self-satisfied smile.

Ferdy's complacence shook Val more than he cared to

admit. "She has a temper," he cautioned, recalling the slap on his cheek that had almost sent him reeling.

"Well, as to that, I believe we could rub along well enough together so that would not be a problem. I am very easy to go along with, you know." Ferdy leaned back in the chair, with an impish gleam in his eyes, beaming a broad smile at Val.

Recalling how the straw damsels adored his large and amiable friend, Val was forced to nod agreement. "I know," he confirmed, unconsciously echoing Ferdy.

"She would have no worries on any account." Ferdy picked at a bit of lint on his breeches, then drummed his fingers on the padded arm of his chair.

"I doubt she'd tolerate your having a mistress," Val said quietly.

"Somehow I doubt that would be a problem," Ferdy intoned solemnly. At Val's hostile look, he added, "I said she's a pleasing lady. I sense passion under that prim exterior. I do not think a chap would be required to look elsewhere were he to nurture what was in his own bed. Besides," he added with a faraway look in his eyes, "I have found those fair charmers to be somewhat lacking as of late."

"I agree." Val crossed the room to lean on the back of the chair where he had been sitting earlier. He stared at Ferdy. The fellow seemed serious in his intent. Val was not certain how he felt about this development, but he had pointed out all possible objections, so he supposed there was little else he might do now one way or the other.

"You might wish me luck," Ferdy said with a wistful grin. "Do I come to you for her hand—should things progress to that point? I would wish to do what is proper and I know she is an orphan. That is how she is so aware of knowing how to care for orphans, being one herself. Poor girl. She has not had an easy life," he concluded with a pious expression.

Val stiffened. "I doubt if I have a thing to say about her future. If there is anyone who might lay claim to that, it would either be Popham or possibly my aunt, who is the one establishing her dowry. I had not realized that you were so far along in your interest."

"When I make up my mind about a matter, I move right along," Ferdy said with conviction.

Val knew his friend meant what he said. "Then I suppose I must wish you well."

If there was a distinct lack of enthusiasm in these words, it did not appear to bother Ferdy in the least. He rose from his chair, clapped Val on the back with one hand, while setting his cup on the sideboard next to Val's. "Good coffee—a nice change from wine," he observed. "I believe I will head on down to a jewelry shop. Most ladies like a little trinket, and I would find something for Phoebe. Perhaps a silver thimble or nosegay holder."

"Phoebe, is it?" Val said in dismay. The knowledge that Ferdy felt so secure that he intended to buy a trinket for Phoebe alarmed Val. A chap bought such a thing for a lady only when betrothed or married.

"As I said, she is a delightful lady," Ferdy offered with a broad wink, then bid Val farewell before sauntering from the room and out the front door to hail a hackney.

Val poured himself another cup of coffee, returned to his chair, and sank into reflection that lasted for quite some time. What was he going to do now?

"It was a splendid boat, Great-aunt Latham," Anthony said with proper deference.

"We had a lovely time, Aunty," Doro said, offering a moist kiss to her great-aunt, whose full title she often failed to use.

"Yes, indeed," Phoebe said while helping the children off with their outer clothes and straightening their garments, her hands fluttering about Doro to brush down her dress and fluff up the ruffles. "Lord Andrews had everything well in hand. Not only did Anthony sail his perfectly splendid boat, but we had a picnic of sorts with little ginger cakes and lemonade."

"That *was* thoughtful," her ladyship said, while watching Phoebe's face with a sharp gaze. The absence of pink cheeks and dreamy eyes was not missed.

"I sailed the boat all the way across the river," Anthony announced to his fascinated great-aunt. "And Cousin Val came to watch us."

"Did he now?" her ladyship queried. The sudden flare of rose in Phoebe's cheeks and a decidedly flustered demeanor were duly noted.

"Well, he was riding and paused to see what we were about. He did not seem very pleased, I must say," Phoebe said crossly. "I thought it most admirable that Lord Andrews was so considerate. The children adored sailing the boat and enjoyed the lemonade and cakes immensely."

"Bachelors tend to be that way when they think their territory is being encroached upon," Lady Latham observed, partly to herself.

"I beg your pardon, ma'am?" Phoebe said, puzzled as to the intent of that comment. Surely it could have nothing to do with Lord Latham's regard for her. Perhaps he was annoyed that Lord Andrews invaded what had been the other's interest heretofore. Which reasoning so confused Phoebe that she put the entire matter aside to consider later on.

Smedley entered the room, bearing a sumptuous tea tray with extravagant biscuits and cakes and tiny sandwiches to tempt the children after their outing spent chasing a sailboat. The butler smiled fondly on the children and Miss Phoebe, when he thought himself unobserved.

This effectively ended the discussion of Lord Latham—or Val—as Phoebe more and more thought of him. Valentine was the most unlikely name for him, she decided. That name seemed more given to romance and love, and she could not think of any man in this world less inclined to love or romance than Valentine, Lord Latham. Oh, she'd heard wherever gossips gathered, evidence of his interest in the ladies. There was always someone who felt that Phoebe should know more about the twins' cousin. If they guessed that Phoebe harbored a deeper interest in Val, it wasn't hinted at.

"Will Lord Andrews be coming to call again, do you know?" Lady Latham asked, when the twins had settled with carefully poured cups of tea laced with milk and a plate of cakes and biscuits.

"He asked if we plan to attend the special concert at Vauxhall when it opens. 'Tis early this year, I understand." Phoebe looked at her ladyship with inquiring eyes.

"Indeed," Lady Latham said. "Although several weeks off, I suppose we might consider buying tickets for it. Where is it we go this evening?"

Phoebe was not fooled for a minute that her ladyship had forgotten their social plans. "We attend a card party at Lady Rosbury's home, I believe."

"Card party! Dashed dull entertainment," her ladyship grumbled. "Cannot think why I accepted."

"Lady Rosbury is of the highest *ton*, my lady," Phoebe reminded. "I fancy one declines her invitations at great risk."

"True. And once in a while she offers unexpected diversions," her ladyship said, brightening with such a look of glee crossing her face that Phoebe wondered if they might not do better to remain at home after all. "I believe the gossip must be dying out if you are invited there. It seems Society has decided you are innocent of any wrongdoing—most likely because of your proper behavior."

"And your sponsorship," Phoebe added fondly.

As it turned out the evening was quite acceptable. Although Phoebe was but an indifferent whist player, she was able to contribute something of interest on nearly any topic for anyone who desired conversation. Those who chanced to chat with her, pronounced her a prettily behaved miss, and wondered at what the gossip was all about. For surely any young woman who had excellent manners and was sponsored by Lady Latham—who was known to be a high-stickler when it came to such matters—must be acceptable. After all, she had attended Almack's, and if those dragons of Society cast a vote in Phoebe's favor, who were they to argue?

However, something occurred to capture the eyes of those who sought interesting bits and scraps to pass along to those not fortunate enough to garner an invitation from Lady Rosbury.

Lord Andrews—wonder of wonders—attended Lady Rosbury's card party. He usually avoided such tame doings like the plague. Not only did he attend, he paid court to Miss Phoebe Thorpe from the moment he entered the drawing room, where she was seated with one of the dowagers.

Dressed in shades of fawn and brown, Ferdy was as fine as fivepence and looked distinguished in spite of his large size. He bowed to the dowager, then somehow managed to draw Phoebe away without her knowing quite how he had done it.

"Thing is," he confided, "dragons terrify me half to death. I depend on you to save me, Phoebe." He made other comments equally nonsensical, bringing laughter gurgling forth from a delighted Phoebe.

She fastened her gaze on Ferdy, somewhat dazed at the look of devotion fixed in his hazel eyes. He reminded her of the spaniel she'd had as a child, with that eager-to-please zeal of a pet. Only, Ferdy was scarcely a pet.

"It is a blessing that I am not playing whist at the moment," she confided as they drifted away from the dowager and those earnestly playing cards. "I should be utterly undone with that expression of yours."

He didn't seem to take amiss at her words, merely grinned and said, "I cannot think what you mean. Surely all gentlemen of discernment admire you—just as I do, fair lady."

She did not believe him for a moment. It did not seem likely that he would abandon his lifelong bachelorhood in an instant, and for Phoebe, of all people. Was it Val who had remarked about his friend's interest in opera dancers? Phoebe was no opera dancer.

Ferdy insisted upon escorting them home and when the three left together, the gossips took note and the word took wing.

But in the days that followed, Phoebe began to wonder if perhaps he might indeed be serious. Daily floral offerings brought a look of speculation to Smedley's fond gaze.

"Place looks like a floral shop," her ladyship grumbled, darting a look of delight at her own dear girl.

"They are acceptable gifts, dear ma'am."

"Well, I did wonder about the silver thimble Lord Andrews gave you." Her ladyship gave Phoebe a look intended to be one of reproach. "And those dainty pearl ear bobs."

"He said they were to replace the one I lost when we

were at the theater the other evening," Phoebe reminded her ladyship of the precise circumstances. "I ought not have complained, but I do not have so much jewelry that the loss of an ear bob does not vex. I thought it exceedingly kind of him. He is most thoughtful."

"Yes, he is, indeed," her ladyship replied, then smiled when her nephew strode into the room, looking for all the world like a thunder cloud.

He gave the room, with its abundance of floral tributes, a dismayed look, then turned to Phoebe. "You are making a byword of yourself, I trust you know."

Nothing could have been more calculated to raise Phoebe's ire than his censure. "Actually, I think the posies are charming. As charming as the gentleman who brings them," she added with a demure smile.

"You cannot be serious," he exclaimed, clearly disturbed by this turn of events.

"And why not, I should like to know?" Phoebe demanded, rising from her chair to gracefully drift across the room until she confronted his lofty lordship. "You said I need a husband."

"Because . . . well, because you simply cannot choose Ferdy," he said without his usual aplomb, appearing almost flustered.

"Do you go to Almack's this evening?" Phoebe inquired, toying with one of the tassels that decorated her cuffs.

"I suppose you mean to attend with Ferdy in tow. Lord, the gossips will have you down the aisle if the two of you go there together." Val cast Phoebe a distracted look, then turned to his aunt. "Why do you not do something?" he demanded. "Talk some sense into the girl."

"I think she is highly sensible," her ladyship countered. "And I will be at Almack's with her, you know. She does not attend alone."

"Are you sure that all this traipsing about does not overtire you?" Val said with a frown.

"Nonsense," she said stoutly. "Phoebe makes me feel young again. I had forgotten so much," she said with a look of fond reminiscence.

Seeing that any word of caution would not be acceptable, Val refused a glass of sherry, asking for coffee instead, thereby raising his aunt's eyebrows. He settled in one of the chairs near Phoebe, with the air of one who has come to stay for a time.

Smedley brought in a tray with the required coffee plus the tea and ginger biscuits Lady Latham favored. He exchanged a questioning look with her ladyship, who merely shrugged in return. Val accepted the coffee with gratitude and even took one of the biscuits.

"I have heard little of you lately, nephew—no races, no wild bets, no outrageous dalliances, and not even the introduction of a new fashion in cravats. I fear you are becoming a dull dog."

"Well, I suppose I have been a trifle preoccupied as of late. Have not had time for that sort of thing," Val replied easily, avoiding his aunt's direct and quizzical gaze. He sipped at his coffee with an oddly reflective air.

When Smedley ushered in Lord Andrews, Val smiled at the cozy family scene presented to Ferdy. Val sat comfortably ensconced at Phoebe's side—more or less—looking quite at home. Ferdy did not look pleased, which brightened Val's countenance considerably.

"Well, this is a surprise, old chap," Ferdy said to Val, while accepting a glass of claret from Smedley. Then he took a second look at Val. "Coffee again?"

"Haven't had much taste for the other as of late," Val admitted with a frown.

"Hmm," Ferdy said with a considering expression settling on his kind face. Then he turned to Lady Latham and said, "I trust we go to Almack's this evening as planned?"

"Come for dinner first. Then we can use my town carriage, for if this mist turns to rain, it will be better." At first she ignored Val's stare, then took pity on him. "Would you join us as well, Nephew?"

Unwilling to watch Ferdy court Phoebe, Val shook his head, albeit with obvious reluctance. "No, I thank you. I shall see you there, however."

Phoebe expected to see Val depart after this and was surprised when he remained, sipping coffee and mostly watching Ferdy while he entertained the ladies.

At last he left, inviting Ferdy to join him in a stroll down Bond Street to view a particular item seen in a shop window. The two left together at Ferdy's amiable acceptance of the offer.

"They are like two dogs after the same bone, each trying to outwit the other," Lady Latham murmured.

Phoebe did not feel much like a bone, but she had to confess that she found it intriguing nevertheless to be the object of such devoted attention.

Ferdy presented her with a nosegay of violets and white rosebuds when he came for dinner. He had another nosegay of red rosebuds and tiny snowdrops for Lady Latham, that sent her into raptures.

"Dear boy, I am so pleased that Phoebe has the good sense to enjoy your company," her ladyship cooed.

Anthony and Doro had been allowed to make an appearance in order to discuss a planned outing to the park with their large friend. The splendid boat was to be launched once again and Anthony clearly relished the thought. Doro wistfully inquired about ginger cakes and lemonade. Phoebe watched over all with a benevolent eye, while Lady Latham kept a sharp gaze on all to estimate the affections of those concerned.

Almack's was crowded as usual although, for once, they did not have to wait an interminable time to leave the carriage. There was but one other group ahead of them on the stairs, so Phoebe was swept up and into the assembly rooms before she had time to catch her breath.

Lady Sefton and Countess Lieven were joined by Mrs. Drummond-Burrell in the receiving line. Phoebe curtsied prettily and blushed when the countess made some reference to Ferdy. The gentleman might be dancing attendance on Phoebe, but never had he given a hint of any permanent intentions. Which was just as well, for Phoebe had to admit that her affections were not seriously engaged.

"Well, will you look at that!" Lady Latham whispered in a scandalized aside to Phoebe as they wound their way through the press of people along the side of the dancers.

"What, dear ma'am?" Phoebe whispered back, and then she saw. Val was in the center of the room with the candlelight of the magnificent chandelier overhead lighting his amused face. He danced with Lady Jersey in a very elegant version of a quadrille. Other than the few involved in that set, the rest of the dancers had withdrawn somewhat to give the eight sufficient room. They performed in a highly smooth, flowing manner, gliding through the figures with breathtaking gracefulness until the last of the four parts of the dance, the *Finale*, was reached.

"Shocking, positively shocking," her ladyship declared, still in a whisper, while smiling and nodding to those of her friends that she happened to see before finding seats.

"Well, the quadrille is most acceptable if Lady Jersey performs it, for all it is new, you know," Phoebe said. The pang that assailed her at seeing Val dancing in such a way with the elegant Lady Jersey was foolish. Val might not approve of her encouraging Ferdy's interest, but he did nothing to catch her himself. She was fast losing patience with the man. In fact . . .

"Well," Lady Latham said when the dancers bowed and curtsied to one another at the conclusion of the quadrille, "I had no notion that Val had studied ballet steps when he attended the opera. I always thought he went for other reasons."

Ferdy broke into a fit of coughing that necessitated a trip to the refreshment room. He promised to return with the ubiquitous lemonade for Phoebe and orgeat for her ladyship.

"Do you know, dear ma'am, I believe I will return to the country. I fear I am becoming too soft in London." At her ladyship's look of astonishment, Phoebe went on. "All these parties and dances and dashing about the city, not to mention the jaunts in the park, are doing me into a frazzle," Phoebe temporized. "And we have imposed upon you for far too long. You must yearn for peace and quiet once again in your lovely home. I do thank you for everything," Phoebe concluded with a hint of wistfulness in her voice.

"I will find that house a mausoleum with you and the children gone. Surely you might wait until the Season is over. Have you told anyone else of this ridiculous notion?"

"It just occurred to me, my lady," Phoebe admitted.

"I see," her ladyship replied with a considering air.

Nothing more was said, for Ferdy appeared with the lemonade for Phoebe and orgeat for her ladyship.

"There are the usual stale bread and butter and elderly cakes. I thought you could do without them," Ferdy explained. "Why Willis cannot manage to provide better fare for his patrons, I do not know," Ferdy grumbled.

"What a quaintish notion, Ferdy. You know very well that the members of Society so blessed as to obtain vouchers for this select assembly delight in complaining about the paucity of the fare."

"Well," Ferdy said in a confiding voice for Phoebe's ears only, "'tis as dull as a dinner at Boodle's. And speaking of dull, here comes Val. Cannot think what he is about. He purchased a buhl table at Baldock's the other day that must have set him back a pretty penny. And I have never seen the like of the set of Sevres he bought at Jarman's not long ago. Next he will be bidding on pictures at Christie's and rare books at Evan's. He reminds one of a gentleman intent upon furnishing a home."

Phoebe gave Ferdy a desolate look, then turned to face Val, wondering if he had an announcement of significance to make.

"The next *contre-danse* is forming, Phoebe. Will you do me the honor of partnering me?" Val said.

"I do not know if my grace is sufficient," she said, hating the note of pique that colored her voice.

"You are grace personified, my dear," he replied with his normal polish.

While not considering herself his "dear," Phoebe accepted his beautifully gloved hand and walked at his side until they reached the center of the dancing area. The music was sprightly and the dancers all quite adept. The others in their set were skillful, which made the dance more enjoyable.

Phoebe remained silent, concentrating on the steps until they were finished. Then, while Val escorted her in a promenade about the room, she said, "I intend to be returning to Beeches soon. I feel we have imposed on your aunt quite long enough. The dear lady claims she enjoys our company, but she must long for peace again."

It said a great deal for how much Val had altered his opinion that Phoebe was out to cozen Lady Latham out of a fortune, or that she was undoubtedly not fit to care for the twins, that he had such a curious reaction to her statement.

"You cannot be serious. Why, she would be devastated."

"Well, I must return someday and it had best be soon."

"Does Ferdy know?" Val inquired as they approached his aunt and friend, who had danced with no one else this evening, a turn of events noted by the tabbies with glee.

"No. I have not mentioned my plans." She caught sight of Miss Oliphant across the room and tightened her hand on Val's arm, wondering if it bothered him to see the woman he had once intended to be his bride. The young woman was now betrothed to an elderly peer.

"Just hold off on announcing your decision. There surely is no rush, is there? You told me that Popham managed well with the bailiff."

"Indeed. Anthony will have a fine estate when he comes of age."

No more was said, for Ferdy stepped forward to claim his second dance of the evening. Val watched glumly, wondering why his life seemed to have been turned upside down as of late. Women and wine—two things that had been mainstays of his life heretofore—pleased him no more. And he found himself oddly drawn to the elegant and beautiful objects to be found at the various dealers of the rare and priceless in London. That he kept wondering what Phoebe would think of this or that bothered him. The lovely young woman was occupying his thoughts far too much. If she left London, he might be free of her. And yet—the notion of Phoebe going faraway into the country to the remote Waring estate was unthinkable.

He noted that the young sprouts were now clustering about Phoebe like bees around honey-dripping eglantine. Val did not bother to ask for a second dance. He most likely could not battle his way to her side. His departure was watched by several of the ladies present. Phoebe pretended to be not affected in the least.

Her ladyship watched everyone: Ferdy, Phoebe—and Val—and drew her own conclusions. Her crafty look would have alarmed them all had they witnessed it—particularly Val.

Chapter 15

"Rosbert, I have reached the conclusion that something is seriously wrong with me," Val confided to his valet the following morning.

"Indeed, milord?" the prudent valet replied while completing the task of arranging his master's cravat in the elegantly simple style they both preferred. "I had not observed anything amiss."

Once free of his valet's able ministrations, Val commenced to pace back and forth across his pleasant bedroom. He paused to stare out of the window a moment, then turned to fix his gaze on Rosbert.

"You would think that I would be overjoyed at the thought of Miss Phoebe Thorpe retiring to the country estate belonging to her nephew. Correct?"

"Indeed, milord," Rosbert agreed.

"Yet I am not. And I shamelessly conspired with Lady Mary to lure Lord Clark away from Miss Thorpe—that was highly successful, for he displays great attention to Lady Catherine Stanford. There is nothing in the betting books regarding it. Their coming marriage is considered a sure thing."

"Lord Clark is pleased, so I see no problem there."

"Quite so. But I wonder if Phoebe had her heart broken." Val gave Rosbert a guilty look, then resumed staring out of the window.

"I believe you mentioned a determined pursuit by Lord Andrews, milord?" Rosbert said while unobtrusively going about the room, straightening it up, putting things away. "It would seem that her heart must be whole if the young lady consents to such a courting by your good friend."

"He is, isn't he? Courting, that is. Some friend he is,"

Val said in derision. "Why he had to decide after all these years that Phoebe would be his choice is beyond me. He said she is the first woman who made no comments on his height or size. Now you must admit, that is scarcely a reason to ask her to be his wife."

"Indeed, milord," Rosbert said, giving Val a curious look. "But you remarked that something was wrong with you."

"Because," Val said patiently, leaning against the fireplace mantel while considering the matter, "I find I neither want her gone from London nor wed to my friend. Dashed peculiar, if you ask me."

"If I may be so bold to inquire, precisely how do you feel regarding Miss Thorpe?" Rosbert discreetly occupied himself in the interior of the massive mahogany armoire.

Faced with this perplexing question, Val sank down upon a chair and studied his hands. He stretched out his legs before him and studied the high polish of his boots, inspecting the toes for signs of wear. But all the while he thought about Phoebe.

Miss Phoebe of the black curls and blue eyes, he had dubbed her upon first sight. And indeed, she possessed glossy black curls so thick it made him long to thread his fingers through the soft mass. And as to those eyes, well, they were incredibly expressive. If he paid attention to her eyes, he realized, he would know the state of her affections.

"I believe I am exceedingly fond of the lady, Rosbert," Val said with customary understatement.

"Indeed, milord," the valet said, withdrawing from the depths of the armoire to survey his employer without the least suspicion of surprise in his voice.

"How long have you been aware of my partiality?" Val said with more than a hint of irritation in his voice.

"It has been coming on for some time, sir. I daresay you have been unaware of it, for I understand that is often the case." Rosbert stood at attention by the armoire, hands linked behind him in an attitude of respect and not a little liking for his longtime employer.

"The question is now: what do I do about it?" Val rose from his chair and resumed his pacing about the room, turning from time to time to give his valet an annoyed look.

"As to that, milord, I believe the thing is to cut out Lord Andrews as neatly as you did Lord Clark,"

Val nodded. "That makes sense. Thing is, Ferdy does not have a convenient cousin, nor is there a budding beauty in the wings awaiting his tender care."

"Well, milord, perhaps you had best consult Lady Latham. I shouldn't wonder if she might have a notion or two."

Val gave a bark of laughter at that quiet understatement. "I believe I shall seek out Butterworth. He might have an idea. Need to be armed before I face my aunt."

Rosbert nodded, dropping his gaze so that Val missed the look of fond esteem in his valet's gray eyes.

Val ran lightly down the stairs, asking Priddy where the secretary might be found. Once located in the depths of the library, the question posed to him, the secretary gave Val much the same advice received from Rosbert.

After explaining the situation and hearing Butterworth's reply, Val stared at his secretary, wondering if the servants had talked about this matter behind his back. He decided they most likely had touched upon it—seeing as how it might affect their lives—and grimaced wryly at Butterworth.

"I see you are as helpful as Rosbert. I shall have to face my aunt with no ammunition," Val grumbled. Then he left the house, taking his gloves, cane, and hat from Priddy with the absentminded courtesy that was part of what made his servants like him so much.

At his aunt's establishment on Mount Street, he found all was strangely peaceful. The reason was—and he would swear she took great delight in the telling—gleefully made known to him in a trice.

"Phoebe is off to the park with Ferdy Andrews. They took that perfectly splendid boat and a little picnic, and went off to do a bit of sailing. Anthony is very partial to Ferdy," her ladyship observed with an astute eye on her nephew's reaction to her words.

"And how does Phoebe view my former friend?" Val asked dryly. He had a feeling of stepping into unknown waters and wondered how deep he would sink.

"She appears to like him well enough," Lady Latham

said in a considering manner. "And what do you mean—former friend? I have heard nothing about you two having a falling out." She rose from her place on the sofa to cross to Val's side, putting a gentle hand on his arm. "What is it?"

Val gave her a slightly embarrassed look, like a schoolboy caught out in snitching an apple from a neighbor's tree. "I find that I harbor rather strong feelings for your guest, Miss Phoebe Thorpe. Amusing, is it not? After all I have said and done to rid you of her presence and take the children from her?"

"And when did you first realize this, Nephew?"

"When I wanted to throttle Ferdy for dancing attendance on her these many weeks. The man is making a byword of himself, fussing over the children in particular."

"And you wish you had thought of the boat first, is that it?" she said with a sly smile.

"It does seem to enchant those little beggars," Val admitted ruefully.

"Well, as to that," her ladyship said while taking a turn about the room with her nephew in tow, "I seem to recall Anthony wistfully yearning for a puppy. And Doro has several times in my hearing longed for a kitten. I should think you might easily outdo Ferdy, for the boy cannot keep the boat—it being far too valuable for a child. A puppy and a kitten, both easily found this time of year, would be something else, and guaranteed to earn you not only their gratitude, but Phoebe's as well. You have heard that the way to a man's heart is through his stomach. To reach Phoebe, you must first reach the twins."

"A puppy and a kitten! Dear heaven," Val muttered. "And what about Phoebe? Once I get past the twins, how do I reach her?"

"If your imagination cannot cope with that task, you do not deserve her, my boy," her ladyship scolded.

"I should say that truly puts me in my place." He took his aunt's hand and smiled down at her with obvious fondness. "You are a dragon, you know, but a very nice dragon for all that. I am off to locate a puppy and kitten. You had best alert the staff, so that all are prepared. My memories of puppyhood are of puddles and worse."

"Puddles! Dear me," her ladyship replied with a trace of laughter in her voice.

Val paused at the door before leaving. "I do not intend to lose, you know."

"I would disown you if you did," she said tartly.

He gave her an arrested look that promised her he intended to inquire about that remark later on.

In the park, Phoebe fondly watched while the twins scampered about chasing the boat and sending it on its way again when reached.

"They will grow up very fast, if my sister's brats are anything to go by," Ferdy commented quietly to her. To Anthony's delight, he sent the boat across the lake again.

"I suppose so. If you say one word about my being alone once they are grown and wed, I shall have hysterics," Phoebe cautioned. "I am quite aware of the future. I would not wish it any other way. Anthony needs to marry and continue the line and care for the estate."

"In the meanwhile, you do the work of both parents. It is vastly unfair and asking a great deal of one so young," Ferdy observed while he poured her a glass of lemonade.

"Oh, pooh," Phoebe said, secretly pleased at his concern. "I agreed to the task quite willingly." At her great age of two-and-twenty, it was lovely to be thought too young for something. Yet she did not wish to encourage Ferdy to continue this courtship of her, for she well knew that all of society was abuzz with his partiality. She accepted the glass from his large, strong hand, thinking it a pity that she could not love this gentle giant.

Why she had to fall in love with the most contrary man in all of England was beyond her understanding. But . . . love him, she did. Little good it did her. He had not danced with *her* as he danced with Lady Jersey. Not but what Lady Latham would have had strong palpitations if he had dared to do such a thing. The quadrille might be accepted at Almack's, but it was still deemed a scandalous dance by many matrons.

He had been so incredibly graceful performing that dance with a practiced skill. Somehow she had not expected him to be so smooth and elegant in his movements.

It may have been due to his rounds of sparring at Gentleman Jackson's, or perhaps he fenced—a sport that required much grace and balance.

"Penny for your thoughts," Ferdy said, intruding on her mental ramblings.

"I was thinking that we had better return to the house. If I am to prepare for this evening at Vauxhall, I shall need a bit of time. Thank you, dear friend," she said, giving Ferdy a direct, open look that expressed more than she realized.

He seemed to sigh with relief—which was odd when she thought about it later. For now, she was grateful that he accepted her end to the afternoon. He rose from the rug, where he had sat so close to her. She watched while he cleverly rounded up the children, stowing the splendid boat in the carriage, before assisting her, then the twins inside.

Before the twins could think of a good argument for remaining, they were bowling along the road from the park, observed by a number of gossips. The grouping was promptly noted and expressive looks exchanged by all.

Vauxhall was utterly splendid, far more so than Phoebe had expected. The ladies were finely garbed in evening gowns of every hue, and the gentlemen were elegant in smart black, corbeau, and midnight blue coats.

The walks, of which she had heard so much, were neatly graveled and diversions abounded everywhere. She found the crowds along the walkways particularly fascinating.

When Ferdy rescued her from the danger of an excessively happy party, Phoebe found she was grateful that she had so large a protector. Even if she might have preferred the attentions of the one she loved, Ferdy offered soothing consideration.

"Well, we have seen the new tightrope walker, viewed the new puppet show, and I doubt if we have missed anything else to be seen. I, for one," Lady Latham declared, "am run off my feet. May I suggest we find that box that Lord Andrews reserved and enjoy a glass of something cool. Having a delightful time can be more fatiguing than one would believe."

"Indeed, ma'am. I apologize. I should have seen that you were tiring," Ferdy said after taking his eyes away from

Phoebe's lovely figure garbed in pink and silver tissue. Tiny pink rosebuds nestled in her curls, and she carried a silver mesh reticule that flashed when she walked, catching the eye if she failed to impress.

Ferdy noticed that his lovely partner had captured a good many glances on their stroll through the famous pleasure gardens. In particular, he had caught sight of his erstwhile friend, Val, who appeared to be skulking about in the shadows while keeping an eye on Phoebe. Ferdy stifled a grin and led the ladies to their booth

"Shaved ham, roast chicken, *and* a dish of beef? Extravagant," Lady Latham declared while nibbling at the fare heaped on her plate by their generous host, who had insisted this was to be part of his treat.

Phoebe sipped her lemonade, thinking it a trifle bitter. She glanced about her, inadvertently leaning against Ferdy as she turned and caught sight of a familiar face.

It was. None other than Lord Latham was in attendance. How curious. But then, she had spotted a duke, several earls, one or two viscounts, and any number of other members of the *ton* dressed to the nines and appearing to enjoy the pleasure gardens immensely. Only Val did not seem to be enjoying himself. Ferdy offered her more ham and she turned her attention to the occupants of the booth once again.

Across the walkway, Val compressed his lips. Why had he not thought about the Vauxhall opening? Had his wits gone begging? Never in his life had he pursued a woman with so little finesse. He was more like a bumbling fool than a member of the Corinthian set. Of course, he would most likely be declared out of fashion since he had taken to neglecting the design of his cravat and the arrangement of his fobs.

Did his aunt not warn him that he was in danger of becoming a dull dog? Well, he had best remedy that at once. He caught sight of a lovely young matron who appeared to be with a group of friends, and no husband in attendance. He strolled over to her side, slipped a proprietary hand beneath her elbow, and smiled into her face.

"La, my lord, how you surprised me." Lady Ilbert batted her lashes at him so furiously that Val wondered the breeze did not blow his cravat out of shape. He forced his smile to remain and strolled along at her side as though he had been a part of the group from the start.

They passed the booth where Ferdy and Lady Latham sat with Phoebe. Val bowed to the ladies—not releasing his hold on Lady Ilbert's arm. He gave Ferdy a freezing look before sweeping past the booth to find an advantageous spot for the fireworks display. Once there, he melted back into the crowd, leaving Lady Ilbert to wonder what had happened to him.

"Everyone appears to be heading in that direction," Phoebe said, once she found her voice again. It pained her to see Lord Latham escorting a pretty woman. Ferdy said she was married. That made it no less hurtful, however. That she sat by Ferdy and had appeared to lean against his broad shoulder did not impinge upon her awareness.

Lady Latham consumed the last bite of chicken on her plate and delicately blotted her mouth with the pretty napkin provided. "Fireworks," she explained when able to speak again.

Ferdy surveyed the table, then the strained face of the young woman sitting quietly at his side. "I think you would enjoy the fireworks and this is not the best place from which to view them. Shall we go?"

Suddenly glad to be doing something, Phoebe eagerly hopped up from her chair and helped her ladyship with shawls, her reticule, and hunted around for a missing handkerchief with good will.

They joined the milling crowd headed in the same direction. It took only a moment for Ferdy to bend his head to hear something Lady Latham was saying, and Phoebe to gaze upward at a remarkable statue for the trio to separate.

When she realized she was alone, she refused to panic. "Surely Ferdy will look for me as soon as he realizes I am not with them." She slowly continued to walk in the direction she thought the others had gone, searching the crowd while scolding herself for her rising fear.

The crowd seemed almost frantic and utterly unmanageable. Men buffeted her from one side or the other. Women seemed to laugh and give her knowing glances—quite as though she were some doxy—one of their sort, she realized with horror. Her feet slowed, her mind in turmoil. What was she to do? Where was Ferdy? What would happen to her if she was not rescued soon? Darkness had fallen while they ate and now the sky had become a velvety black. Lamps were lit, true, but this walk was still alarming.

She had almost drawn to a halt in fright, reluctant to stop but unwilling to continue when an arm snaked about her waist and she was pulled to one side of the graveled walk.

Her scream was cut off when a firm hand was clapped over her mouth and Phoebe wondered if she would faint. Never in her life had she been so terrified. Jostled and carried willy-nilly was bad enough, but she could not see a thing of her captor.

Propelled into the shadows of a niche to one side, she found herself freed . . . almost. Her captor continued to loosely hold her and that firm hand was replaced by a warm mouth when she found herself somewhat ruthlessly swept off her feet and kissed.

At first she fought him, pummeling him with her small fists. Then her senses recognized this man. His scent, his touch, and most certainly his kiss revealed him even if they were in deep shadows. She drew back and gave him an angry look.

"Val, do you realize you frightened me half out of my wits? How dare you kiss me like that?" She placed her hands on her hips and glared at the man she had thought she loved. Now she was not so certain. "How could you do this to me?"

The arrack punch he'd consumed had given Val a bit of Dutch courage, and he swiftly pulled Phoebe to him again. "Kiss you, my sweet? Simple. 'Twas like this." He demonstrated his expertise with a skill that not only left Phoebe breathless, but to her utter shame had her longing for more.

Her fists uncurled and her hands rested lightly against his midnight blue coat of the softest, smoothest superfine. One hand actually had the temerity to gently caress that firm jaw, fingers dared to thread through those careless locks.

Then she recalled herself, and where they were, and she twisted in his arms, fighting him to release her.

He set her on her rather unsteady legs, retaining a light

hold on her. It seemed he feared she might faint—or collapse. Small wonder if she did.

"Val, you are the most outrageous man I have ever met," she declared in ringing tones.

"Shh, my love. You do not want to call attention to us, to your somewhat compromising position—do you?" He cocked his head to one side and gave her a beguiling—if slightly tipsy—grin. "I might have to use my admittedly effective method of silencing you again. You would not wish that—would you?"

Since there was nothing Phoebe desired more, she remained silent, content to glare at him. Then reason began to return to her muzzy brain. "Ferdy! And Lady Latham!" she cried, heedless of his warning to keep quiet.

"Indeed. Ferdy is to escort my aunt safely home after the fireworks. The crowd is impossible. I told him that I knew where you were to be found and that I would return you to the house, safe and sound."

"You have a strange notion of safe and sound, sirrah," she said with a fulminating look. "And precisely how could you find me when Ferdy did not know where I was. I missed the fireworks," she wailed.

"You did not miss a great deal. We provided our own fireworks," he observed, in what Phoebe deemed was a rascally manner. "And I felt sure you would have concern for my elderly aunt. She tries so hard to partake in everything, but she really is fragile."

"True." Phoebe was forced to admit he had the right of it in this instance, as much as it galled her to admit it. As to the fireworks he mentioned, she was sorry to have missed the spectacular display. "I am sorry I missed the rockets and Catherine wheels. I did hear the explosions."

"Were there explosions? I thought it was merely the effect of kissing you," he teased.

Phoebe found he was drawing her closer, so she quickly turned aside to search the area. There was no sign of Ferdy or Lady Latham. "We had best leave now, if you please."

"So prim a request? I like the fire within, Phoebe." He touched her chin with his fingers, turning her face toward him. He studied her as though memorizing each feature, an experience Phoebe found unsettling.

"I believe you have imbibed far too much punch," she said. "I was told it is very potent. Is it?" She tugged at his hand, drawing them along into the walkway and toward the entry gate.

His grin was endearing, if a trifle wry. "Not as potent as you, my dear."

"You must not say such things," she scolded. Yet she could not help but be secretly pleased he seemed so taken with her. Pretending to be unaffected, she retorted, "And what happened to the lady I saw you with before? Ferdy said she is Lady Ilbert. You should be shamed to be flirting with a married woman."

"Do not be a scold, Phoebe. It ill becomes you," he said in reply. He pulled her hand, whirling her about to face him. They were virtually alone but for a few people some distance away. The lamps flickered through the trees; shouts of the wherrymen drifted in from the river.

Phoebe knew a flicker of alarm. She'd not seen him like this before. Usually he was suave, polished, and in complete control of himself. Now he had become a different being, a stranger—a very dangerous stranger.

Again he touched her chin, tilting her face up to his. She ought to turn aside. She did not. And she knew a touch of annoyance when all he did was to place a feather of a kiss on her lips.

"Now we shall go home," he said firmly, escorting her from the park without further ado.

She was bundled into a waiting carriage and heard Val instruct his coachman to drive them to his aunt's home as quickly as may be.

"The more respectable element has left, so the crush of carriages has thinned out considerably, and we should not have any difficulty in crossing the bridge." He settled in his corner opposite where she leaned against the squabs.

Phoebe found to her great dismay that she wished he had continued what she knew was no more than a light dalliance. He had not even sat next to her. Had she given him such a disgust of her for her utterly wanton behavior? She turned her gaze to the passing scene outside of the carriage, thus missing the look of yearning in Val's eyes.

He deposited her in the entry hall with no more than a

pleasant good evening, then left. Phoebe stood there a minute, dazed and feeling lost. Then she collected herself and marched resolutely up the stairs to her room, while behind her Smedley locked the door for the night. This would never do—mooning over that dratted man like a schoolgirl.

The following morning, a bouquet of flowers to outdo any bouquet that ever might be arrived early. The maid brought it up to Phoebe's room with wide-eyed amazement. Actually, the bouquet was nearly as large as the girl and Phoebe stifled the urge to giggle at the sight of the bouquet that appeared to walk of itself.

"I think your gentleman friend bought out the flower sellers in all of London," the maid observed before leaving the room.

Phoebe had a hunch who had sent the extravagant arrangement that must have contained every color and sort of flower to be found. A glance at the card and the bold scrawl of "Latham" across the white paper confirmed it. He had also written, "Sorry."

Now whatever did he mean by that, for pity's sake?

"Cousin Phoebe," Doro cried, "what a lot of flowers!"

"Indeed, love." Phoebe crossed to give the girl a quick hug, then patted her shoulder. "Run along and finish your breakfast and perhaps we can take a walk in the park."

"I wish we could have our own boat," Doro said softly. "I should like something to play with all the time, and not just with Lord Andrews."

"I know, dear. We will see what can be done." Phoebe did not promise anything. She would have to explore a toy shop and see if she might find something of interest.

Once dressed and downstairs with the twins in the morning room, she was not terribly surprised when Lord Latham followed Smedley into the room. They were followed by two servants who carried mysterious covered baskets.

Anthony and Doro stood quietly, watching with wide eyes as Phoebe rose to greet their cousin. The twins exchanged a look of communication when they saw how Phoebe turned a pretty pink and Cousin Val gave her a fond look.

"Am I forgiven?" Val said quietly.

"For all the flowers?" Phoebe said pertly.

"Liberties," Val admitted.

"Oh, liberties," she echoed, unsure of how to handle the matter. Could she scold him when he made such a lovely atonement?

The mysterious parcels yelped and mewed and wiggled dreadfully. Anthony and Doro approached, curious as to what the baskets might contain.

"I decided that while a sailing boat might be fine—when you are allowed to play with it—it might be more jolly to have something of your very own. Anthony, here is a fine beagle puppy for you. I believe his name is Toby, if I make no mistake." He whisked off the cover over one basket to reveal a long-eared pup with melting brown eyes that quite captured Anthony's heart immediately.

"And Doro, do not think I have forgotten you." He pulled off the cover to the other basket tied with blue ribbon. Inside was a precious little gray-and-white kitten. "I was told its name is Tom Kitten. He is yours to play with and care for, so mind you learn well."

The children were enchanted with their presents.

Anthony shouted, "Champion, Cousin Val. How did you know I wanted a puppy? And this is a good little fellow. Thank you very much," he said, suddenly mindful of his manners.

Doro thanked her Cousin Val with a smacking kiss.

They turned their attention back to the new pets, while Val drew Phoebe to one side. "I wish I might accept thanks for the flowers in the same way, my dear."

Phoebe turned a pretty shade of pink and wondered how to cope with this impossible man. With lips compressed—lest she chuckle—she held out her hand and shook his most properly.

"I see I still have a steep hill to climb."

Phoebe did not quite know what he meant, but she longed to find out.

Chapter 16

Phoebe watched the twins play with their new pets while enjoying a bit of sun in the park. She'd chosen Green Park this morning, but away from the cows and milkmaids. Anthony had run with Toby until the puppy dropped of exhaustion, and he now sat quietly beside the dog, petting him. Doro trailed a piece of riband for Tom Kitten to follow. All of which left Phoebe to mull over her problems.

Every instinct urged her to flee London for the country. She had been rather shocked by Val's kisses while at Vauxhall. Not that there really was anything so terribly improper with those kisses, she supposed. That is, if one were accustomed to receiving kisses—which she was not.

Ferdy had not attempted anything beyond holding her hand, which she fancied was all he wished. This also perplexed her. Surely if he had such a partiality for her, he might attempt a kiss, if only on the cheek. She picked at the grass, pulling up one blade at a time. Perhaps Ferdy's interest was naught but pretense? She recalled that sigh of relief when she termed him a good friend.

Val, on the other hand, had shown disdain for her, believing she might try to cozen his aunt out of a fortune, then declaring Phoebe unable to care properly for the twins by herself. Well, she had done her best, just as she had promised George, their father. It had not been easy, but one cuddle of those precious babies and she had gladly given up a chance of a Season in London, possibly a home of her own. She had been desperately needed, and had given of herself without a thought of compensation. Val's final shot had been to insist that she needed a husband. Quite as though one just picked a husband from a tree—like a piece of fruit.

She was suspicious of his latest behavior. Surely the outrageous bouquet of flowers was no more than a grandiose apology? As for his cryptic words in parting, she could offer no explanation. What did he mean, "a steep hill to climb"? Where? It did not make sense. Of one thing she was certain, Val had no serious intentions toward her. And this knowledge was what prompted her to plan her retreat to Beeches.

She would begin immediately. Lady Latham might take a bit of convincing, for she had taken to the twins with surprising affection. It seemed unfair that her ladyship be deprived of the delight of her grand-nephew and niece merely because her nephew was a bit of a scoundrel and an utterly impossible man—as contrary as might be.

She welcomed the assistance of the maid when it came time to return to the house on Mount Street. A sleepy puppy, a tired kitten, and two worn-out children were bound to be fractious—which they were. Once they were settled in the nursery, the pets in their little baskets and the children with mugs of hot chocolate and biscuits, Phoebe sought out Lady Latham.

In the morning room she found her ladyship nodding over a volume of verse.

"The children enjoying Val's presents?" Lady Latham inquired, sitting up and pretending that she had not been caught napping.

"Indeed, as you might well know. I believe Anthony ran as much as the puppy, and Doro is quite entranced with trailing a riband for the kitten." Phoebe crossed the room to take a seat close to where her ladyship sat. Pleating the skirt of her muslin gown between fingers that revealed how ill at ease she was, Phoebe continued. "It is all the more reason for us to return to the country. Pets need to run about out-of-doors, I should think. And it makes for a great deal of bother for your staff—all those puddles, you know. Puppies and kittens take much patience."

"Has anyone complained?" her ladyship said with a narrow look at the door beyond, where servants passed from time to time.

"Of course not. They are wonderful and all cooperate

completely. I believe they are as fond of the twins as you, dear ma'am. But the fact remains that I believe it is time for us to leave." Phoebe could not bring herself to look directly at her ladyship. That canny soul saw far too much.

"Oh, rubbish. Things are just becoming interesting," her ladyship grumbled. Dropping her book on the floor with no regard for the delicate binding, Lady Latham rose from her chair with a stiffness that revealed she was in pain again. Slowly straightening, she took a hesitant turn about the room, coming to a halt before Phoebe, with a sad expression on her face.

"Are you all right, ma'am?" Phoebe said, rising to place a comforting arm about the older woman's shoulders.

"No, I am not," her ladyship confessed, training her gaze on the floor. "I ache dreadfully and I wish for some of your soothing potion. Perhaps you might rub my neck for a bit. It helped me so much the last time you did it. In truth, I do not see how I can manage without you, dearest girl."

Phoebe was utterly dismayed by this admission from one whom most people termed a dragon. "Of course, my lady," she said softly, walking at her side up to her ladyship's room.

"I like to imagine I shall live long enough to see those darling children next summer, but the way I feel now, I do not know . . ." Her ladyship's steps faltered and she placed a trembling hand on Phoebe's strong arm.

Phoebe felt absolutely dreadful that she could be so heartless as to place her own wants before the needs of a woman who had been so kind and gracious to her.

"Will you promise me to stay a trifle longer, my dear?"

"Of course, I will," Phoebe said promptly. "I could not leave you now if you truly need me."

It was as well that Phoebe could not see the crafty gleam in the soft brown eyes as her ladyship leaned against her while she helped the old lady up the stairs.

Once the neck rub had been tenderly given and Lady Latham tucked under the down covers of her bed, Phoebe hurried back to her room to contemplate what she must do now. No point in ordering her trunks brought down from the box room, nor in writing to the housekeeper at Beeches with instructions regarding their return. A rap on the door brought Doro with a request for a story. Phoebe set aside her difficulties to entertain her young cousin.

Val read the hastily scribbled note from his aunt a second time in an attempt to make sense of it. "Best go over there to see what bee she has in her bonnet now."

Smedley informed Val that he was to go directly to her ladyship's room without making himself known to anyone else. The look he exchanged with Val offered a clue that something dubious was afoot.

Val rapped softly on her bedroom door, then entered when he heard her summons.

"I am impressed," she said from where she was ensconced on her chaise longue and covered with a pretty shawl. "You came directly you received my message. What a good boy you are. Sit down. We must talk."

The "boy" smiled wryly, and at her negligent gesture, settled on a surprisingly comfortable chair. "I await your pleasure, dear Aunt."

"Phoebe insists she must return to Beeches at once. What on earth did you do to make her think she must flee to the country? On second thought, do not tell me. My heart most likely could not stand the hearing. What are you going to do about it?" she demanded. "I tricked her into remaining a little longer. Poor darling believes I am about to drop short. No, no, I am not about to go aloft," she said in response to the look of alarm from her nephew.

"Then I fail to see what you are about."

"Nodcock. How you ever came to be deemed a lady's man is beyond me. I am keeping her in London so that you, dear Nephew, will have time to court the girl."

"In my defense, may I say that I never cared about any of those other women. As you rightly guess, I do care about Phoebe. Although she is not quite what I had in mind for my baroness, being far too independent."

"You must court her properly," her ladyship commanded.

"I confess that is something I've not done before." Val gave his outrageous aunt a look of amusement. How she adored conspiring over something.

"You overdid the flowers. Made her suspicious, I should

imagine. You ought to bring her pretty little things, posies, little gifts."

Val grimaced. "I would rather toss her across Valiant and ride off to a parson."

"And you claim to be a Corinthian? A dashing man about town?" Her shocked look was almost Val's undoing.

"They usually are not courting a shy, suspicious young lady who seems to take umbrage at the least thing," he pointed out in his defense.

"She approved the puppy and kitten," her ladyship reminded.

"For which I was given a firm handshake. I believe she was mistrustful of that as well, dearest Aunt." Val leaned back in his chair, quite amused with the look of frustration that settled on his aunt's face.

"Young people today simply do not know how to go about things. Why, when I was young . . ." She gave Val a sheepish look. "I always vowed I'd not say such words, and here I am."

"The problem remains, however. I thank you for your advice and will take it to heart." He rose from the chair and walked to the door. Before he left, his aunt called out to him.

"Val . . . I must know. What dreadful thing *did* you do that required buying the contents of all the flower shops in London?"

Val's grin lit up his handsome face. "I kissed her . . . twice." With that, he slipped around the door and was gone.

A wily smile crossed Lady Latham's wise old face and she rubbed her hands with glee. "There is hope for us yet."

When Phoebe took the children down for an afternoon romp in the park with their pets—more to get the animals outside than because the twins needed the air—she found Smedley accepting a charming nosegay of spring blooms from a boy at the door.

"Ah, miss. Flowers for you, if I make no mistake," the butler said with a kindly look.

Phoebe accepted the nosegay, studying the attached card

with curious eyes. "Your Valentine," it was signed. It was scarcely Valentine's Day, but that was *his* name.

"Who sent the flowers, Cousin Phoebe?" Doro demanded, cuddling her kitten to her chest.

"Cousin Val, dear," Phoebe said absently.

The twins exchanged looks, then trotted along with Phoebe to the lovely expanse of green grass and shade trees.

Phoebe found a comfortable spot beneath a spreading oak and watched the nursery maid assist the children in playing with their pets. Then other matters intruded. What was that scoundrel up to now? Sending her flowers—first an enormous bouquet, now a dainty nosegay.

A study of it brought forth a wistful smile, for it held her favorite pink roses and forget-me-nots—though where anyone found them at this time of year she couldn't imagine. She wondered if he had to resort to the nosegay after having depleted the flower supply of the city's florists. That thought was unworthy of her, she admitted to the dainty bouquet she cradled in her hand. The flowers may have been an excessive gesture, but they were nevertheless a charming one.

A man on horseback cantered across the grass until he drew so close she could identify him. He must have been conjured up from her mind, for it was Val. She greeted him with wary hesitancy.

She sat up straighter when he dismounted, then joined her at watching the children. "They are doing splendidly, I believe," he said softly. "Do you agree with me? You have said nothing to me other than hullo. Surely you have forgiven me for Vauxhall by now?" He gave a pointed look at the flowers she held in her hand.

"I am surprised you beg my forgiveness. Your aunt seems to think you can do no wrong," Phoebe said tartly. "I pity the woman you take to wife." She absently twirled the nosegay in her fingers.

"No," Val said in what she could see was mock horror. "But then, what do you know of my choice of a wife?"

"At one time you thought to wed Eustacia Oliphant," Phoebe reminded him. She placed the nosegay in her lap.

"Please do not remind me of past folly," he said.

When Phoebe turned to meet his gaze, she found herself captured by the look in his eyes. What was he trying to convey to her? Earnestness? A plea to understand him? She did not think she could. Understand him, that is.

"What may I do to please you?" Val said lightly.

"You have already pleased me," she replied, turning to look at the twins. "See how happy they are with their pets. That was a lovely thing for you to do. I am amazed at how perceptive you were."

"That cuts to the bone, Phoebe," he protested. "I did not know that you thought so little of me."

Since this was far from the truth of the matter, Phoebe blushed and shook her head. But she could not bring herself to tell the dratted man that she was in love with him. "You seem a fine man—most of the time. Ferdy says you are becoming a dull dog, what with buying Sevres porcelain and paintings at Christies. You add to your furnishings?"

"A few things. I'd not have you think me a fribble."

"Never that," she exclaimed, then rose in a flutter of muslin. She held the nosegay in one hand, while she brushed off bits of grass and leaves with the other.

At this promising point Mr. Pippin-Jones and Lord Ackhurst rode up with a flourish and dismounted to make their bows to Phoebe. Val cast them an irritated look and resigned himself to a patient wait until the boorish chaps gave up and left Val and Phoebe in peace.

Rather than join in their inane chatter, he crossed the lawn to see how the twins fared.

"Cousin Val," Doro said in her piping voice, "do you like Cousin Phoebe?"

"Why, of course," Val replied, while he scratched behind Toby's long ears.

"We thought so. Do you want to marry her?" the child persisted.

"Do you think I should?" Val countered, wondering where this line of questioning was going.

"Yes. Anthony and I 'cided we would like you and Cousin Phoebe to be with us always. And Great-aunt said Cousin Phoebe would have to marry you first."

"I see. So what do you propose?" Val said, highly diverted by this line of conversation.

"We could help you," Anthony offered, for the first time putting in his two pence.

"Indeed? How so?" Val said with a delighted grin at his would-be conspirators.

"You should ride off with Cousin Phoebe like the knight in the story she read me," Doro said with a nod that made the bonnet on her head wobble dangerously.

"Great-aunt disapproved of that," Val said solemnly.

"Oh." Doro was clearly disappointed that such a practical and dashing solution could not be used.

"I promise that if I think of something you might do, I will let you know. I must say, it is nice to think I have you on my side," Val concluded with another grin. He ruffled Anthony's hair and then picked up Doro to whirl her about so that she squealed with delight.

This resulted in Anthony's plea for the same and Val found himself taking turns swinging the twins about in the air. To his surprise he found it a pleasant experience—playing with the children. He had not expected that to be the case.

Pippin-Jones and Ackhurst finally took their departure, casting pitying glances at Val as they rode off.

"What was all that about?" he said when Phoebe joined him.

"They wanted to know if I attended the Vauxhall affair. I was forced to be evasive," she said, flashing a look at Val that he found impossible to interpret.

"I will not apologize again for something I thoroughly enjoyed" he said quietly.

He would swear a smile quivered on her lips, although she made no reply.

Clouds had begun to gather. Phoebe glanced at the sky and turned to the nursery maid. "It looks to coming on rain. We had best head for home."

"Are you actually contemplating forsaking the delights of London for the remoteness of Beeches?" Val said while swinging Anthony up to ride with him on Valiant.

"I promised your aunt to stay for a while longer, but, yes, I intend to leave as soon as may be. There seems to be nothing for me in London." Her direct gaze fell before the intensity of Val's smile.

"We shall see about that," he murmured.

At least, Phoebe thought that was what he said. She hastily gathered the children's things, helped Doro with her kitten, and handed Toby to the nursery maid.

Val walked his horse at a pace to remain beside Phoebe and the others. He held Anthony comfortably close to him, easily accommodating the boy. Odd, he had not given much thought to a family of his own, but now it felt strangely right to be with Phoebe and the twins. What would it be like to have his own children? His and Phoebe's? The very thought warmed him. However, it seemed Phoebe still held deep reservations about him.

Val had always considered being a member of the Corinthian set an advantage. It was something of a shock to learn that there was a woman who did not yearn for a dashing, polished gentleman of the highest stare of fashion. That he had a reputation for being somewhat of a lady's man appeared to be to his disadvantage as well.

How was he to overcome her qualms in this regard? Instinct told him that it would not be easy. The idea of losing Phoebe after realizing that she was the woman for him was enough to send him into a cold sweat. He refused to accept defeat. He must win. But how?

All she talked about was returning to Beeches. Courting her at Beeches, deep in the countryside, would not be impossible, but it would not be a simple matter either.

"Here we are, my lord," Phoebe said intruding on his contemplation.

Anthony, who had remained in blissful silence all this while, spoke up. "I should like to ride my pony with you one day, Cousin Val."

"I fear the pony has been somewhat neglected with the arrival of Toby," Phoebe said, flashing Val a rueful smile.

"Happy the little beggars enjoy their pets," Val said while assisting Anthony to the ground. He watched the group straggle up the steps, then into the house. Phoebe had said nothing more to him, other than a faint farewell.

Val sighed. Not only did he have a steep hill to climb, there was no great promise that he might actually achieve his goal—which was marriage to Phoebe.

After returning home and submitting to a change of garments, Val sauntered along to his club, here to listen to others chat. He inserted questions now and again, always in the direction of how they managed to marry their choice. The results of his afternoon were distinctly depressing.

Most of the men he knew had arranged marriages, with fathers and solicitors handling details. Many were caught in those marriages of convenience that Val thought rather cold and unrewarding. None seemed to have married for love.

All of which brought him to consulting with his aunt once again that evening. They happened, by mere chance, to both attend a rather dull dance at the Hemmingfords'.

"I gather you have met with little success," Lady Latham said acidly when she saw her nephew's face.

"If you refer to my pursuit of a certain person, I would agree," he said discreetly. He glanced about the room to note that Phoebe was dancing with Ferdy. The sight made him gnash his teeth.

"Graceful, is she not? Lord Andrews as well." Her ladyship tapped Val sharply on his arm. "I cannot believe you have not swept her off her feet by this point."

"I might, if I could manage to find her alone," Val admitted. It was galling for him to reveal just how vulnerable he was in respect to Phoebe Thorpe. All his polish was for nothing in the face of a woman who cared not a fig for it.

"The twins, eh?" Lady Latham said. "Well, I suppose if one might arrange for a special treat for the twins, one might manage to accomplish just that," she mused aloud.

"Alone," Val repeated. While he watched Phoebe and Andrews progress through the paces of the country dance, he took note of the respectful look on Ferdy's face and the polite expression on Phoebe's. A feeling of triumph rose in him when he realized that Phoebe did not love Ferdy. There was no glow on her cheeks, no sparkle in her eyes—other than delight in the dancing. He began to have hope he might succeed.

Alone. Where could he propose they go that Phoebe would accept? He wanted to avoid crowds—so that eliminated anything like a museum or such place were people gathered and it was permissible to take a young lady.

She liked the country. And that was when it came to him.

He smiled at his aunt, who gave him a rather startled look in return.

"What are you up to, Nephew? That is a distinctly suspect expression you wear."

"Indeed," he murmured and went off to claim the next dance with his intended.

Fortunately it was a dance where he had a chance to exchange a few words with Phoebe while others performed their part of the pattern.

"Would you consider a ride in the country one of these days?"

Her alert expression warned Val that he had to be careful in his approach. "Country? I thought you did not care for the country."

"Not so," he replied easily, then took her hand to lead her through their steps.

"Where?" she asked, then smiled. "The twins would adore an excursion into the countryside."

Val had no intention of taking the twins, but merely smiled. "A picnic, I believe. Would you enjoy that?"

"We all love picnics." But her glance was still wary and Val knew his path was fragile.

"Leave everything to me. I shall make the arrangements and all you need to do is to be ready. Wear that smashing Gypsy hat you have. I like that on you," he said before leading her through the remainder of the dance.

Phoebe glowed to think that a gentleman of his stature would recall her favorite hat. A picnic. The twins liked picnics. Every now and again, Phoebe packed a little basket with a lunch and they had wandered along the stream that cut through Beeches so they might enjoy an al fresco meal in the sunshine.

When he returned her to his aunt's side he murmured, "Until then, dear Phoebe."

"Did you enjoy your dance?" her ladyship said with an innocent glance at Phoebe.

"Umm," Phoebe murmured. "He suggested a picnic in the country."

"Sounds romantic. Did not know he had it in him," her ladyship muttered.

It was two days hence that all came together. The

weather cooperated by being warm and sunny. A friend of Val's had agreed to repay a debt owed to Val by taking the twins along with his young brother to the Tower of London.

When Val appeared at his aunt's home, it was to find a distracted Phoebe awaiting him in the morning room. He introduced his friend Atherton and his young brother. They proceeded to whisk away the twins for the entrancing treat of viewing the lion and seeing the ravens. Before they left, they exchanged a knowing look with their Cousin Val, then scampered off in high spirits.

Phoebe was speechless, which Val minded not in the least. "Shall we go? I have the carriage waiting for us."

She adjusted her Gypsy bonnet and walked at his side, but not without protest.

"I vow this is most peculiar. I had thought we were to take the twins along. Are you certain this friend of yours is respectable? Will he look after the children well enough?"

"What a mother hen you are," Val complained.

Phoebe blushed and allowed that she was being a trifle worrisome.

Handed into the carriage she darted side glances at Val while he turned onto the pike road and soon was headed out of London. They jogged along at a smart pace, until Val turned off the main road and finally halted by a pretty stream.

He removed a large hamper from the back of the curricle—where a groom would have sat if one had come along—and placed it not far from the stream.

They were alone. Utterly, peacefully alone. Not so much as a carriage or a street hawker or anything that smacked of the city could be heard.

"There is not a child to claim your attention, nor an aunt to demand attendance. I have you all to myself," Val said with evident pleasure.

"I fail to see why that is necessary," Phoebe said primly, perching on the edge of the rug he placed on the ground while maintaining a prudent distance. She had not forgotten a moment of those bone-melting kisses. And they were now alone. She had thought long into the night about this man and her love for him. Might they actually have a future together? This solitary picnic seemed auspicious.

Val fished into a pocket, then pulled out a tiny package. Phoebe felt her heart take wing.

"I have a trifle for you. Open it."

Her fingers fumbled with the wrapping and when she snapped the little box open, she saw a tiny jeweled rose. "A pin!" she exclaimed with a mixture of pleasure and disappointment. She pinned it on her pelisse, then smiled and said her proper thank you.

He seemed not to notice her lack of true delight and went about serving up their little repast with the flair one expected of a Corinthian. He toasted her with a delicate white wine, then ate with a relish that she simply could not match.

When replete, Val leaned back against the tree beneath which he had settled them and appeared to enjoy listening to the birds and the stream and the quiet of the country.

"Well?" she said at last. She found it hard to accept that he did not have some ulterior motive for the picnic and she longed to know what he was about.

"You must, you know." He was fishing about in his pocket again and pulled out another item.

"Must what?" Phoebe ached with curiosity, but turned her gaze to the distance, refusing to let her interest show.

Then Val gently pulled Phoebe into his arms and did what both of them had yearned for all this while. He kissed her with all the expertise he had acquired during his years on the town, until Phoebe thought she would dissolve completely.

"You must marry me. The twins want it. My aunt wants it. Last but not least, I have discovered that I want it very much, my dearest Phoebe of the black curls and blue eyes. Please say you want it as well," he pleaded.

"I do, for I love you terribly," she replied with stunning simplicity, giving Val a direct look that revealed what was deep within her. Her heart's desire had come true at last. That he could love her as she loved him was beyond anything wonderful. He would be a good father to the twins, something they needed very much, and a good father to their own children—which thought made her cheeks even pinker.

After which, Val pulled her back into his arms and continued on as begun, thinking that he had done well after all.

"You know," he said thoughtfully some time later with Phoebe cradled in his arms, "my aunt is going to take complete credit for this marriage. I suspect she has schemed from the beginning to bring it about. She admitted as much to me the other day." He decided not to tell her that he also suspected Ferdy had played the attentive swain with the same end in mind.

"What a crafty soul she is," Phoebe said with a chuckle, snuggling closer to her love. "But I do love her."

"Good, for she will keep an eye on the twins while we take a wedding trip. I have no intention of sharing you with anyone for a time." After which, he demonstrated one or two of the reasons with Phoebe's wholehearted cooperation.